DAY OF THE WHALE

DAY OF THE WHALE

RACHEL DELAHAYE

SCHOLASTIC

Scholastic Australia
PO Box 579 Gosford NSW 2250
ABN 11 000 614 577
www.scholastic.com.au

Part of the Scholastic Group
Sydney • Auckland • New York • Toronto • London • Mexico City
New Delhi • Hong Kong • Buenos Aires • Puerto Rico

First published in the UK by Troika Books in 2022.
This edition published by Scholastic Australia in 2023.

ISBN 978-1-76129-857-8

Printed in China by RR Donnelley.
Scholastic Australia's policy, in association with RR Donnelley, is
to use papers that are renewable and made efficiently with wood
from responsibly managed sources, so as to minimise its
environmental footprint.

23 24 25 26 27 / 2

To Mum, and to Australia,
where my own story begins

MAP OF CETACEA

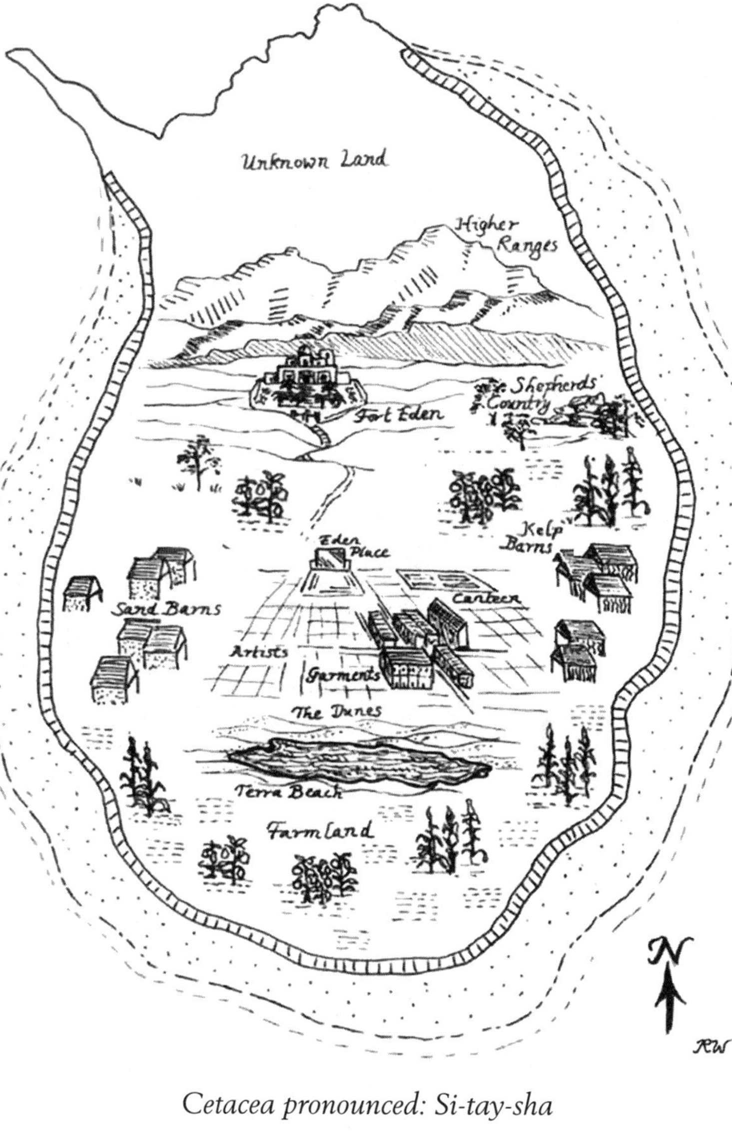

Cetacea pronounced: Si-tay-sha

'Truth is not afraid of questions.'
– Paramahansa Yogananda

CHAPTER I

Big Blue

A single note soared over the island – a high-pitched yawn that cut through the thick, sticky heat. Cam stopped scrubbing and waited, hoping another would follow. Hoping with all his might . . . Seconds later it came: a long, mournful bleat. A summoning call.

'Big Blue's coming!'

Cam dropped his brush and ran out of the barn and into the open yard where he fell, sprawling on piles of seaweed. The workers around him laughed and pretended to prod him with their rakes, but he picked himself up and kept going, dashing through the tight alleys of the kelp district, his green tunic flapping like sea lettuce in a storm.

When he hit the main streets, crowds of people were oozing through them already, slow and thick like lava. He bounced on his toes, watching as the throng thickened. If he was swallowed up in that sluggish tide, he'd be stuck at the back, lucky to see anything at all.

And he had to see. He had to.

Crowds were now building up behind him; he was running out of time. Cam looked for an escape. To his left was a breeze tunnel – a gut-pinch alley between two houses, barely wide enough for a possum. He sucked in his tummy and slipped into it sideways, edging through it like thread through a needle to the other side, where he found himself in the network of small alleys that criss-crossed the districts. The backstreets were cool and empty, and Cam sprinted through them, zigzagging towards Eden Place as fast as he could.

Eden Place was at the heart of Cetacea: a square so big, it could hold everyone on the island. It was half full by the time Cam got there, and hot – the stone baking like an oven under the vicious southern sun. People scurried to pockets of shade and squabbled over the auditorium seats on the east and west sides.

That's where Cam and his dad had always chosen to sit. Not for the light breezes, like most, but for the clear view of the screen that towered over the north side of the square. It was almost as big as Eden Place itself, and from up there, at the top, when Big Blue came, they could see all of him, tip to tail. Cam recalled his dad's excitement, how his fidgeting hand would tap Cam's knee and he'd say, 'Take a good look him, Cam. See what he is.'

What he was, was a blue whale. And when Big Blue appeared, magnified and magnificent on the giant screen, it always took Cam's breath away.

Take a good look him, Cam. See what he is.

His dad had always urged him to look harder. And over the years, Cam had done just that. He'd memorised the whale's markings, colours, scars and barnacles; he knew the contours of the creature better than he knew his own face. He thought he knew everything there was to know, but it turns out he didn't know anything at all. Not about Big Blue. And not about his dad.

Because he never thought his dad would leave.

'If I don't come back, follow Big Blue and find the truth, Cam. Understand?' His father had gripped his arm and nodded as if to nail the words into Cam's forehead. Then he stepped through the door and was gone. He didn't return that day or the day after, and, as the weeks turned into months, Cam took those last words and distilled them into an oath.

Follow Big Blue. Find the truth.

There was something else he needed to know about Big Blue – some truth – and when he found out what it was, then he'd find out where his dad had gone.

It seemed simple enough at first. But four Big Blue sermons had passed since then. Four times, Cam had rushed to the top row of seats and stared so hard at the Eden Screen his eyes dried up – inspecting the whale from mouth to tail fluke, from dorsal to belly – and each time he learned nothing new. Now, he suddenly realised how pointless it was. Pointless doing the same thing over and over again, expecting a different outcome. If he hadn't seen the 'truth' in the last four sermons, why would it be different this time?

He was going to try something else.

Instead of scrabbling up the scaffolding, he headed into the standing area, where people were surging like shoals of fish towards the slim shadows. Some fell due to the heat, or from sheer exhaustion after starting dawn work shifts. Others pushed and shoved. The pit was always like a tureen of boiling carrots.

Cam twisted his body through the tiny gaps that opened up between elbows and shoulders, pushing his way forward bit by bit until he found himself in the one area of Eden Place that everyone else avoided.

The very north side of the square was in full sun and right under the screen. The view was terrible and the noise unbearable. But that's what he had come for: the sound. If he couldn't see the truth, perhaps he could hear it. *Feel* it. Anything was worth a try.

He shook out his green tunic, scraped back his damp brown hair and climbed on to the wooden stage beneath the screen, positioning himself cross-legged in front of a noise box. When sound came, it would be unbearable; the vibrations would play his bones like a xylophone. But he hoped Big Blue's voice would sing right through him and leave a message under his skin.

As he waited for it all to begin, he recited the *Birth of Cetacea* laws, hoping Big Blue would somehow notice his devotion.

We do not speak of the dirty past –
the past destroys the future.
We will work hard –
we must sustain ourselves and clean the world.
We do not consume more than we need –
greed is our downfall.
We do not eat animals – all creatures are equal.
We stay away from the sea – we will trespass no more.
We work together. We eat together. We live together.
We obey the whales. Long live the whales.

The crowd suddenly *aaaaah*-ed. Cam leant back a little and saw above him the Eden Screen had blinked on. It was filled with blue. Fish now flickered this way, then that. Sun pierced the water in shimmering spears. Like magic, it had become a porthole into the Cetacea Sea.

Applause rippled through the square and Cam knew that somewhere in the ocean blue, a dark shape was emerging. They clapped harder and cheered. He was coming.

Big Blue, the Master Whale.

Cam couldn't see clearly from his position, but he knew it by heart – how the giant appeared from the deep, swimming closer and closer until the grooves along his throat were as big as the plough lines in the fields. So close, it looked as if he might break through the glass and swim right into the crowds. And then stopped and hung there, suspended, gazing out at them with a patient eye.

Cam gritted his teeth. 'This time, Dad, I'm going to find the truth. I promise.'

The sound box buzzed to life and vibrations spread through his skin like a shower of pins. Then a voice flowed out of it, rich and slow like syrup.

'Good morning, Cetacea.'

On a platform to the left of the screen, fifty metres above the stage, a curtain was pulled back to reveal Byron Vos, the greatest whale expert the world had ever known. The founder of Cetacea. The only person on the planet who could talk to whales.

Next to the giant master whale his body looked tiny, but his presence was huge; he always drew everyone's attention.

Byron raised his arms to the sky and the crowd began to chant.

'Byron! Byron! Byron!'

His voice soothed. 'Everyone, please be still.'

The applause evaporated. Eden Place fell silent. The whale-talker focused, and Cam braced himself.

A groan burst through the noise box and slammed into his body. The sound boomed; it twisted, yawned and throbbed like earache. Cam squeezed his eyes shut against the pain and tried to imagine the whale call wrapping itself around his heart.

'What truth? Tell me!' he yelled, but Big Blue fell silent and Byron's voice took over.

'Big Blue says welcome, citizens of Cetacea . . . Because of your dedication, the seas surrounding your island are abundant with life. Fish have begun to fill the reefs. The waters are awash with nutrients . . . The sea gardens will soon be restored to glory.'

'Yeah!'

Cam turned his head to see who had spoken. Behind him, a boy was standing in the pit, his arms resting on the stage. About the same age, with light brown skin and blond hair, wearing the yellow tunic of the sand workers. The boy was smiling right at him. Cam wondered why, but he couldn't be distracted, not now. He couldn't miss a thing. He turned back to face the noise box.

Big Blue continued his sermon with wide, hollow bleats that strummed Cam's throat and shook his bones. But as the call faded and Byron began his translation, Cam was left with nothing but a churning stomach.

'You are making progress, but you are yet to rid the oceans . . . of waste created by thousands of years . . . of human neglect. Look after the Earth and the Earth will look after you.'

Look after the Earth and the Earth will look after you. Those were always the final words. So, just like that, it was over. The shortest sermon in years.

A sob escaped Cam's chest as he looked up and saw the blurred image of Big Blue drifting like a giant monolith into the steely distance. The Cetacea Sea faded too, along with Cam's hope that this time would be different. He wanted to slink away and scream with frustration, but the session hadn't finished – not until Byron said so.

The whale-talker's upper half now filled the screen. His linen top and long sandy hair fluttered in the thin breeze and his hands were positioned in front of his chest, wrists pressed together and palms apart.

'Adopt the whale tail,' he prompted.

Everyone placed their hands in the whale-tail position for their silent promise to reject the dirty past and live for a clean future under the guidance and laws of the whales. Cam usually loved this part. But today he was agitated. His body was still shaking from the noise, and his mind was maddened. The truth – whatever the truth was – had evaded him again. He felt his father slipping further away.

'Thank you, all.' Byron Vos's bright green eyes seemed to look at each and every one of them in the square. 'Let us remind ourselves. Who caused the floods?'

'*We caused the floods!*'

'What must we do?'

'*Clean up the Earth!*'

'Who saved our souls?'

'*The whales saved our souls.*'

'The whales are our masters. Long live the whale!'

'*Long live the whale. Long live the whale.*'

Chapter 2
The Boy

It was over. The image of Byron Vos dissolved, the screen went blank and the magic vanished. The crowds filtered back through the myriad lanes, taking their time to gossip, delaying their return to work as long as they could.

Cam didn't usually try to avoid work – he liked his work, he *believed* in it. He tried to be the first in and the last out. But with his mind and body aching, he moved slowly towards the kelp district.

Suddenly, someone crashed against his shoulder and he was knocked off-balance. He stumbled sideways. He was shoved again, and again, until he was on the ground.

'Hopelessly devoted to Blue,' a voice teased. 'He doesn't even know you exist, loser.'

It was Matteo. Others behind him echoed like lyrebirds. *Loser. Loser.*

The bullying never normally affected Cam – his dad's words had always been like an invisible talisman, keeping his chin up, keeping him strong; he didn't need to be liked when there were bigger things to think about. But now, the words unexpectedly stung.

Matteo pulled a face as the gang passed by. 'If whales are so great, why don't you ever look as if you're having fun, Cam?'

Cam waited for them to turn the corner before he got up. He watched Matteo's long hair bounce out of sight and wondered, not for the first time, what had gone so wrong between them. A sense of loneliness swelled inside his chest.

Then, a scuff of shoes on the stone caught Cam's attention. There was a figure watching him from the shade of a wall. Wide face and straw-blond hair. It was the boy in the yellow tunic.

'Are you following me?'

The boy stepped forward and grinned. 'Yeah, it looks like I am.'

'Why?'

He shrugged. 'Just curious. Never seen anyone get on stage during a sermon before. Hey, Big Blue's voice was awesome, wasn't it? Sounded like it was coming from the centre of the Earth.'

'Yeah, I suppose it did . . . Who *are* you?'

'Banjo.'

'Like the instrument?'

'Like the frog. You?'

Cam tried not to laugh at the idea of being named after a frog. 'I'm Cam.'

'As in camouflage?'

'No.' Cam laughed out loud. 'Just Cam.'

'Why did those boys say mean things to you?' Banjo rubbed his eyes, and Cam noticed they were red, typical of sand workers, who squinted twelve hours a day, separating plastic and metal particles from the grains.

'It's a long story.'

'I got time.' The boy's smile was wide, crammed with white teeth. His brown eyes, though sore, sparkled.

'I haven't. I've got to get back to work.'

'You're kelp,' Banjo said, pointing at Cam's green tunic. 'Whale work, like me.'

'Yeah. Look, I've got to go. I'm late.'

'Okay, see you around.'

'See you.'

Cam ran to his kelp barn as fast as he could. He was the last one in, but the manager pretended not to notice. Mr Freedman was rarely angry. He hardly ever raised his voice, and Cam had never seen him use the strap, not like some managers. Nevertheless, Cam set to work, determined but numb, hardly feeling the sting of sea water on his cracked hands.

Washing kelp was tough; all day, every day they scrubbed the long weed ribbons to dislodge the microscopic plastics, so they could be replanted in the clean sea gardens. It was 'whale work' – a planet-protecting job, like sand sorting. But where the sand sorters had sore eyes, the kelp cleaners had gnarled hands. The salt water damaged the skin, and workers often snagged each other with their hard bristle brushes.

Cam's workstation was opposite Dean. The bully's brush instantly caught his hand, knocking the tender scabs.

'I saw you sitting in front of the noise box,' Dean said. 'That's just weird. What were you doing?'

Cam gave him a hard stare, trying to grab on to that inner strength he once had, muster some confidence.

'Hey? I asked you a question, weed-brain.'

Dean's brush smashed into Cam's knuckles again, ripping back the skin like paperbark. Cam chewed the inside of his mouth to stop himself crying out. He couldn't let Dean win.

There'd be another sermon. Another chance. Stay strong.

'Why?' Dean persisted.

'None of your business.' Cam flicked his brush across the table, nicking Dean's wrist.

Dean yelped and drew his fist to his mouth and sucked the scratches. 'You're a little freak,' he hissed. 'You're crazy.'

Cam wondered if the bullies might back off if they understood *why* he was obsessed with Big Blue. But he'd tried to talk to Matteo about it, hadn't he, and Matteo had stuck his fingers in his ears and told Cam to shut his mouth. Since then Cam hadn't told a soul, and he sure as tides wasn't going to tell a moron like Dean. He'd rather put up with the insults and the cuts. One day, when he found what he was looking for, everything would be better.

When their shift finished, the other barn kids ran out honking like geese. Cam hung back and crawled under the tables to collect the seaweed everyone had dropped in their hurry to get to mid meal. He did it to help Mr Freedman, and to put some distance between himself and the gang. But Mr Freedman pulled at his tunic.

'Get going, Cam. There's a replanting boat going out later so they'll be here any minute to collect the kelp, and they won't want you in their way. Treat your hands and get to the square, now, before you miss all the food. You know there's never quite enough for a full belly. If you dally any longer, you'll be lucky to get a crumb.'

'But –'

'Go, or I'll have you transferred.'

It was a joke, but Cam didn't want to take a chance on that. On the Eden Screen, he'd watch their lush forests of clean, replanted kelp, providing shelter for sea life and calming choppy seas. Restoring the whales' watery home made him happy. It was a small link between him and Big Blue. Him and his father. He didn't want to work anywhere else. And Mr Freedman was right – he had to get a move on. There was never enough food to feel fully satisfied; people taking more than their share was the cause of most fights.

He washed his cuts and ran to Eden Place. The clatter of metal pans rang through the alleys, and with every corner he turned, the chitter-chatter grew louder, like flocking cockatoos. In the square, people sat either side of colourful cloth runners, a hundred in every row, as the canteen crew weaved through them like hummingbirds in their bright blue tunics. They had a system. Everyone had a system. Cetacea ran on systems and rules.

Cam looked about desperately for a place to sit.

'Cam, over here!'

An arm was beckoning. It belonged to Lindy. She was probably the kindest of all the kids in his kelp barn, but he was wary of her – she camouflaged herself like an octopus so as not to stand out. Matteo had done that too, changed to fit in with a new gang. He never used to be such a bully.

Cam walked towards Lindy and immediately regretted it when he saw the others all sitting alongside her, attacking the food like wild dingoes. Taking more than their share.

Pip was whining. 'Mum says the whales will drown me in bad luck.'

'We'll just sneak away for a few hours,' Dean said. 'Freedman probably won't even miss us.'

'If he does, we might get transferred to Harvest or Hygiene.'

'Who cares? Whale work is rubbish.'

'No, it's not.' The moment Cam said it, he knew he shouldn't have.

Matteo laughed. 'Look who it is. Cam Solomon. Are

you called that because you're always on your own, Solo Man?' He was pleased with his joke.

'Matt,' Lindy warned. 'Why *are* you so obsessed, Cam?' Her voice was sweet, but Cam could see she had changed colour again.

'You know – look after the Earth and the Earth will look after you,' he muttered.

'Yeah, because your mum won't.' Pip smirked at the others. 'She looks ready for the grape fields.'

They all choked with laughter, apart from Matteo. Cam saw him shift uncomfortably. Lindy patted the ground next to her, telling him to sit. But no, they'd gone too far this time. His dad was gone, and yes, his mother had begun to disappear too, right in front of his eyes. Every day she faded a little bit, and some days she was barely more than a ghost. But to say that she was ready for the grape fields, ready to be put in the ground? That was just nasty, and none of those kids had lost a parent. They didn't understand grief.

Cam's eyes watered as he gazed across the square, looking for somewhere else to sit, trying to forget that once upon a time David Solomon would have been sitting here too, saving a space for his son.

'Hey! Hey, Cam!'

There was a flash of yellow and Cam saw a nimble figure jumping towards him in wallaby hops. Banjo. The boy landed at his feet and quickly pushed something into his hands – a banana leaf stuffed with curry and rice.

'Here – I saw you looking like a stranded turtle,' Banjo said. 'And food's disappearing fast.'

Cam opened his mouth to talk, but his stomach spoke first with a roar of hunger. Banjo threw his head back and laughed, and Dean and Matteo looked up. Banjo saw Cam's unease.

'Them again, hey? Let's get out of here. Follow me.'

'But . . .' Cam nodded to the food parcel. Somehow, the community always found out about those who disobeyed the 'eat together' rule. For them, and their neighbours either side, it meant a full day with no food. Sometimes two.

'Trust me, no one saw the food. I'm quick as a tiger beetle. And you're slow as a slug. Come on!'

They scurried round the runners and nipped down a side street. Cam scoffed the contents of the banana leaf as they ran, digging his fingers deep into the stew and pushing handfuls into his mouth. When he'd finished, Banjo took the leaf and threw it in the gutter.

'You don't want to be carrying that around.'

'Why?'

'It's evidence, dopey. You don't want a community helper knocking on your door. You're skinny enough, and your neighbours'll hate you.'

'Where are we going now?'

'Terra Beach. You've got food on your face.'

Chapter 3

The Pontoon

Cam and Banjo ran in single file through the tight lanes and out into the southern scrublands. Ahead of them, the white dunes shivered in the heat. When the rocks gave way to dust and sand, they slipped off their shoes and leapt like lizards across the scorching ground to the top of the closest dune.

Below them, the bright blue of Terra Beach glittered like broken glass: a basin of sea water, brought in from the coast through underground pipes, surrounded by a band of blinding sand. Older grown-ups whispered that Terra Beach was the next best thing to being on the coast. For those born on Cetacea, it was all they knew. The whales said the ocean was not for humans any more.

A group of young farm workers sped past them, tumbling down the sand hill and hitting the water at the bottom with a sigh. They were grabbing a few minutes of relief before another six-hour shift, toiling in the red earth. *Slave labour,* Cam had heard his dad say once. He didn't know what that meant.

'Come on, then!' Cam said. 'Last one to the bottom's a rotten skink.'

They skidded down the slope, their out-of-control legs pulling them haphazardly towards Main Beach, where sensible beachgoers huddled beneath straw umbrellas and the foolish roasted like carrots under the hot sun. The air was filled with the sweet smell of sunscreen, made with oils of walnut and coconut.

'There's an umbrella free over there,' Cam said, pointing.

Banjo tugged him along. 'Nah, let's get away from the crowds. Let's keep going.'

They followed the shoreline towards the far dunes, the air around them rippling in the heat, the sand sizzling hot under their feet.

'Can't go any further,' Cam panted.

'Then we'll stop here,' Banjo said. 'Last one in the water's a dozy wombat.'

They whipped off their tunics and sprinted into the sun-warmed water. It wasn't refreshing but it soothed their dry skin. Banjo dived under in a perfect arc, breaking the surface with barely a ripple, and through the crystal water, Cam saw him flipping along the sandy bottom. Then he shot up again, shaking his head and spraying water like a wet dog.

Cam retaliated, slamming the water with his forearm and sending a wave crashing over Banjo's head. They fought until their eyes stung with salt and their throats were raw with laughing.

Banjo pointed to a pontoon, bobbing way out in the middle of the lake. 'Race you.'

Despite all the swimming lessons he'd had with his dad, Cam found it hard to keep up. Banjo moved through the water as if he'd been born in it. He was also a foot taller than Cam, with limbs as long and flexible as kelp. He was a natural, and he knew it.

'Keep up, mate!' he shouted, and his laugh sounded like a mountain river after rain.

They heaved themselves on to the wooden pontoon and flopped, catching their breath. Out there, so far from land, the people on Main Beach looked like red ants, and the only sound was the plop and smack of the water under the deck. They baked in silence, feeling the salt crystallise on their skin. Above them, the sky stretched forever – a vast shawl of palest blue, as if the sun had bleached away the colour.

The atmosphere was easy – it felt like they had done this a hundred times before – and Cam turned to look at the strange boy who had adopted him. He was about to ask why, when Banjo suddenly spluttered and coughed.

'Damn flies. What are they even doing out here!' He sat up and spat the offending insect on to the deck. It was then Cam noticed the markings on the boy's back. Lines and circles, woven around each other to make a shape that seemed ghostly, yet solid. There, but not there. It was a whale.

Banjo seemed to sense his interest. 'Want to see it? Here, look. It's a humpback.'

He turned fully to show Cam the whale diving down his spine, the tail licking the nape of his neck.

Cam gasped. 'That's amazing.'

'Thought you'd like it,' Banjo said, twisting to give him a smile. 'Makes me even more glad I chose you.'

'For what?'

'To be my friend, stupid. I'm usually a bit picky, but I reckon you're alright.'

'Thanks.' Cam smiled awkwardly, but he couldn't take his eyes off Banjo's picture. He'd never seen anything like it. It drew him like a spell.

'Why is it made with dots?'

Banjo spun back to face Cam and fixed him with his dark, round eyes. 'It's Dreamtime art. The art of the First Nations, the Aboriginal people. That's why it's on my back – so my ancestors are behind me all the time.'

Cam's tongue froze. It wasn't allowed. Talking of old cultures and the Long Ago. *The past destroys the future.* The whales had told them. It was in the Birth of Cetacea rule book, the one they were taught along with nursery rhymes. He knew it word for word.

'I know what you're thinking. It's forbidden.'

'It *is* forbidden,' Cam said seriously. 'You just . . . shouldn't.'

'No one can hear us out here.' Banjo drummed the pontoon with his palms. 'Look, can I tell you something?'

Cam nodded. 'Yeah, alright. Quietly, though.'

Banjo's voice dropped to a whisper. 'I've got adoptive parents now. My real mum and dad got sick and died a few years back. When I was little, they whispered stories about the Dreamtime to me in my bed. It's all I have left of them. I reckon I should be allowed to keep that.'

'I understand,' Cam said, thinking of how he kept his own father's words so close. 'What's the Dreamtime?'

'It's like all of creation and life – a hole that stretches in every direction, filled with memories of the past, present and future. *Everywhen*, that's how my mum described it. Everywhere, throughout all of time. Everywhen.' Banjo rubbed the salt off his arms. 'Mind you, the First Nations people never called it Dreamtime. It's how white man tried to explain it. Doesn't really work. Can't put all of existence in one word like that, really.'

'But what's that got to do with a whale?'

'The Darkinjung people – that's my ancestors – well, they believe that the sky father, Baiyami created all things that give us life. Toorongong the Whale was one of his special creatures that helped make the Earth. Before it went to live in the sea, it spread togetherness and connections between family and friends across the land. It's how the world as we know it began.'

Dreamtime, whales and Everywhen. The words were like fireworks in his brain, but Cam was supposed to be following Big Blue and that meant obeying his rules. He could listen to Banjo, but he couldn't take part, couldn't encourage it.

Banjo noticed his silence and smiled sadly. 'Why don't you tell me about you, instead?'

'What do you want to know?'

'Why you were sitting in front of the noise box like a dopey possum?'

'Just seeing what it was like.'

Banjo clicked his tongue and shook his head. 'Nah, it's got to be more than that. I came to have a listen and it nearly took my ears off.' He waggled a finger inside his left ear. 'But you don't have to tell me if you don't want to.'

Cam looked at Banjo. His eyes were kind and his smile was warm. He didn't seem like the sort who'd take a secret and shred it up in front of you. Besides, the boy had given him information that Cam could've taken straight to the community leaders, but Banjo had trusted him; maybe he should trust back. That's how you started making friends, wasn't it?

Cam nodded. 'Alright, I'll tell you.' After the failure of the day, the story felt sore as it climbed from his heart to his mouth. 'Two years ago, my father vanished. Before he disappeared, he told me to follow Big Blue and find the truth. Since then, I've tried to understand what he meant. I've watched the sermons so hard, I could tell you everything about that whale. Twenty-six barnacles.

Eighty-six grooves. Two blowholes. This time, I thought I'd try listening instead.'

'And?'

'Nothing.'

'What is this truth about?'

'I don't know.'

'Hard to know what you're looking for if you don't know what you're looking for,' Banjo said. 'Where did your dad go?'

'Nobody knows. My mother says he's with the whales.'

Banjo blinked and smiled sadly. 'Toorongong might be looking after him, hey?'

They sat in peace until the sun beat them back into the water, where they swam round and round the pontoon, and dived down as far as they could before their ears crackled with the pressure. As they played, Cam's eyes kept returning to Banjo's curious whale – it moved with his muscles and shone in the light, as though it was alive. Something to keep him company even when he was alone.

'Does it ever come off?' Cam asked as they trod water, gulping air.

'Toorongong? Nah, it's a tattoo. It's forever. Do you want one?'

'Maybe,' Cam said cautiously. But he did. He knew it instantly.

'Have you got a shift this afternoon?'

'Not until later. Got some hours off.'

'Want to meet the man who drew it? He's cool.'

'Yeah, alright.'

They swam back to shore and threw on their tunics, which were scratchy and brittle with salt. When they reached Main Beach, it was thick with people. Everyone had come for a dip after mid meal. Matteo was wading in the shallows. As they passed, he looked at them both with a strange expression. Then Dean pounced on his back and he disappeared underwater.

Cam and Banjo shrugged and laughed and then scrambled back up the dunes, clutching at grasses to help them climb. By the time they reached the top, they were hot again. They rolled the tops of their tunics down to let the air reach their skin, and wandered westwards towards the art district. Every now and then, Cam dropped behind to look at Toorongong rippling across Banjo's back. There but not there. Moving but not moving.

'Hey, Banjo, I can't have a tattoo of Toorongong,' he said. 'The Dreamtime story belongs to your people.'

'You have to have something that feels right. You can't rub it out.'

'What shall I get, then?'

'Something will come to you.'

'I didn't know tattooing was a job,' Cam said.

'It's not. Fixing things is his day job. Tattooing is his life work.'

Residential districts were named after the nearby

workstations, like Kelp, Canteen or Garment, but anyone could live there. The art district was different. There was a clay barn in the middle, and the huddle of alleyways around it only attracted the likes of makers, painters and potters. It had a reputation for being shady, as if people who make art might also make trouble.

Cam's mother had always forbidden him to go to the art district. She said he'd get tangled in the streets and lost in its secrets. But shc said a lot of strange things these days. Cam dragged his feet as he absorbed the colours and sounds.

Paintings hung like laundry, drying on lines strung across streets. Pottery mistakes were placed on doorsteps for people to take. There was hammering and scraping inside some of the houses, metalwork and woodwork, the chink of brushes in pots, the hum of people singing. The air was filled with clay dust. It smelled musty, like dry riverbeds.

Banjo prodded him. 'We're here.'

The tattooist's house was different from the others. Art wasn't spilling from open windows like its neighbours'. There were no puddles of colour or buckets of terracotta on the doorstep. There was no whistle or song. Instead, a curtain was drawn across the window and the wooden door was pulled tight shut. In Cetacea, people left doors and windows open to create a through-draught to blow away the stifling heat. This was strange. Unfriendly.

Banjo knocked. 'Arlo, it's me. Banjo.'

A second later, the door opened a fraction and an eyeball pressed against the gap. It rolled left and right, looking at Cam and then at Banjo. Then the door shut again, briefly, before it swung open. A hand beckoned them to hurry in. Banjo stepped into the house as if this was totally normal. Cam followed.

Chapter 4
Arlo Fox

Like most houses, Arlo's was poky. Downstairs there was a storeroom for basics and a tiny living room with a single chair, a desk and large wall shelves, which were stacked with little pots, pens, brushes and needles. Black sketches on white paper were stuck to the wall. They flipped like moth wings as Cam walked past.

'Arlo, this is Cam. Cam, this is Arlo Fox.'

The man was tall and slim with high cheekbones that poked through weathered skin. His hair was scruffy – black with shots of silver – and his grey eyes shone like smooth pebbles. You got to know most faces on Cetacea, but Cam was sure he'd never seen this man.

'Pleased to meet you, Cam.' Arlo Fox held out his hand. It was stained. Ink had seeped into the creases in his skin, like tiny black rivers. Cam shook it.

'He wants a tattoo,' Banjo said. 'Will you give him one?'

'That depends what he wants and why he wants it,' the

man said, putting his hands on his hips. His sleeves rose up a little and Cam noticed colours on the skin beneath.

'What tattoos do you have?' Cam asked politely.

Arlo held out his arms, twisting them one way then the other. On his right arm was a colourful bird, and a date beneath it.

'A parrot,' Cam said.

'Yes. A rosella, to be precise.'

'What's the date for?'

Arlo ignored the question. 'And this one is home,' he said, nodding at his left arm. It was a low building with gum trees in the yard, in browns, greens and reds. A miniature landscape painting on a patch of skin. It didn't look anything like his house, but Cam didn't want to say so.

'And what's that – a wave?' Cam pointed to a tiny black tick in the crook of his wrist.

Arlo pulled his sleeves down and crossed his arms over his chest.

'And you want one, do you?'

Cam nodded. 'I really do.'

'A tattoo has to have meaning. The skin has to beg for it. Anything else is vandalism.' He paused. 'Do you love anything enough for a tattoo?'

'I love whales,' Cam mused.

'Whales,' Arlo said flatly. He rolled his eyes. 'A Cetacea-born that doesn't like whales is like a bird that doesn't like seed. Any whale in particular?'

'Not Toorongong. That belongs to Banjo.'

Cam turned to smile at Banjo, and his eye caught a picture on the wall behind his friend's head. It was a simple sketch. A few slick lines. Arcs and grooves. A whale with an almond-shaped eye, just like Big Blue.

'That one,' Cam said.

Arlo followed Cam's gaze and his face hardened. 'That one's taken.'

'What do you mean?'

'I said, it's taken. You can keep the picture if you like. Stick it on your wall.'

Cam's heart dropped. He didn't want it on a wall, flat and lifeless like the snakeskins the little kids traded. And Arlo must have been a magician, because his skin begged for it. Suddenly, strangely. He remembered the loneliness in his chest, and how it had felt, just for a while, as if he'd been abandoned. If he had that on his skin, he would carry it everywhere, the bond between him and Big Blue and his father.

He stared at the image and drank it in. The room was silent.

Arlo's voice was kind. 'You think you've made a connection, but it's just a picture.'

'It's not just a picture,' Cam said. 'It's . . . it's . . . never mind.'

'Alright, then. Why don't you convince me?'

Banjo mouthed, 'Tell him'. The man's gaze held steady.

'My father loved Big Blue. He talked about the master

whale all the time. So, it would mean a lot.'

'Cam's dad isn't here any more,' Banjo explained.

Arlo tutted. 'I'm sorry to hear that. How did he die?'

'I don't know that he died for sure. He just vanished,' Cam said. 'Over two years ago.'

Arlo raised an eyebrow and stood back. 'Cam *Solomon?*'

'How do you know my name?'

The tattooist caught his breath. 'I – I knew your father, that's all.'

In the evenings, his father's friends had come to play cards on their doorstep. Arlo had never been one of them. Cam would've remembered.

'Did you know him well?'

'No, no. Just in passing.' Arlo turned away then spun back again, wearing a smile that was thin but kind. 'I will give you that tattoo, if you'd still like it. Son of David Solomon.'

'Now?'

'If you like.'

Banjo clapped his hands. 'I knew you two would get on! I've got to go. The sand is calling me. I'll catch you soon, Cam. Bye, Arlo.'

Arlo closed the door firmly behind Banjo and pulled out the chair from under the desk. He motioned for Cam to sit down. Cam looked nervously at the collection of inks and the pots of needles, points so sharp they tapered into thin air.

'Will it hurt?'

'Only a bit. Not as much as that mess on your hands.'

Cam looked down at his knuckles; it looked as if he'd been punching fire. He patted his shoulder.

'Here, do you think?'

'Why not here?' Arlo laid his large hand over Cam's chest. Cam wondered if that's what the truth would feel like, when he found it. Lying solid and warm on his heart.

Arlo hopped his chair closer. 'Tell me more about your father and Big Blue.'

Cam hesitated. Most people just didn't understand – including his mother. The way she'd reacted when he told her! She'd drowned him out with the motto – *look after the Earth and the Earth will look after you* – over and over, like she was stuck on a loop. And after what happened with Matteo . . . Over time it became something he thought he should keep to himself. Except with Banjo. But Banjo was different.

Arlo sat back. 'Are you having second thoughts? Why don't you come back another time, when you've thought about it a bit more? It's never a good idea to rush in.'

'No. It's OK.'

It *was* OK, wasn't it? Nothing bad had happened when he told Banjo, and Banjo trusted Arlo . . . Arlo was waiting, his face furrowed with lines, not one of them impatient.

'Dad talked about Big Blue all the time – what he

looked like, how he swam, how he spoke with those moans and wails. He used to say, "Imagine being able to understand any of that!" But I think he *could* understand it, because he went to see Big Blue. The whale was going to tell him something. A secret.'

'What do you think it is?'

'Something big, I reckon. I don't know. I've been trying to work it out for so long and today I felt like giving up. But then I met Banjo and when I saw his tattoo, I knew it was a sign to keep going. I'm going to find out. I'm never giving up.'

'Giving up what, Cam?'

'My promise. To find out more about Big Blue. Maybe that way, I'll find out what happened to Dad, too.'

Arlo nodded and wiped the back of his hand across his eyes.

'How long will the tattoo take?' Cam asked.

'A while.'

Cam settled into the chair and Arlo wiped his chest with a damp cloth.

'Alcohol to sterilise. You don't want to get an infection. If you die, my reputation will be in tatters.'

Cam wasn't sure if Arlo's jokes were making him more or less nervous, but all he had to do was look at the drawing. He could see all the world in that one knowing eye. *What did it know exactly?*

'You must love whales, too,' Cam said. 'You draw them so well.'

'They certainly have meaning.' Arlo reached behind him and dipped a needle in black ink.

'Arlo, can I ask you a question?'

'Not now.'

The first prick was painful, but Arlo worked fast and soon it was nothing more than a scratching sensation. In a funny way, Cam enjoyed it. He liked the peacefulness of Arlo's concentration and his room, with its warm papery smell. It all felt like the beginning of something. Like the wind before a storm, which came from nowhere and sent ripples speeding over the water at Terra Beach.

Half an hour later, Arlo leant back and inclined his head, examining his work. 'I've just done the outline for now – you'll have to come back for the colouring-in another time.' He wiped it with a damp cloth. 'Keep your tunic loose, let the air get to it, not too much sun.'

As Cam pulled up his tunic, Arlo reached for a thick battered notebook.

'What's that?'

'A logbook. I keep a record of all the tattoos and their stories. It's a hobby of mine. So, *Cam Solomon, Kelp worker, Blue Whale* . . . Reason? Looking for the truth?'

'Yes.'

Arlo raised his head to look at Cam. His eyebrows were low, stern. 'How serious are you about all this?'

'I won't rest until I find what Dad wanted me to find. And I won't rest until I find out what happened to him, too.'

Cam saw Arlo's eyes searching his. For what, he didn't know, but it struck Cam that he had never said the word *truth* to Arlo. He'd said *secret*. He narrowed his eyes.

'Arlo, is there anything else you can remember about my father?'

Arlo smiled sadly. 'I'm afraid not.'

'Do you have a bad memory?'

'Something like that.'

Cam looked at the logbook and wondered if his dad was in there – if that's how they knew each other. But Cam recalled his father's skin as being smooth, unblemished, the colour of tea-stained wood all over. If there had been ink, he'd have seen it. But then again, he hadn't noticed any tattoos in the crowds at Eden Place and there were plenty here in the book . . . Perhaps they were on private patches of skin, hidden beneath clothes.

'Why do people come to you for tattoos?'

Arlo wiped the ink from the tip of the needle and held it in the flame of his lamp to sterilise it.

'Many reasons. Sometimes a person loves something so much, they want it to be part of them. Or they want a picture or a symbol that reminds them of the Long Ago.'

'But the law says –'

Arlo slowly raised a finger to his lips. 'The Great Silence is cruel.'

'The Great Silence?'

'People who wanted to settle on Cetacea had to throw away everything relating to their past – all their possessions. As you know, they were not allowed to talk about it either. But memories don't hurt, and sometimes they're all people have.'

'Like Banjo.'

'Yes, like Banjo. Banjo is remembering something, but he's also keeping it alive. Perhaps that's what you're doing, with your whale.'

There was silence as Arlo's words sank in. It was true. He *was* trying to keep his dad alive. That's what his oath was all about. And with the whale drawn across his heart, he'd never give up.

In the distance, the calling horn sounded. Late meal.

'You'd better hop along now.' Arlo held open the door and placed a hand on Cam's shoulder as he stepped through. 'Your father was a good man,' he said.

The door shut with a firm clunk.

Chapter 5
Stealing Bread

Cam pulled on a fresh green tunic. The other one was salt-stained from Terra Beach; he'd have to remember to wash it. When his mother worked in the garment barns, she could sneak home replacements, but now she was in Food Quality he only had two, and there'd be no more until he'd outgrown them.

His mother was slow to get ready, but eventually she appeared dressed in her tunic, which was orange like mango. Cam joked that she was the fruit and he was the leaf. They walked to Eden Place and found a runner with enough space that they could sit next to each other. He ate with her whenever he could, just to make sure she got enough food, but the early meal was easiest as they could go together from home. At other times of the day, it was difficult to find each other in the throng, and sometimes she didn't go at all – she hated the noise.

As they picked at breads and fruit, Cam tried to talk to her, but it was hard. She used to be chattier than a budgerigar, but since David Solomon had vanished she said little and her voice was barely a whisper. She had withered like an un-watered flower.

Cam knew his dad would be sad to see her this way. He had fallen in love with her 'verve', he said. Cam would spy on them together when he was supposed to be in bed. His mother would dress up and twirl in colourful rags she'd brought home from the garment district; his father would call her his Leading Lady and say how he wished he'd seen her name in lights. Cam didn't know what that meant, but there was no light now.

The calling horn sounded. All eyes turned to the screen.

'Morning, everyone!' Byron's wide smile embraced them all. 'No need to stop eating. Let's have breakfast together.' On the screen, Byron raised a peeled banana and bit into it and slowly blinked his electric-green eyes. 'Today, my team and I have work to do in various parts of the island. We don't want to get in the way of the good work that you do – we all have our systems. So those in the sand and kelp barns will have the day off.' Byron adopted the whale-tail position. 'Long live the whale!'

'Long live the whale!'

Eden Place immediately filled with discussions so loud, Cam wondered if Byron could hear them from his home in the hills. There was an excited babble from those who had unexpected free time, and groans from those who didn't. He saw the sand and kelp children rushing together to make plans.

'What are you going to do with your day?' his mother asked, reaching out to him. Cam helped her to her feet.

'We could take a walk? Your shift doesn't start for another few hours.'

She shook her head. 'No, no . . . it's not a good day.'

Not a good day could mean she was sad again, or anxious. Or sleepy. She slept a lot. The herbalist had given her St John's wort and lavender teas to help her moods, but all they seemed to do was fill the house with meadowy smells.

'OK, Mumma,' Cam said. 'Do you want help getting home?'

She shooed him away. 'I'll be fine. Go and enjoy yourself.'

She walked away slowly as if her legs were filled with rocks. When Cam was little, she used to dance everywhere. It was embarrassing at the time, but now he'd give anything to see her like that again. *Ready for the grape fields*. His heart thudded painfully.

A day off now stretched ahead of him. What would he do with it? Sit and wait for the Eden Screen to come on, he supposed. Every hour, for ten or fifteen minutes, it showed the reefs and seas round Cetacea. Just short bursts of activity to remind the islanders what they were working their fingers to the bone for – all the life that they were bringing back from the edge of oblivion after the dirty past. Sometimes the screen would show lobsters, other times cuttlefish. Bigger creatures like dolphins and rays, if they were lucky. Occasionally it would show the depths, with its sharks and whales. Shapes gliding in the dark blue.

Cam never understood how they got Big Blue and his beautiful sea on to the Eden Screen. His dad had said it was Long Ago technology, like the noise box and the microphone; things only Byron was allowed to use. What did technology even mean? Cam had persisted, but his father hushed him when he did and said it was too hard to explain. *Just accept, Cam, it's easier.*

But *he* hadn't accepted. He'd gone in search of something. And Cam would, too.

'Cam!' He heard his name ring against the stone. 'Oi, dopey!'

Banjo was standing on the other side of the square. Cam grinned. That afternoon on the sunny pontoon had felt like a dream. He'd made a new friend he wasn't sure he'd even see again. But it was all real, and Banjo was now springing across the pit towards him on bandy legs.

'Hi, Banjo. Woah!'

Banjo swallowed Cam in a big hug, knocking him off his feet. 'Let's see! Come on, show me the tattoo.' Banjo tugged at his tunic. 'Awesome. *Awesome*. He must really like you.'

'Really? Why?'

'Didn't he tell you? It's his lost brother's tattoo. Hey, want to hang out?'

Cam blinked away the strange significance of the

tattoo and Arlo's parting words, which suddenly returned to him, bubbling like a stew. *A good man.*

'Yeah. Terra Beach?'

'Nah, I'm going to take you to the caves.'

'What caves?'

'Secret caves, over east, towards Shepherds' Country.'

'I didn't know there *were* secret caves.'

'That's because they're secret, dummy!'

Banjo rested his elbow on Cam's shoulder and they walked like old friends, heading north-east, sticking to the cooler streets and leaping over dozy ibis birds with their old-man necks and sickle beaks. Banjo insisted on taking a shortcut through the canteen quarter – a hustle of lanes with kitchens, bakeries and food stores – which was strictly out of bounds. But he seemed to know where he was going. All Cam could do was follow as Banjo weaved through the deafening kitchens, ducking the plumes of hot steam that burst from their doorways and leaping over the boiling trickles that snaked along the gutters.

Banjo motioned for him to slow down. Up ahead, trays of bread rolls were cooling on tables.

'Ready to run?' Banjo winked. He kept low and crept closer. Then he snatched two bread rolls and sprinted, juggling them as they burned his skin.

Cam scrambled after him, heart racing. Cutting through the canteen was bad enough, but stealing food? That was definitely against the law. But he was in the thick of it now, and he sped to keep up with Banjo, who was careering round corners, sending pigeons and mynah birds screeching into the sky.

When they got to the eastern scrubland, they stopped and doubled over, catching their breath and looking around to see if they'd been seen. But the only eyes watching them were those of a large red kangaroo reclining in the grass. Its chest muscles were huge, and it was propped up on one elbow like an off-shift farmer lying on the sand at Terra Beach.

'We'd better watch that fella,' Banjo said. 'Just in case.'

Big Reds could gut you with one swipe – slit you open like you were nothing more than a teddy bear. They rarely caused trouble but, still, the threat was there.

'Give me one of those rolls, then,' Cam said, holding out his hand. He wasn't hungry, but he wanted to get rid of the evidence.

Banjo shook his head. 'They're not for us.'

'What are they for, then?'

'You'll see.'

They walked on a dust track into the low bushlands. Banjo pointed out nature that was important to his Darkinjung ancestors: glossy black cockatoos with dramatic dark crowns; a tiny fairy wren with electric-blue feathers; golden wattle, a plant used for hygiene.

'These things are all alive right now,' he said, 'so we're not breaking any laws talking about them, right?'

He picked up a dry snakeskin – a crinkly, translucent tube. 'Brown snake. One of the worst.'

'So what lives in the caves, then?' Cam asked, trying to hide his nerves. Could it be a wild dingo? There had been talk of recent attacks. Their incisors could tear through flesh like fingernails through mango.

'You'll see. We're nearly there.'

Banjo stopped where the forest became denser and the path petered out into a scrabble of ferns and fallen branches. And from there he walked on, planting each foot firmly on the ground as if he were counting. But instead of counting, he sang.

We are walking the trail
Of Toorongong the whale,
Who leads us day and night.
Pass the gully on the right,
Then twice around the bend
To the big gum, and my friend.

Cam saw the gully below them on the right, and the ground beneath them became soft and damp underfoot from the overflow of an old trickle creek, banked by gums, tree ferns and mountain ash. The way ahead was strewn with more fallen branches and skinny brambles.

Banjo stopped singing and wrapped his arm round the trunk of a big old gum tree. 'This is the one.'

The gum looked just like all the others, but Banjo

swung himself round it and stepped left, up the hill and into the bush. Cam followed. They walked for a couple of minutes through a thicket until they reached an outcrop – a clump of rounded, grey granite boulders. Some towered above them, smooth as bald heads, while others sprouted grasses and gorse bushes.

Banjo stopped, cupped his hands around his mouth, and called. 'Coo-ee.'

It was a flat sound that flicked up at the end like the cry of a whipbird. It cut through the thick eucalyptus air and echoed against the high green canopy.

'Like a whale call,' Banjo said, looking at Cam's perplexed face. 'Travels long distances.' He paused. 'Coo-ee.'

Cam smiled. It *was* like a whale call – singing through the branches, penetrating deep into the forest. When the sound vanished, it was followed by silence. The quiet brought out the rustle and shuffle of echidnas and rodents in the bushes, and Cam wondered whether the next big noise would be dingoes or boar or the wild horses that no one could catch. Banjo's gaze was pinned on the highest rock.

A couple of minutes later, a young voice shouted from somewhere high up. 'Banj, is that you, y'old dog?'

'Yep, it's me. Got someone you should meet.'

The grubby face of a girl, their age, maybe older, appeared over the top. She scrabbled down, leaping from boulder to boulder, confident as a rock wallaby.

'We brought you some bread,' Banjo said. 'Freshly baked.'

'Delish!' The girl jumped down the last few stones and squatted at their feet, taking the bread and tearing into it like an animal. She looked wild, too, with long, straggly dark hair and cheeks covered with rust-stain freckles. 'Who's that?' she said, her mouth still full.

'New friend,' Banjo said. 'His name's Cam.'

She looked at Cam curiously and nodded. Cam looked at her clothes: a kelp green top over a skirt made with blue linen and a red belt. It was a mish-mash of districts.

'What work are you?' he said, thinking he should make conversation.

She rolled her eyes at Banjo and swallowed hard. 'I'm not defined by *work,* y'know. Not like you lot. I'm just Petra.'

'She doesn't have a workplace and she doesn't live in any district,' Banjo explained. 'She lives here.'

'In the bush?' Cam asked.

Petra looked at Banjo. 'Sure we can we trust him?'

Banjo slowly reached across Cam's body and tugged down on the neck of his tunic, revealing the blue whale on his chest. 'Arlo did it. It's *that* one.'

Cam didn't understand, but the girl's huge smile and twinkly eyes made him think whatever it was, it was a good thing.

She whistled high, then low. 'Arlo must think you're

something special,' she said. 'Alright then, if you're a friend of Banjo and Arlo, you must be alright.' She started climbing back up the rocks.

'Come and see her place,' Banjo said, nudging Cam. 'It's going to blow your mind.'

They climbed up after her, but Petra was fast and sure-footed and left the boys behind, struggling to get up the huge stones. Even Banjo with his bendy limbs had trouble with the smooth surfaces of the giant marbles. Cam fell about laughing as his new friend slid again and again, losing ground instead of gaining it.

'You should've just gone round, y'idiots!' Petra's teasing voice drifted down from further up. 'There's a path, y'know!'

'Following a path? Where's the fun in that?' Banjo shouted back.

Chapter 6
Petra's Caves

The outcrop was embedded into the hill and on the other side of it there wasn't such a drop – just a gentle slope with tracks that wound through scattered rocks and boulders. There was no sign of Petra. Banjo led Cam across a clearing that was sunk into the ground like a giant footprint. On the other side of it was a large square hole. It went deep, straight down into the earth. Its mouth was strengthened with wooden slats and there was a metal ladder on one side.

'Old mine,' Banjo said. He sat, legs dangling down, then flipped himself over and began to descend. 'It's a bit dark, but your eyes'll get used it.'

His figure melted into the gloom and Cam climbed after him, slowly, down, down, the outside light fading like a fall into sleep. When he reached the bottom of the hole, it was pitch black. He blinked and blew on his hands, which were sore from gripping the rusty old ladder.

'Banjo?'

Nothing.

'Banjo!'

Then he heard singing. Petra's voice, like a chime.

In the middle of the dark
On the left we pass a spark;
On the right, we pass two more.
Turn left and follow the floor.
Turn right and crouch down low.
To the very end we go.

Cam felt the space around him. The nothingness beyond his outstretched arms told him there was a horizontal tunnel ahead. With his back to the wall, he edged along it sideways, like the crabs that made it through the pipes to Terra Beach. He followed the sound of the voices ahead, ignoring the breaks in the wall, which led to dark caverns on either side of the main tunnel. He passed one on his left that was full of tiny blinking stars. He stopped. *The song.* He listened carefully as Petra repeated it from somewhere deep inside the caves.

In the middle of the dark
On the left we pass a spark;
On the right, we pass two more.
Turn left and follow the floor.
Turn right and crouch down low.
To the very end we go.

They were directions! He shuffled forward, passing more sparkling caves – one, two, then he turned left, right and ducked as the song said to, down the final tunnel. At the end of it, he was relieved to see Banjo and Petra, sitting together in the dull light of an olive oil lamp.

'He made it!' Banjo shouted.

'Y'passed the first test,' Petra said.

'What test?'

'The mapping song.'

'Did you see the glow-worms?' Banjo asked excitedly. 'When I first saw those, I freaked out. P told me they're flies with fire in their bums.'

'Not fire, Banj.' Petra laughed. 'It's a chemical or something, Arlo said. Anyway, you're here. Sit down, Cam.'

Cam sat, noticing how Petra had created a comfortable space with pillows, blankets and cushions made from old tunics. There were pieces of paper pinned to the walls with twigs. It reminded Cam of Arlo's wall of sketches, but Petra's drawings were of birds, buildings – strange, tall things. And they were so good. Better than any drawings he'd ever seen before.

Banjo took Cam's hand and squeezed it tightly. 'Go on, Cam, tell Petra your secret.'

'What? Why?'

'Because you have to trust her with something now. She's let you into her house. You have to give back.'

'Wait, you actually live *down here*?'

Petra rolled on to her back and kicked her legs in the air before swinging herself upright again. 'The look on your face! Only Banjo and Arlo know. And you. *You* know.'

'Doesn't your family miss you?'

'Nope. They died in a farming accident a few years ago, and I got put with some neighbours. I ran away.'

'What was wrong with them?'

'They properly believed in punishing themselves for the Old World's mistakes. No singing, no dancing, no laughing. I felt like my head was being crushed.' She screwed up her face as if she was in pain. 'But it's OK, I'm free now.'

'How do you get food?'

'I steal it.'

Cam whistled and looked at Banjo with wide eyes. It was bad enough breaking a Birth of Cetacea law once. But to do it every day? There was enough on the island for everyone, but only so long as everyone stuck to the rules. If everyone worked to the system, the system worked for everyone.

'So, enough about me, Cam. What about you?' Petra patted him on the arm. 'What's this big secret y'got?'

'It's not really a secret – I seem to be telling everyone recently.'

'Just me and Arlo,' Banjo corrected.

'Yes, just you and Arlo. It's about my dad and this whale,' he said, patting his chest. Cam admitted to himself that he was enjoying the attention. He'd been starved of it for so long. He hadn't talked this much in years.

'Go on.'

'My dad vanished two years ago, but before he left, he told me to follow Big Blue and find the truth.'

'Whoah! So, what's the truth?'

'He didn't say. That's kind of the problem.'

Banjo rubbed his hands. 'Maybe it's the answer to the universe. The meaning of life.'

'I thought it might be another island,' Cam suggested. 'What if Cetacea's sinking and we need to find new land?'

'Or perhaps Byron's missing something,' Petra said. 'Some message the whales want to give us about the planet, and he's not translating it right. That's a possibility.'

'But if Byron can't translate it, then how could my dad? He didn't do whale-talk. I'd know.'

'Perhaps he saw something no one else did,' Banjo said.

Cam thought of the times his father had stared at the screen, unblinking, as if he was reading every wrinkle on Big Blue's skin. *What do you think, Cam? Do you really think they're talking to us?*

'What are you going to do about it?' Petra asked.

'I'm going to do what he did. Find Big Blue and discover this truth,' Cam said.

'And we'll help you, won't we, Banj?' Petra said.

'Absolutely. I'm pretty good at moral support, and finding stuff is Petra's speciality,' Banjo said. Cam thought he saw something meaningful pass between them. 'Go on, show him the treasure.'

Petra got up and walked into the gloom behind, returning a moment later with a long, flat wooden box. She placed it next to the lamp and flipped open the lid. It released a musty sweet smell of old leaves. Cam peered inside to see a bundle of small pictures in the bottom. They were so realistic. So lifelike.

'Did you draw these? They're amazing.'

Petra laughed and Banjo pushed her. 'What else would he think?'

'Think about what?' Cam asked, looking from one to the other.

'These aren't drawings. They're *photos*. In the Long Ago, they had machines that snatched real-life moments from the air and put them on to paper. Like a rubbing.'

Cam thought of the crayon rubbings he'd done of snakeskins, stone and bark. You could do that with life, too?

Petra made a frame with her hands and held it in front of Cam's face. 'They could put y'face on paper. Just like that. See?' She rifled through the box and pulled out a picture of a woman, smiling. She had a large floppy hat on her head.

'Who is it?'

'I don't know. Someone from the Long Ago.'

'Why do you have these?'

'They're in the caves. Scattered everywhere. Arlo said that after the last floods, anyone who wanted to make their home on Cetacea had to hand over everything they owned. Photos, books, papers. It was burned and dumped down here. Not everything burned properly though.'

'The Great Silence,' Cam remembered.

'Yeah, the Great Silence. Shocking. Hey, look at this one I found. For Banjo.'

It was a page torn from a book – a photo that showed people with dark brown skin, their bodies decorated in long chalk-white lines. On the other side of the page was a picture he already knew. A painting. He looked at Banjo, his mouth open. 'Toorongong?'

'Arlo copied it from that.' Banjo turned the paper back over. 'And the people on the other side are Aboriginal people.' He tilted his head proudly, inviting his friends to find a likeness.

Petra laughed. 'Sure, I can see the similarity between you and your great-great-great-great-grandmother, Banj!'

'Yeah, well, it's what's in here that counts,' Banjo said huffily, tapping his chest.

Cam felt his head spin. On Cetacea, there were sketchbooks and notepads, of course, and the Birth of Cetacea rule book in every household. But not books with letters written out all in perfect rows; not books with information from the Long Ago. *The dirty past.*

'Are there any more?'

Petra shrugged, casual about the whole thing. 'Ah yeah, there's loads of stuff down here in the tunnels. I go looking when I've got enough oil for my lamp. Most things are burned but I got a few story-books, photograph books, books about birds –'

'Aren't you scared at seeing stuff that was supposed to be destroyed?'

She looked at his confused face. 'I'm scared about *not* seeing stuff, Cam. Life is like a desert. Every way y'look, nothing but the same view. These?' She pointed around her at the papers. 'They're like signposts. They show me which direction the past was in. They make sense of the desert ahead.'

Cam nodded, but he didn't really understand the bit about signposts in the desert. It was almost as confusing as Banjo's talk of Everywhen.

'Ever wondered where the curlews go after summer?' she continued. 'They migrate. It says so in a book I found, called *Avian Flight Paths*.'

'What's migrate?'

'It's when animals go to the other side of the world for food or warmth. If I could migrate I would, just to get off this island.'

'But this is your home,' Cam said.

'The way I see it, it's only a home if you're free to leave it.' Petra's lips formed a pout.

'Show Cam the whales,' Banjo prompted.

She shuffled through the pages in the box and pulled

out a thin glossy sheet of paper, slightly torn. It was a photo of a blue whale underwater, light rippling on his back. Just like Big Blue. Cam's hand shook as he picked it up. *This was all real?* Maybe it was still out there. His dad had once told him that blue whales could live for nearly a hundred years.

'You can keep that, if you like,' Petra said.

'Get the other one, Petra. The amazing one.' Banjo rubbed his hands together. 'Wait until you see this, Cam.'

Petra ran her hands through the pictures like a lucky dip. Cam watched as the photos fell on to the blankets – rubbings of people, places, bridges, things he didn't understand. They could have been pictures from the future, for all he knew about the past . . .

'Aha!' She plucked out a small photo on card.

Banjo made a funny squeal of anticipation as Cam peered at the crumpled image: a white-sand beach with a crystal-blue sea on one side and forests on the other. The coast. The *real* coast. Two enormous lumps glistened like giant wet boulders at the water's edge. But the grooves were unmistakable. These were whales. Whales had *visited land.*

'They came to shore?'

'It looks like it,' Petra said. She looked at Cam, the black centres of her honey-coloured eyes huge in the low light. 'And I've got an idea.'

'She's good at ideas,' Banjo said.

'We know that the whales can come to land, so let's

call them, ask them to come again. *Meet* them.'

'How?'

'We go to the beach.'

'But whales can't get into Terra Beach. They'll never fit down the pipes.'

'No, the *real* beach, silly.'

'What are you talking about? You're crazy!' Cam laughed.

'*Why* shouldn't we be near them? Byron Vos gets near them. He speaks with them. He probably even swims with them. We're all supposed to be equals here on Cetacea, remember?'

Cam felt the tug of responsibility. 'But it's about respecting the whales. Leaving them alone. Admiring them from afar. It's the law *they* made.'

'It will be from afar, unless the whales are having a campfire on the beach. And if they are, we'll say sorry.'

Cam snorted at the image of whales round a campfire. Petra smiled, dimples appearing at the corners of her mouth.

'And if they do come to see us, then it'll be because they want to. We won't be making them. We're not doing anything wrong. Cam, if they come, you can ask about this truth. They might know where y'dad is.'

He wasn't used to this – kids his age trying to include him, make him part of something. He remembered Pip's worried words as Dean persuaded her to skip work. *The whales will drown me in bad luck.* He never thought he'd be in the same position. It felt dangerous but exciting.

'I want to, but . . .'

'Look, I'll do you a deal. We don't go in the water with the whales. Just the water's edge.' She tapped the photo. 'We'll speak to the ocean and ask the whales to come. Wouldn't it be mind-blowing if they did?'

Cam bit his lip. Before he knew what he was doing, he was nodding, and he couldn't stop. 'Alright, alright. How do we do it?'

Petra lifted the lantern so the light glowed on their cheeks. 'We're three misfits. No one notices us when we're here – so they're sure as tides not going to miss us when we're not. We leave when it's dark.'

'When?'

Banjo's eyes gleamed in the light. 'Tonight.'

Chapter 7
The Edge of Cetacea

They ducked beneath windows and scurried round corners like runaways, but they didn't need to. After a full work day, most people were too tired to raise an eyebrow, let alone care what a few children were up to. And if they had announced it to the whole of Eden Place, no one would have believed it. There was a time when Cam wouldn't have believed it, either. But here he was, being drawn by excitement and adventure, and there was another feeling, too. Anticipation. Something was about to happen. Finally.

They headed south to the coast, circumnavigating Terra Beach and the farmlands behind. They tiptoed round the crops of corn, peppers and aubergines and ran between fruit polytunnels that loomed like ghostly scrolls in the dusk. Every noise they made was amplified in the still night air. Their breathing rasped and their laughs cracked loud as thunder. The further they got from the districts, the less it mattered and they started to whoop and whistle, their excitement electric.

It ended abruptly when they hit the sea wall: a giant barrier that penned in the town and its people, keeping human feet from Cetacea's sacred coastal edge. They knew it was there, of course, but they'd never been this close. They had always assumed it would be badly built or crumbling, just like the buildings in the town. They'd imagined loose bricks and easy footholds. Instead, it towered above them, high as a house, smooth as glass.

'What are we going to do?' Petra asked, sounding deflated. 'We can't *float* up it.'

'Wait here.' Banjo ran back into the darkness of the farmlands. While they waited for him to return, Cam paced and Petra jumped at the wall to see how high she could go.

'You should save your energy,' Cam cautioned.

'I *never* run out of energy,' she grunted. 'I'm *made* of energy. See?' She grabbed his hand and squeezed it with excitement, jogging on the spot.

The difference between this and when he was with the kelp barn kids was like comparing pouring rain to stifling sun. This was rain, fresh and free. His skin tingled.

Banjo returned, dragging a huge ladder that was at least four times his height.

'Where did y'get that?' Petra asked.

'Fruit tunnels. They got plants big as tree ferns in there. I guessed they'd need a way to get up them.'

They pulled the ladder upright. It rocked on the

uneven ground and it didn't reach to the top of the wall, but Petra immediately started to climb. With her feet on the highest rung, she jumped, caught the lip of the wall with her fingertips and dragged herself up and on to her stomach. She settled on the top, facing them.

'No looking at the beach until we're all up there, OK?' Banjo said. 'That wouldn't be fair.'

'And how are *we* going to get up there?' Cam said. Petra was taller than both of them. And she was used to climbing tall rocks.

'Watch.'

Banjo took a few steps back then sprinted up the ladder, quick as a huntsman spider. His feet ran on, past the top rung, as if he was weightless. His hands caught the top of the wall, and within seconds he was sitting alongside Petra. He reached down to Cam.

'Climb to the top. I'll pull you the rest of the way. Strong as a Big Red, I am.'

Cam balanced precariously on the top rung of the rickety ladder and reached for his friend's hand. Banjo had ridiculous strength packed into a few lean muscles, and pulled Cam, with Petra helping at the end, up and over the edge. They had done it. They were at the top. And behind them, the ocean waited.

They heard it before they saw it, rumbling like a huge beast shifting in its sleep.

Careful not to fall, they turned. Then, in silent awe, they reached for each other's hands.

Boxed in by grids of streets, work barns, hills and districts, they'd never seen so much empty space. A deep purple canopy began at the horizon and stretched way over their heads, holding a bright three-quarter moon; and below them stirred an inky sea. Shallow, scrolling waves travelled towards them, fizzing as they hit the beach.

'I'm going down,' Banjo said. 'Who's coming?'

Cam looked at the drop on the other side, so high it could break their ankles. But that wasn't the only problem. Something glinted in the moonlight.

'No, wait.' Cam held his friend back with an arm. 'Look.'

They had been so mesmerised by what was ahead, they didn't see that the beach directly below was covered in rolls of thick wire, studded with cruel spikes. Rolls and rolls of it, reaching left and right along the shore as far as they could see.

'We're bound to get cut,' Petra whispered.

A nasty cut could mean death if the herbs didn't work. And how would they explain their injuries to the herbalist? Those spikes would stick deep. Nothing else in Cetacea would create such a puncture. It was hopeless.

'Argh!' Petra roared with the unfairness of it all. 'We were so close!'

'We still are,' Cam said. 'I never thought I'd be this close to the sea. We haven't failed. Just look!'

'He's right, P. Let's just sit here a while and watch,' Banjo said. 'There's not a lot else we can do.'

Petra blew a sad raspberry. Eventually she said, 'What do you think's going on down there?'

No one replied, but Cam pictured a water paradise at night, where the tropical fish slipped in and out of the corals and somewhere deeper, further out, were whales. Hundreds, maybe. Perhaps even Big Blue himself. His heart ached as if it had been opened up and exposed to the night air.

'Why don't you say something to the whales?' Banjo whispered.

Petra patted his back. 'Yeah, go on, Cam. That's what we're here for.'

'Alright.' Cam got to his feet. His friends wrapped their hands around his ankles to keep him secure. He didn't know what to say. Perhaps he didn't need many words. After all, his dad had only given him a few. 'Um . . . I'm Cam Solomon,' he called. 'Big Blue, I follow you. I wash your kelp and I listen to your sermons. Everything I do is for the whales and the sea. Please look after David Solomon, my father. And please show me the truth he was looking for.'

A wave scratched at the beach. Cam looked at the sand, bluish in the moonlight, smooth and cool. But there was no message there. There was no change in the air, either, nor in the ebb and flow of the sea.

'Let's wait and see if something happens,' Banjo said. 'It might take time.'

They stayed for they didn't know how long – time seemed irrelevant, tricked away from them by the rhythm of the waves. They scanned the waters for shapes, every now and then mistaking a wave for a fin, or a slick patch of water for a rubbery back. The sky grew darker.

'They're not coming,' Cam said softly.

His friends stood up alongside him and wrapped their arms round his middle. Their warmth felt like a blanket and he didn't want this evening to go cold or end in disappointment. He didn't want it to end at all.

'Let's walk along the wall for a while,' he said boldly. 'If we can't go on the beach, let's follow the wall until it stops, or until we reach the districts. Just to see some more of the ocean. Just for fun. We may as well make the most of it.'

'Yeah, alright,' Banjo agreed.

'I'm in!' Petra said, raising her arm.

They walked the top of the wall towards the west, sighing with the sea breezes. Coastal winds didn't penetrate the district mazes, not like this. Cam stopped and held his arms out either side of him, letting the gusts rip through his clothes, drawing the sharp sea scent into his nostrils.

'Take an air bath!' he said.

The others copied, and they laughed as they inhaled and expelled the air with an 'Aaaaah,' all at the same time. They continued, giggling and whispering and air-bathing, until Cam gave a hard 'Sshhh!'

'What's that?' He pointed north-west.

In the distance, a string of white lights stretched out

to sea like a glowing antenna, their reflections smudged on the water. It didn't look like any part of Cetacea they recognised.

'That's got to be beyond the Ranges,' Cam said. 'It has to be. Is it land?'

'I don't know, but those lights are too bright for oil lamps,' Petra said.

'They look like stars that fell into the sea,' Banjo said.

'Spaceships!' Petra gasped.

Banjo tapped Cam's shoulder. 'Maybe it's the sand boats. Or maybe the kelp boats, replanting. Do you think, Cam?'

On unsettled sea, the boats would bob. And there wouldn't be so many. Not in a line like that. 'No, they're not kelp boats.'

'There's got to be an explanation.' Banjo sighed.

'There is one explanation,' Cam said quietly. 'It's a secret we're not supposed to see.'

A wind sliced through them, making them wobble and there was a sudden change in the air.

'We should go.' Petra's voice was shaky. 'We can't risk getting caught. You'll be strapped or sent to the fields, and I'll be . . . We just can't get caught, that's all.'

Cam looked out at the dark ocean and felt his heart implode. He didn't want go back into the suffocating alleyways of town. He wanted to stay on the edge of the whales' world. On the edge of truth.

'My dad might be somewhere out there,' he whispered.

Banjo placed a hand on his back. 'Somewhere, yeah.'

'If he is, then he's free, isn't he?' Petra said, although it wasn't a question. There was a longing in her voice, as if the world beckoned.

Without warning, Banjo leapt to his right, off the wall, and dropped into the darkness.

Petra and Cam held on to each other. 'Banj?'

There was a splutter. 'Down here. Compost heap. Smells like roo poo, but it's a soft landing.'

'Kangaroo poo it is, then!' Petra laughed.

Cam held her hand and they jumped, plummeting into the rotting organic matter on the other side. They clambered out, moaning with disgust and picking compost from their cheeks.

'I can't go back to the caves stinking like this,' Petra grumbled. 'It'll suffocate me, or attract animals or something.'

'We can swim it off at Terra Beach.'

Banjo slapped Cam's shoulder affectionately. 'He might be small, but he's got big brains.'

'Brilliant idea,' Petra said. 'Night swimming!'

They walked back through the crop fields, grabbing and peeling heads of maize and crunching on the sweet kernels. Even Cam. It was as if, in this moment, the rules didn't apply to them. They felt blessed and invincible. They had dared to approach the world's most magnificent creatures, and although the whales hadn't come to shore, they hadn't been angry, either. In fact, the night was so magical, it was almost as if they'd been rewarded for their bravery. They felt it in the cool breeze and the lightness in their hearts and heads.

At Terra Beach they ran into the salty water, still bubbling with excitement. They splashed and laughed in the moonlight, and it felt like madness and happiness rolled into one.

'This whole night has been incredible,' Banjo said, floating on his back.

Petra waded ahead of them, dancing her fingers on the water. 'Arlo told me it would be alright.'

'Arlo knows about this?' Cam struggled to place his feet on the sandy bottom.

'He doesn't know we're here right now. But going to the wall was his suggestion. He said if I could see that there was space outside Cetacea, it might make me less frustrated.'

'Frustrated with what?'

'Rules, fences, cages. Being in one place.'

'How do *you* know Arlo? Do you have a tattoo as well?'

'No!' She laughed. 'He caught me trying to steal food. I ran away with a tureen. Except I ran straight into him and dropped it on his foot. He knew right away I was the missing child. They'd made "missing" leaflets.'

'Oh yeah . . .' Cam now vaguely recalled papers being left out on the runners, people reading and tutting sadly.

'He helped me. To make people give up the hunt

for me, he started a rumour that dingoes had been seen close to town. It worked. They thought I'd been taken.' She clawed her hand and scratched the air and laughed. 'Most adults would have dragged me home, but not Arlo. He's different. He notices everything.' She swam out into the lake and turned to float on her back, wriggling her toes through the surface of the water. 'You can't tell anyone, remember. If they stick me back in that house with those people, I'll go and find a dingo and I'll feed myself to it.'

'Cam won't tell, will you, Cam?' Banjo said.

'Of course not.'

When their fingertips were wrinkly, they pulled themselves on to the sand and lay on their backs, staring up at the sky. The purple had turned to black and the stars had multiplied – sprayed across the sky, some as big as lanterns and others as tiny as the tip of a tattooist's needle.

'Have you noticed how stars always come back to the same place?' Banjo said. 'They stay in the same shapes, too. That's my favourite, there.' He pointed at a cluster, where five stars glowed blue. 'So if they come back to the same place in the same patterns, it means our ancestors will have looked up at exactly the same stars. It's like home.'

One night to connect with the past would be OK, Cam thought. Especially if it made his friend happy. 'Everywhen, Banjo,' he said.

'Yeah, that's right. Everywhen,' Banjo repeated. Cam could feel his smile.

They drifted back to town in the early hours of the morning. It was quiet, apart from the occasional shuffle of possums and potoroos. At Eden Place, they had a group hug that seemed to last forever. Then Petra broke away and ran round and round the square like a bush fly in a bubble.

'What's she doing?' Cam whispered.

'Just being Petra.'

'She's not exactly keeping herself a secret,' Cam said.

'She can't help it. Anyway, there's no one here. Uh oh, here she comes.'

They stifled their laughter as Petra cut diagonally across the square towards them, her dark hair flapping behind her like a bat.

'Cam, Cam,' she panted. 'I don't want you to feel disappointed about not finding the truth.'

'OK!' He laughed.

'If the whales didn't punish us for going to the sea wall, perhaps they were inviting you to look harder.'

'But I have looked,' Cam said. 'The rule book, the sermons . . .'

'So you need to look somewhere else, obviously!' She went back to running round the square.

Banjo patted Cam's back. 'She has ideas, but not *all* of them are great. Probably one in ten. Something like that.'

'No, she's right,' Cam said, suddenly struck by

something. 'I've been looking in the wrong place.'

'Where else is there to look?'

'Tonight, Banjo, we discovered something, didn't we? We don't know *what* those lights are or even *where* they are. We only know about them because we looked in a place we weren't supposed to look.'

Petra zoomed back and flung her arms around them. 'What are you looking so serious about?'

'He's thought of something,' Banjo said. 'Go on, Cam.'

'Maybe Byron Vos knows the truth and he's keeping it from us.'

'Are you going to *ask* him?' Banjo whispered disbelievingly.

'No. If he's hiding something, why would he admit it?' Cam froze as his mind worked through the problem. 'People work up there at Fort Eden, don't they? People clean and cook. If I got a job up there, maybe I could take a look around.'

'Oh my tides, that's a brilliant idea!' Petra gasped.

'And how are you going to get a job? Walk into the Whale Station and ask for one?' Banjo shook his head and chuckled.

'Why not? It's where you go if you want a job swap, isn't it?'

'I love your spirit,' Petra said, patting his cheeks with both hands.

They turned at the sound of footsteps behind them.

A figure stepped back into the shadows and then ran into the darkness of an alley.

'Matteo?' Cam was certain it was him. Right height, long hair.

'Who was that?' Petra said, nervously.

'Just a kid I know. Don't worry. It's dark. He won't know who you are.'

Petra's face relaxed. She took their hands. 'You know what the best thing is about tonight? We have a secret that binds us, and because of that all our secrets are safe. Say it with me: our secrets are safe.'

'Our secrets are safe,' they whispered.

'We'd better get home. Back on shift tomorrow morning, and we've hardly time to sleep.' Banjo yawned.

Before they parted ways, they promised to meet outside Petra's cave in the afternoon.

When he got home, Cam dozed on a cushion in the living room, dreaming of sitting on a pontoon with Banjo, laughing as Petra danced around it, rocking it from side to side like a boat on the waves. Before sleep took him away, he saw a reflection of the stars on the wavy surface of the dark ocean. A pattern of dots and shapes that looked like a giant blue whale.

Chapter 8
How to Be Noticed

Cam stood in a queue outside the small stone building, round the corner from Eden Place. He'd woken up still buzzing with the excitement of the night before and had decided to take action. But in his rush, he hadn't thought things through. What would he say? Would they want to know why he wanted a job swap? He hadn't even asked Mr Freedman if it would be alright. Nerves began to tumble inside him and his skin prickled in the hot morning sun.

The Whale Station was the community hub – a place that held all the residents' documents and files, and where anyone could talk to a community advisor. Most people in line were there to snitch on law-breaking in return for a 'whale gratitude' – usually a basket of fruit – or they were there for job swaps. Doing the same thing for too many years could cause unrest, and people were encouraged to move around. Cam had been cleaning kelp since he was the work-age, seven; he was now thirteen and he'd never worked anywhere else. The humid barns sometimes made him dizzy and his hands wept like blood oranges, but he would never want to do anything but whale work. Until now.

When it was Cam's turn, he shuffled into the building, still unsure of what to say.

'Name, work and reason for visit?' A badge said the advisor's name was Drake.

'Cam Solomon. Kelp. Job swap.'

Drake rifled through a box and pulled out a file, which he opened out on the desk. His eyes widened. 'Cam Solomon, son of David and Daisy.' He nodded slowly. 'Never swapped. If you're unhappy in kelp, I'm sure there won't be a problem getting you transferred. Is there anywhere in particular you had in mind?'

'Yes. I want to get a job with Byron Vos.'

Cam heard Drake's sharp intake of breath. His eyes twinkled with amusement and he clasped his hands in front of him on the desk. Before his hands closed together, Cam thought he saw a mark on Drake's wrist, beneath his bracelet. A black tick like Arlo's.

'That's a very unusual request. Can you tell me why?'

Why? *Why*? Cam had to think fast.

'I want to be a whale-talker.'

'I see.' Drake didn't move, but the corners of his lips twitched.

'Eventually, I want to be a whale-talker,' Cam added, realising how silly it sounded. 'But for now, I'll do anything. I'll clean his house. Anything.'

Drake clicked his tongue. 'I don't want to be the bearer of bad news, but there is no such thing as a job swap when it comes to working for Mr Vos. He hand-picks all his workers.'

'Oh.' Cam's shoulders dropped in disappointment. 'How does he pick them?'

'I'm not really sure,' Drake said brightly, sitting back in his chair. 'I think he *notices* people. Yes, I suppose he just has to notice you. I'm sorry I can't be of more help.' His eyes fell on Cam's knuckles. 'Goodness, they look bad. Go to the herbalist right away. You don't want an infection. Next!'

A woman pushed in front to talk about her noisy neighbours and Cam left the Whale Station, instantly forgetting about knuckles and herbs. The community advisor hadn't handed it to him on a banana leaf, but it wasn't impossible. He just had to be noticed. And that's what he was going to do. He was going to get inside Fort Eden, home of Byron Vos. He was going to uncover the truth.

By the time he got back to the kelp barns, he was late – so late he deserved to be strapped. He even exposed the backs of his knees for the whip, but Mr Freedman shooed him away. Cam hoped that his punishment wouldn't come in a different form, such as bad luck sent by the whales. But his father had always told him not to believe those superstitions. *Whales can't see what's going on when their eyes are underwater, can they?*

Although they had come on to land. Cam wished he could tell his father that. But perhaps he already knew. He knew *something*.

'Cam, Cam, Cam.' Dean repeated his name over and over until it got annoying. 'Cam, Cam, Cam.'

'What, Dean?'

'You're a freak.'

Cam stopped and looked the boy in the eye. 'Dean, why are you so obsessed with me?'

Dean's cheeks turned purple. Cam continued scrubbing, trying to suppress a triumphant smile; his confidence seemed to be back! With the visit to the beach, his new friends, and now a plan to get to the truth . . . It made him feel reignited. And the talisman of strength had a shape: a whale on his chest.

He worked as hard as he could to make up for lost time, and after the wild excitement of the night before, the monotonous scrubbing felt soothing and familiar. It suited his lack of sleep. The rhythm was like the roll of the waves, and now that he'd seen the sea with his own eyes, he felt an even stronger connection to the kelp forests he was cleaning.

When the mid meal horn sounded, kelp workers threw down their scrubbing brushes and rushed for the exit, and Cam didn't hold back. He couldn't wait to tell Banjo about Drake and the Whale Station, and if he got to Eden Place fast enough, they could eat and walk to the caves together.

'Cam, wait a minute, will you?'

Cam closed his eyes and gritted his teeth, but he couldn't show his annoyance. Mr Freedman wasn't only the manager, he had also been one of his dad's friends. Since the disappearance, he'd been easy on him.

'Yes, Mr Freedman.'

'That table's got wobbly and I need to tighten the screws. If you could just help me turn the thing over?'

'Of course, Mr Freedman.' Cam cleared the kelp from the tabletop and then helped upend the table on to the floor. Mr Freedman got down to his knees and twisted the screws tight.

'How are you doing, Cam?' he grunted, his arms turning and tensing.

'I'm OK, thanks.'

'Your mum?'

'I don't know. She doesn't say much any more.'

'It's tough on you both. If you ever want to talk about it, I'm here. You know how much I loved your father.'

Curious, Cam looked for tattoos as the man worked, but his brown arms bore only freckles and moles. 'Where do you think my dad went, Mr Freedman?'

'I don't know, Cam. All I know is that he was last seen heading up to the Ranges. Now,' – his voice dropped to a whisper – 'if you ever need some time off, just ask me.' He took Cam in a quick hug before pushing him away. 'Go on, be gone.'

Eden Place was already bulging with people and noise.

Cam walked the runners, up and down, but looking for a friend was like trying to find a needle in a haystack when the square was this full, with people milling around and squabbles breaking out over food and spaces. When there was no sign of Banjo, Cam took the nearest free spot he could find, sitting alongside people he didn't know. The meal was flatbreads and aubergine stew. He shovelled it in, thinking of how Petra never got to eat like this. She never had a guaranteed meal, yet she had all that energy.

He looked around him: his neighbours either side were busy chatting, and the man sitting opposite had eyes that were white and smoky with blindness. Unseen, Cam selected the biggest flatbread from the basket and filled the centre with stew. He rolled it, folded the ends and tied everything in place with fibre shreds from a banana leaf. He rested the parcel like a baby in the crook of his arm and covered it with a fold of his tunic.

He left Eden Place and headed east, skirting below the canteen district. It took longer, but he couldn't risk meeting an angry chef. From the eastern scrubland, he took the dust path into the bush, noting glossy black cockatoos and kookaburras, and the red flash of a king parrot.

When the overgrown path started a steep ascent into the bush, he realised he was in unfamiliar territory – he'd come too far. He didn't remember passing the big gum, but then again, they all looked the same. How was he supposed to know? Getting lost in the bush was stupid – you could turn in circles for days and die of thirst. They'd been taught since kindergarten not to go adventuring there. He should turn back and go home. But he didn't want to. He wanted to see his new friends.

Cam laid the flatbread carefully on the ground in front of him then cupped his hands around his mouth. He hoped it would come out right. Low-high. A whipbird. A whale call.

'Coo-ee. Coo-ee.'

His cry melted into the forest. He waited and waited, laughed at by a kookaburra somewhere high in the gums, his skin prickling at the thought of being sniffed out by boar or dingoes. Then out of nowhere there were thuds on the ground. Cam jumped to the side, fearing a Big Red – upright, they stood taller than a man – but this figure was a lot shorter and a lot less dangerous.

'You frightened me, Banj!'

'That was the idea!' Banjo said with a mischievous smile. He ran forward and grabbed Cam's hand, and Cam only had a second to scoop his food parcel off the ground before they were running into the bush.

'It's a shortcut back. You came too far along the path,' Banjo explained. 'As soon as you get to the undergrowth, you've got to sing the song. It leads you to the gum, and *then* you turn left.'

'A mapping song – of course!' Cam panted.

When they got to the top of the outcrop, Petra was sitting above ground in the crater, eating a flatbread full of stew. Banjo had already thought of it, of course he had. Cam handed her his offering.

'It's a bumper meal!' she said, swallowing hard. 'Thanks, Cam.'

She belched so loudly it startled a cockatoo, and they laughed as it flapped to a tree for safety. Cam paced backwards and forwards, waiting for a moment to speak.

'What's on y'mind?' Petra asked.

'Well, I went to the Whale Station –'

'You didn't!' Petra gasped.

Banjo chuckled and shook his head in amazement. 'I thought there was no way you'd actually . . . Thought it was just sea air,' he added, tapping his head.

'No, I'm deadly serious about finding out what's going on. Anyway, the man said that there's no job swap that would get me into Fort Eden –'

'Knew it.' Banjo sighed.

'But he did say that I just needed to get Mr Vos's attention. He just has to *notice* me.'

'Right, get noticed, I see.' Petra nodded slowly, as if she was chewing the information along with her food.

'You could turn up at Fort Eden with a chicken on your head!' Banjo said. 'You'd have to notice someone with a chicken on their head.'

Cam laughed. 'I'm only going to get noticed once, so it needs to be for the right reason. A chicken hat is not the right reason. No, if I go up to Fort Eden acting like a stupid galah, I'll definitely get turned away.'

'Then make him come to *you*!' Petra cartwheeled across the crater then held her bloated stomach. 'Shouldn't have done that.'

'But how? I'd have to be something really special or interesting to get him to come down to the town just to see me.'

'But you are special and interesting,' Banjo said. 'You love whales.'

'Yeah, but *everyone* loves whales.'

'Not like you. You have a connection. You know everything.'

Not everything, but he and his dad had often talked about the shape of the dorsal fin and the horizontal tail with a vertical swish, and the echo of the whale call, which sounded so empty and yet carried complex messages. Thanks to his dad's obsession with Big Blue, he had spent his childhood wondering about the infinite wisdoms in those incredible brains.

'Even if he did find that interesting, how would I get him to know about me?'

'Shout about how great they are. Or something.' Banjo shrugged.

'That's boring,' Petra said, shaking her head. 'Where's the fun in just talking about whales?'

If whales are so great, why don't you ever look as if you're having fun?

Cam's cheeks flushed as he recalled Matteo's taunts. Whales. Fun. Whales, *having fun*. The answer sailed right into his brain. 'I've got it!'

'Tell!' Banjo sat next to Petra on a rock and clapped his hands impatiently.

'What if I invent a day of fun for everyone – a day off for the whole island?'

'You *invent* a day off for no reason?' Petra repeated flatly. 'I don't think it works that way.'

'Not for no reason,' Cam said. 'For the whales. A day off to celebrate the whales.'

'That's good.' Banjo nodded. 'I like that.'

'A whole day dedicated to whales,' Cam continued. 'Spread the word and everyone will start talking about it. Who doesn't want a day off work?'

'If you cause a commotion, Byron will hear about it alright. Arlo told me that the Whale Station sends a report to Fort Eden every day.' Petra flashed a grin and waggled her eyebrows.

'A festival,' Banjo said. 'A big party. Feasting. Dancing. Singing!'

'Genius.' Petra picked a splinter of bark from her palm. 'Give it a name to make it sound like y'thought about it properly. Make it sound grand. How about: The Whale Day?'

'Whales day,' Banjo suggested. 'Day for the whales.'

'Day *of* the whale.' Cam looked up, his eyes shining. 'Day of the Whale!'

Day of the Whale. They repeated it over and over. It sounded big and brilliant. Important, even.

Petra pointed in the direction of town. 'Now all you have to do is spread the word. Go right now. To Eden Place. Stand on the stage and announce your idea. Make it happen.'

'S-stand on stage?'

Petra laughed at his expression. 'Of course. You're a bit titchy and no one'll see you if y'don't find something to stand on.'

'He could go on my shoulders?' Banjo offered.

'You'd look ridiculous,' Petra said matter-of-factly. 'Take him now, Banj, before he possums out and the truth is lost forever.'

'I'll make sure he does it, P!' Banjo said. 'Let's go!'

As they trekked back towards town, Banjo chatted excitedly, imagining Day of the Whale as if it were something that was really happening. He wanted swimming contests at Terra Beach and extra food – Cam *had* to ask for extra food. Cam listened and laughed along, but he was nervous. Everything was moving so fast.

Better than standing still, he told himself. He'd been standing still for years.

When they got to Eden Place, it was nearly empty. Most people either at work, asleep or down at Terra Beach. There were a few people washing their tunics at the far end.

Banjo pushed him towards the stage. 'Go for it, Cam. I'll clap and cheer. It'll lure people over.'

To the sound of Banjo's whoops and applause, Cam climbed up and cleared his throat.

'People of Cetacea!' he called. His voice barely penetrated the thick air. The people at the fountains didn't look up.

'Louder!' Banjo shouted.

'Listen, everyone! Listen to me. I have an idea. A brilliant idea! A party for all of Cetacea!'

A group of older kelp barn teenagers traipsed across the square, and they chortled like magpies as they bounced their ball, drowning out Cam's pleas for them to stop.

'Please stop and listen. Somebody, please stop.' It was pointless. Cam stood in the hot sun, sweat trickling down his face. 'What's the point, Banj?'

'Try again later?' Banjo suggested.

Then came a call. 'Go on, I'm listening.'

Over Banjo's head, Cam saw Drake, the man from the Whale Station. He was strolling across the square, smiling that amused smile. When he got to the stage, he folded his arms across his chest.

'But –'

'I've walked all this way to hear your idea. Don't disappoint me now.'

Banjo winked and gave Cam a thumbs-up.

'Oh, OK.' Cam straightened. His cheeks burned as he spoke. 'Hello, everyone. I think we should create a festival to show the whales we are happy with how they rule us, and that we feel honoured to help them clean the planet. It will be a day off work for all Cetacea to celebrate the wisdom of the whale.'

Drake clapped. 'Sounds good, young man. But without a huge crowd, Byron won't even know that you're here.'

'He's trying!' Banjo said in Cam's defence.

'I have a suggestion. Do it again at late meal, tonight. Let them get their gossiping out of the way – wait until they're tucking in. Then get up and say what you just said to me. Even better, collect their signatures. Make a petition that I can deliver to Fort Eden. I'll leave everything you need on the stage for you.'

Cam gulped. The thought of facing the whole of Cetacea – all those faces, including Matteo and Dean . . .

'It would get you noticed,' Drake said firmly. 'What's two minutes of feeling nervous, if it gets you closer to the truth?'

What? Cam blinked. 'Wait! What did you mean?'

But Drake was walking away. 'See you later, Cam,' he shouted over his shoulder. 'Take the whale by the tail.'

'Did you hear that?' Cam stared at Banjo. But his friend was trying to kick off a green skink that was slithering across his foot.

'Hear what?'

The truth. Perhaps he'd imagined it. 'Oh, my tides. Banjo, there'll be hundreds, maybe thousands here at late meal.'

'If you need strength, look at me,' Banjo said. 'And if you can't find me in the crowd, talk over their heads. Look up, like you're speaking to the stars.'

Cam stared around him. The square was vast – empty now, but in a few hours' time it would be filled corner to corner with people. He swallowed hard.

Take the whale by the tail.

Chapter 9
Planting the Seed

Cam chewed nervously on a hunk of flatbread. Around him, people were busy discussing the dramas of their shift. Garment workers complained about the new thread and how it snapped too easily, and farmers grumbled about cockatoos attacking the crops. They all moaned about their tiredness, how their bodies ached.

But as their bellies filled, the hubbub began to die down, just as Drake said it would.

From the corner of his eye, Cam saw the Whale Station helper drag a microphone stand to the centre of the stage. Technology from the Long Ago, only used for whale business. He had left piles of papers and pots of pencils there, too. He was going to so much trouble to help. *Why?*

It didn't matter. So long as it worked.

And it was time.

Cam slowly stood. His head went dizzy as he swept his eyes over Eden Place. Movement. Colours. Tunics.

Laughter. He felt like a little fish in a colourful reef, and somewhere out there were sharks. He couldn't see Matteo and the others, but that was probably for the best.

Move. Go now.

Cam pulled himself on to the stage, walked to the centre and placed his hands around the microphone. The noise box rumbled. Heads turned, curious. He coughed, and the sound rasped so loudly that anyone who hadn't noticed him before now snapped their heads round to see what was going on. He froze. Everything felt dreamlike.

Someone shouted, 'Come on!'

People were waiting. And out there, somewhere, his father was waiting too. He breathed in deeply and felt himself fill up again, with strength and purpose.

'Hello, my name is Cam Solomon. I'm here to talk to you about . . .' He paused. Gathered his thoughts. 'Cetacea is a special place. It survived the three floods when everything around it sank. It has given us a place to live and food to eat. And it's all because of the whales.'

He was interrupted by a crack of laughter somewhere in the crowd. Dean. Then he heard a voice he recognised.

'Go on, Cam! Go on!'

Thank you, Banjo.

'I think we need a festival to celebrate the whales. A festival that will take an entire day and night, and everyone in Cetacea – together – will have the day off work.'

A voice shouted, 'We'll get a day off when we die!',

and the crowd erupted in laughter. They were ridiculing him.

Cam looked down and saw Drake, three rows back, a smile at the corner of his lips, and next to him was Arlo. His eyes were trained on Cam like a fish hawk. In the bouncing throng, he was as still as a puddle in summer. Cam quickly pulled his attention back to the crowd.

'I haven't finished!' Cam pleaded.

There were shouts of, 'Let him speak!' and the noise died down again.

'The festival will be called Day of the Whale. And we shall have feasting, dancing and singing. We will show the whales how happy we are to have them as our masters. Please, if you support Day of the Whale, then come to the stage and sign the petition. Thank you.'

In the brief silence that followed, Cam's heart beat so fast he thought he might throw up. Then, some people began to chant, 'Day off, day off, day off!' and the square suddenly became a swirling pot of colour as everyone made their way to the stage. Hundreds of people formed queues down the runners, and the pages at Cam's feet filled up with names. Some people reached up to shake his hand, although what he really wanted to see now was a friendly face.

Arlo and Banjo had disappeared into the crowd. And his mother – was she here? Probably not. Eden Place could be too much for her. She said the walls had eyes and the stones had ears.

Cam remained on the stage, guarding the pieces of paper as if they were precious tickets, until everyone had come and gone. It took over an hour. As Eden Place emptied out, he saw for the first time the carnage that was left after mealtime. Of course, it's what they all did – got up and left, abandoning their waste. That was the system. The canteen teams organised themselves into lines, twenty strong, and marched up and down the square, collecting tureens, cups and leaves. If only there had been such a system in the Long Ago, Cam thought, then the planet wouldn't have become such a mess.

That was the dirty past. Things were better now. Nevertheless, Cam felt a stab of sadness and he suddenly longed to see Banjo. Where was he? Maybe he'd gone to tell Petra. The idea of the two of them flooded his stomach with warmth, like a cup of hot fruit tea.

Blue whales formed deep attachments with only one or two others – that's what his dad had told him. *Better to have one friend that'll respond to your call than ten who won't.* Once upon a time, he'd thought that one friend was Matteo. Of course, Matteo denied they'd ever been close – he had denied it in front of Dean, Lindy and Pip and called Cam a liar.

Cam shivered as the old memory collided with a terrible new thought: if you didn't need a reason to break friends with someone, then how would you know when it was about to happen? And where *was* Banjo? By now, he could have gone to the caves and back twice.

A breeze arrived, scattering the petition pages across the stage. He quickly gathered them together, noticing how the sun had dipped and the flying foxes were beginning to flap across the sky. He shivered, but not because it was cold. Banjo wasn't coming. Cam's mission was something he was destined to do alone. He had always known it, and he'd been stupid to think even for a moment that it could be any other way. All the more reason to forget, and focus on the task.

Hoping it was still open, and he hadn't missed the sending of the daily report to Fort Eden, he rushed to the Whale Station. He found Drake still at his desk, flicking through a register by the light of an olive oil lamp.

'Cam.' Drake held out his hand for the petition. 'Well, well. That's a lot of signatures. I thought your talk was very persuasive, by the way.'

'They were only interested because I mentioned a day off work.'

Drake raised an eyebrow. 'Does it matter? After all, it was just a way to get noticed by Byron Vos. Wasn't it?'

'Yes, although it is for the whales, too,' Cam said hurriedly, in case Drake thought he was being selfish. He didn't want *that* getting back to Byron.

'I'll make sure this gets to Fort Eden tonight with the rest of the day's reports, and I'll add a note about the crowd's enthusiasm. Now, go home and get some rest.'

At the door, Cam turned. 'Drake, what did you mean when you said –'

But Drake suddenly got up and disappeared into a back room.

Cam felt strangely uneasy about what he'd done, so he walked home slowly, letting the evening mood settle his mind. Cetacea was beautiful in the daytime – colours so bright they stung your eyes – but at night it was much kinder. The pale blue sky turned to plum, and the last fingers of sun that stroked the tops of the palms and Moreton Bay fig trees were soft yellow. By the time he reached his door they had disappeared, and the horizon was a thin band of gold.

In the evenings, his mother usually sat up playing solitaire at the table, but she had turned the downstairs lamps off and gone to her room. Cam crept upstairs and stood in her doorway. She was propped up in her bed, a low light spilling from the bedside lamp across her face, her eyes half closed. At the sound of his footsteps on the floorboards she leapt up and flew at him, hugging him as if he'd been gone a week. Then her worried expression was replaced by something more ferocious.

She shook him roughly. 'What did you think you were doing up there on that stage? What are you playing at?'

Cam was shocked. She was often sad, but she was never angry with him. Never.

'Mumma, I was just –'

'You were just what? Putting yourself up there for everyone to see? Talking about whales?'

'Protect the Earth and the Earth will protect you,' he quoted. 'Whales are our masters.'

She stamped her foot. 'Of course they are. But just get on with your life like everyone else. Why do you have to stand out?'

'I thought if I could get noticed by Byron Vos, I could –'

'No!' she shrieked. Her voice dropped to a hiss. 'Not another word. Not – another – word. You hear me?' She jumped back into bed, the frame creaking under the weight of her anger. In the dim light, Cam noticed that her eyes were red. Was it the grief monster again? He sat on the edge of the bed and took her hand.

'It's alright, Mumma. I won't say anything else. And I won't stand on the stage again.'

She sniffed and nodded. He wondered if she was losing her mind. He'd heard of people forgetting things or making up problems, but it was usually those who had paper-thin skin and hooded eyes. Cam's mother was far too young. But maybe grief made madness come faster. He looked for something positive to smooth it away.

'Mumma, I've made some friends.'

'You have?' Her anger dropped like a loose mask. 'Tell me.'

'A boy called Banjo, and a girl called –' He wasn't supposed to say anything about Petra. He'd promised. 'I can't remember her name. But she's crazy. She skips and dances everywhere, like you used to, remember? You'd like her.'

'How did you meet?'

'At mealtime,' Cam lied.

'Are they good? Are they good Cetacean children? Do they live by the laws? They're not troublemakers?'

They live by their own laws, Cam thought. 'They're very good, Mumma.' He was glad that in the semi-darkness she wouldn't see the lying blush on his cheeks.

'Good. Good.'

When her eyes closed, Cam snuffed out the oil lamp and left. He had an early shift the next day, but his nerves were buzzing; there was no way he could sleep. Quiet as a mouse, he snuck back out of the house and into the warm evening air.

His dad used to take him for late walks to look for creatures. Since the floods, the animals had fewer places to hide, he'd explained, and the island was like a zoo. When Cam learned what a zoo was, he thought it sounded strange: a place where creatures were fed, but not free.

Together, they had pointed out the nocturnal creatures that crept like bandits through the streets, and tried to identify the barks, peeps and whistles that cut through the quiet sky. And they'd talk. About life, whales, wishes. Cam always got the impression his dad was holding something back. There were times when he'd told Cam to listen to what he was about to say, before falling silent and shaking his head. *Forget it.* Cam realised there was so much about his dad that he didn't know or understand, but he missed him madly. He missed the way he made his mother smile. He missed the noises in the house – the footsteps, morning coughs, yawning stretches. He missed his company. And right now, feeling so alone, Cam needed it.

Cam had been strolling to nowhere in particular, mind caught up in memories, but he found himself wandering the dusty scrubland south-west of the kelp district. The sand dunes loomed ahead. He looked down on the water. Terra Beach basin was no longer a turquoise jewel in the sun but an inky lake, a place you could lose yourself. Strangely inviting. Cam ran down the dune, shed his tunic and dived right in, blinking against the salt.

The temperature of the water had dropped in the night air – it was cool, otherworldly, and he stayed under as long as he could, counting the seconds, slowing his heart as his dad had taught him. *In case the floods come again.* On a good day, he could do sixty seconds, but his anxiety was gobbling oxygen too fast, so he gave up and floated on his back in the dark water, looking at the stars as they popped out above him. There. There, there and there. And there. The forever stars. The ancestor stars.

He'd promised he wouldn't think about friendship again, but as the five-star shape twinkled above him, the thought of Banjo crept back in, and it felt like a stab in the heart. Their friendship had sealed so fast and felt so sure, but that was the thing about friendship: it seemed as strong as rock when you were together, but when you were apart, it could crumble to dust in the blink of an eye.

'Raaargh!'

Cam was suddenly pulled beneath the surface of the water and he thrashed in panic, mind flooded with images of sharks. Stupid, of course. There were no sharks in the basin. He scrambled to the surface and saw Banjo, clutching his stomach, laughing.

'You frightened the life out of me!' Cam shouted.

'That was the idea, dopey!'

'How did you know I was here?'

'I tracked you using my bush skills,' Banjo said. 'Nah, to be honest, I just saw you. But I wanted to shake that boy off me first.'

'What boy?'

'That cockroach from your barn with the long hair. He started following me today. Up to no good, I reckon.'

'When?' Cam wiped the water from his eyes and tried to catch his breath.

'Eden Place. When you were busy with the petition, I ran back to the caves to tell Petra how brilliant you were. But halfway there, I saw him trailing me. Couldn't lead him straight to Petra, could I? So I had to walk right into Shepherds' Country to shake him off. And then I got lost – *me,* a descendant of Aboriginal people, lost in the bush!' He shook his head. 'By the time I found my way out, it was getting dark, and I'll be honest with you, I got a bit scared. About dingoes and all that.'

'I thought Arlo made that up?'

'He did. But it still spooked me out, the thought of it. Stories stick in your head, don't they? They become true even if you can't see the truth of them.'

Cam felt his insides thaw. They hadn't abandoned him at all.

'I wonder why Matteo is so interested in you.'

Banjo shrugged. 'Dunno. Perhaps he doesn't like seeing you with new friends.'

'It doesn't make sense.'

'It probably does, but we just don't know the big picture. Got to have more information so you can join the dots, see?' Banjo turned his back to show Toorongong.

'Very good, Banjo.'

'Anyway, glad I found you. You were great today – I just had tell you that. I'd better get home now.'

'Me too.'

They walked back to town through the garment district. Eden Place was quiet – just a few people washing at the water pumps. But the screen was on. Bright, glaring blue. An eye into Cetacea's bubbling reefs. Cam and Banjo stopped and stared, waiting to see what animals would appear. Cam pointed at a flat fish with blue fins and spots.

He whispered, 'Blue angelfish. My dad used to swim with them as a kid. Imagine that.'

'Not talking about the Long Ago, are we?' Banjo tutted jokily. 'Your dad sounds cool. I bet he was a good man,' he added softly.

A good man.

'Banjo, I've been meaning to ask you something.'

'Anything.'

'You told Petra that Arlo thinks I'm special. Why?'

Banjo tapped his head. 'Arlo thinks most kids on this island are dumb. Not their fault. They just don't think about stuff. He says Cetacea needs young people who use their brains. Like me.' He grinned triumphantly. 'And Petra, of course. He told me to look out for others who use their brains too. That's how we rebuild an intelligent society, he says.'

'Why does he say that?'

'Dunno. He says we've got to find out for ourselves.'

'That's annoying.'

'Yeah, it is a bit. Oh, look!' Banjo pointed at a turtle, munching on a jellyfish.

'That looks *turtly* delicious,' Cam said. It was his dad's joke, but it didn't matter. Banjo creased up, slapping his thigh. 'Why is the reef sunny?'

They looked at the night sky above them.

'Maybe the moon's extra bright over that bit,' Banjo said.

'Maybe.'

Chapter 10
Byron Vos

Mr Freedman was in the doorway of the barn with a woman, their silhouettes punched against the bright light of the yard beyond. A worker further along the line had overheard some of their conversation and was sending whispers down the long tables.

They're talking about Cam Solomon.

Cam's in trouble.

'You're gonna get transferred,' Dean cackled. 'Boo-hoo. Bad luck, kelpie.'

Cam didn't respond in case he was right. Mr Freedman wouldn't transfer Cam if he didn't have to, but Cam had seen the way he looked at his sore knuckles – perhaps his manager thought his hands needed a rest, or maybe his mother had requested a swap. Or Drake. Or anyone who'd seen the state of his scabs.

'Cam?' Mr Freedman beckoned.

Cam put down his brush and wiped his hands on his tunic. He ignored the faces of Matteo and the others as he made his way across the silent barn. Mr Freedman's eyes were kind as always, but the woman's face gave nothing away. She was tall, with bright blue eyes and hair the colour of sunset.

'I'm Dana, assistant to Byron Vos. He would like to meet you. Is now OK?'

Cam spluttered. 'Uh, uh, yeah. OK.'

'Good,' she said. 'Why don't you come with me?'

Without looking back, he followed her out into the yard. 'Are we going to the Whale Station?'

'Mr Vos thought you might like to come and see the gardens at Fort Eden.'

Fort Eden? *This was too fast. Too fast.* Cam put his hand over his chest where his heart was pounding; it felt as if the tattoo was flipping with excitement.

Dana strode towards a dark brown horse tethered to the yard gates. 'You'll get the hang of it,' she said. 'Hook your foot here and when I give you a little push, grab hold of the saddle and pull yourself up. All OK? One, two, there you go!'

Up in the saddle, Cam was at least twice his own height from the ground. He gripped the pommel. Dana gave him a patient smile.

'Don't worry. You'll be safe with me. I've been riding my entire life. Just hold tight to my waist. Shuffle back so I can get up.'

Dana pulled herself up to sit in front of Cam and slid her feet into the stirrups. With a click and a nudge, they were off, clip-clopping through the gates, yard kids gawping. As they trotted through the town, people stopped at the sight of a small kelp boy on a big horse, and although he'd survived public speaking on the stage in Eden Place, Cam wasn't any more comfortable with being stared at. He wished they could go a little faster.

When they reached the soft ground of the foothills, they did. Dana gave a kick and the horse picked up speed – a trot became a canter, which rolled into a gallop. Cam rattled around on the saddle, unable to sit straight. He held on to Dana so tightly that she shouted at him to calm down. He gripped the saddle with his knees and closed his eyes and tried to concentrate on what was ahead.

What would he say to Byron Vos? Where would he look for the truth? He didn't know where to begin. This was his one chance. He wouldn't get into Fort Eden again.

Eventually, the horse slowed down and Cam forced himself to open his eyes. Dana had dismounted and left him up in the saddle with a view of Fort Eden straight ahead – an estate with wide, wonderful gardens, not like the scrubby patches down in the town. This was a pocket of land so lush and exotic, he could barely believe it. It was a beautiful place to keep secrets.

Men approached to take the horse away. They wore white linen and shiny necklaces.

'Come on, Cam.' Dana helped him down. 'This way.'

The Fort Eden house was big and made of thick stone

painted brilliant white: a fortress against the blistering sun. Cam imagined an interior with smooth floors and still, cool air. But there was a front garden to cross first, and it was the size of a pumpkin field. The grass was luscious and there were exotics – ferns, frangipani trees and hibiscus bushes. Slender palms stood like grand pillars, leaves rustling high above them in the breeze.

Cam stopped to look at a bush of strange spiky flowers that looked like birds. He'd seen a few skinny plants around the town, but these were huge and healthy, glossy petals as orange as mango with shots of purple, strutting straight from the stem.

'Strelitzia,' Dana said, seeing Cam's interest. 'Bird of paradise flower. They're a favourite at Fort Eden.'

'Shall we pick one for Mr Vos?'

Dana frowned. 'No, we only pick flowers when they're close to dying, when it helps the plant conserve energy. Why capture nature when it's right here in front of us?'

'Is that what Mr Vos says? He's very wise.' He was sure he heard her tut, but Dana had moved on, leading him on a path that snaked round the house, past the stables on the right to the land behind.

Cam was sorry not to experience the cool interior, but his disappointment soon evaporated. Below them was another enormous, luminous garden. It was hemmed by thick gum forests and outcrops to the left and right, and at the far end a waterfall tumbled down a towering rock face into a large lake. Even from the terrace, he could feel the cool mist.

'Byron's down there.' Dana pointed out a figure in a deckchair. 'He's waiting for you.'

She turned away. Cam didn't have time to worry about why she was so frosty. He was here, and Byron was *there*. The whale-talker. The creator of Cetacea. And the man who was hiding something – possibly the biggest secret of them all. Was this really happening?

Cam's heart fluttered like palm tree fronds. He had no plan. He would have to work things out as he went along. But there was one thing he knew for sure – he had to get Byron to like him. Because if he didn't, there'd be no second chance. No second horse ride up the Ranges to Fort Eden. No more excited planning with Banjo and Petra. He had one chance.

Cam walked across the spongy grass and stopped a few metres behind the deckchair.

'Mr Vos?'

The man stood and turned to face him. His straw-blond hair was pulled into a ponytail and his neck was strung with beads. He was fifty years old at least. Maybe sixty. He was fit and lean, with tanned skin that creased round his eyes and mouth when he smiled. That incredible smile. Those bright green eyes. Byron wasn't as tall as Cam imagined, but there was something overwhelming about him, as if a personality the size of a whale was packed inside this small man.

'Hello, Mr Vos.' Cam offered his hand.

Byron clasped it in both of his. They were warm and soft. His eyes danced with excitement.

'Welcome, Cam. Let's sit here.' Byron squatted on the edge of the lake and swished his hand through the waters. 'The waterfall flows from an aquifer – do you know what that is, Cam? It's an underground water source. That's why the water is always cold. Stick your feet in.'

The lake was clear, with pondweed as green as fresh salad. Cam lowered his feet into the icy water and sighed, just like the farm workers at Terra Beach. His skin tingled. Goosebumps ran up his legs.

'So, Cam. You have come to my attention,' Byron said languidly.

'Have I?'

'Yes. I heard about your speech, and I received your petition.' He reached out a hand to Cam's shoulder and his eyes narrowed, glittering with intensity. 'It ignited something in me. It made me *feel* something.'

Cam blushed. 'Is that good?'

Byron tipped back his head and laughed. 'It's more than good.'

Cam didn't know what to say. He kicked his legs in the water, sending dragonflies skimming.

'Day of the Whale . . .' Byron drifted off for a moment, his chin lifted to the sky. 'Love for the whales isn't what it used to be, Cam. The whales are concerned that people will get lazy and all the good work will be undone. Things break much faster than they mend.'

'Cetacea wouldn't let that happen!' Cam said.

'No, we won't and we can't let that happen. And that's why Day of the Whale is an incredible idea. It will make people remember why we gave our power to the wise ones. *You* are going to be the one to make them see.'

'Me?'

'Yes. You have restored my faith. And the whales will hear of this, I promise you.'

Cam's mouth dropped open. It seemed to amuse Byron, who dipped his hands into the lake and splashed Cam with droplets. Cam rubbed the cold water into his face.

'Just look at those hands!' Byron grabbed Cam's wrists and brought them in front of his eyes. 'I'll have a word with your barn manager.'

'No, it's fine. It's whale work. Whale work doesn't hurt.'

Byron clicked his tongue. 'You truly are extraordinary, Cam. But you need to rest those hands for a while. Day of the Whale is your whale work now.'

'But I don't know how to organise a festival.'

'Dana will be in charge of the event itself. She's good at that sort of thing. All you have to do is make the opening speech – something to inspire the next generation.'

Cam felt his heart race. The festival was just supposed

to get him to Fort Eden, and now it was actually happening. What should he do next?

'Maybe you should do it,' Cam suggested. 'You're the leader.'

'Your voice will appeal to the younger members of our community, and that's what we need. You'll be fantastic.' Byron brushed away his concerns like flies. 'Shall we make it ten days' time? Is that long enough? Dana will start on it right away, but if you have any ideas, I'll make sure she includes them.'

Was that it? Cam had met the leader of paradise, but he hadn't yet seen what he was hiding. And there had to be something. Byron was getting up. *Think of something!*

'What do you think the whales would want us to do for the festival, Mr Vos?' Cam asked sincerely.

Byron settled back down. 'Call me Byron, please. No more Mr Vos. As for the whales, well . . . I'll see if I can speak with Big Blue about it. Perhaps he'll even agree to make a special sermon.'

Cam's heart thudded. He felt it, like rain before it falls: whatever his father was looking for – and what he wanted Cam to find – was closer. Now was not the time to shy away. *Take the whale by the tail.*

'Could *I* speak to Big Blue?'

Byron put his fingers to his lips and smiled with amusement. 'You are *passionate,* aren't you, Cam? Passionate and ambitious. No one has ever asked me that before. Tell me, Cam, if I gave you the gift of whale-talk, what would you say to our masters?'

'Lots of things. I would ask them about their wisdom, about the future of Cetacea and our people, and . . .' Cam bit his lip, worried about his next words. But he had to get a reaction, a clue, something to go on. 'And I'd ask them if they know where my father is.'

'Why do you say that?'

'My father disappeared. Nearly three years ago.'

Byron frowned. 'What is your surname again, Cam?'

'Solomon.'

Byron leant back on his hands and looked up at the sky. Cam swished his feet in the lake and waited for him to say something. But for a long time, there was no sound apart from the cicadas in the bush and the roar of the waterfall.

Then, suddenly, Byron leapt up and clapped his hands. 'Time to hop along now, Cam. I've got work to do.'

Cam scrambled to his feet. He hadn't been inside the house, he hadn't found a single clue that might lead him to Big Blue's truth. And now it looked as if he'd annoyed Byron Vos.

'Thank you for your time, Mr Vos.' Cam turned to go, head heavy with disappointment.

'*Please* call me *Byron*. And Cam? I'll see you at Fort Eden again soon.'

'When?' Cam's eagerness leapt from his tongue. It wasn't over!

'I'll send for you. Now, off you go.'

Byron adopted the whale-tail pose and Cam returned it, trying to hide his excited smile. He'd be coming to Fort Eden again. He had another chance.

He ran back round the house, past the stables, across the front lawns. He saw a few of the men in white linen drifting around the gardens, but Dana wasn't anywhere to be seen. He walked home. Five miles of track. But it was all downhill and it didn't matter anyway, because he was floating on air. On clouds. On the back of a giant whale. Something was actually happening.

I'm close, Dad. I can feel it.

When he got to town, he sprinted into the vast, empty space of Eden Square and stood in the centre, spinning round and round.

'Did something good happen?'

Arlo was collecting water from the pump. Cam ran towards him, bursting with news. 'Yes, Arlo. I went to Fort Eden!'

Arlo straightened, his arm sinewy and taut from the weight of his bucket. 'Come back to mine. I can do the rest of your tattoo and you can tell me all about it.'

They returned to the art district with its puddles of paint and its chalky smells. Again, the streets seemed to sing with colour, and again, Arlo's door was shut. Cam watched as Arlo felt with his fingertips along the top edge of the door frame. He pulled down a loop of string, looked up and down the street, then tugged it. The door swung open. Arlo winked at Cam, as if it was a magic trick. Cam didn't ask why the door was unopenable in the first place.

'If you're wondering, it's a home-made lock. I have to protect my things,' Arlo added, ushering Cam inside. He looked up and down the street again before closing the door. It reminded Cam of his mother. *The walls have eyes, the stones have ears.*

When they were inside, Arlo relaxed. But it took a while for Cam to settle. His heart raced and his mind flickered with snapshots of the day's events – the lake, Byron, Day of the Whale.

Arlo folded his arms, showing impatience. 'Talk. Perhaps if you keep your mouth busy, your body might stay still long enough for me to finish this picture, hmmm?'

The tattooist examined the outline of the whale on Cam's chest and set about inking his needle, first showing Cam the bottle – a deep blue pigment. Cam nodded his approval. A blue whale had to be blue, apart from the tummy, which was sometimes tinged yellow. His dad had pointed that out once.

Arlo waited with his needle poised. 'I'm ready when you are. Tell me about today.'

'I met Byron in person.'

'Mr Vos?'

'He told me to call him Byron, and he says he'll be welcoming me at Fort Eden again.'

Arlo's eyelids fluttered a little; he stopped to scratch the side of his mouth. 'First-name terms and an open invitation, eh?'

'Yup. I was nervous at first, but he's really nice. Nice, and kind of mysterious, like a magician.'

'He made us believe in paradise, alright.'

Cam closed his eyes a while, absorbing the scratch and stick of the tattoo developing on his skin. Arlo told him that most people fussed, flinching and jerking, which made it harder to tattoo straight, but Cam could sit there all day, still as a rock. Arlo seemed to make time stop.

'So you're going to be seeing a lot more of Mr Vos now? Does this have something to do with what you were telling me, about your father?' Arlo paused a moment to twist his wrist and stretch out the cricks in his elbow.

'Maybe,' Cam said with a little smile.

'Did you tell him about your tattoo?'

'No.'

'Good. Best not to. That's between you and me, and whomever you feel a connection with.'

'Alright, but Arlo, the secret might be at Fort Eden, don't you think? Next time I go, I'm going to look for it.'

'Are you sure this is what you want to do?'

'Of course. I made a promise to Dad.'

Arlo continued with the ink fill, and Cam let his eyes wander the little room, taking in the grubby cloths and ink pots, and the sketches pinned to the walls. There were roses, shapes, words. He thought of the parrot on Arlo's arm. 'So, if a tattoo has to mean something, what's the meaning of your parrot?'

'It's not so much the bird, but the name. Rosella.'

'Rosella. Is that an important person in your life?'

'Definitely a very important thing in my life. And the other arm, the farmyard – that's where I grew up. It was just outside a town called Wagga Wagga.'

'Wagga Wagga's a funny name.'

'It's an Aboriginal name.'

'Like Banjo's ancestors.'

Arlo smiled. 'That's right. The first people of Australia.'

'Australia's gone. It's the past.'

'But it's not gone. It's right here, beneath us. Underwater. We're living on a tip of it. It's been renamed, that's all. If I decided to call you Billy, it wouldn't stop you being Cam Solomon, would it?' Arlo reached back to re-ink the needle and sighed. 'I've run out of blue.'

He wiped at Cam's chest with the wet cloth, tilting his head to look at the evenness of the shine, then raised a grimy piece of mirror-glass for Cam to see. The skin was pink with irritation, but the whale was now smooth and blue, all apart from a tail fluke, which remained unfilled.

'I'll finish the tail when I get my hands on more indigo ink.'

'It's brilliant, just brilliant,' Cam said, the words catching in his throat. 'It's Big Blue.'

'I like it on you.' Arlo nodded, and wiped his eyes.

Cam held the mirror-glass in front of his face. He didn't have one at home. He'd never seen his freckles so close up. So many of them. He even had freckles in his blue eyes. He angled the mirror-glass down to the tattoo again. It was beautiful. He couldn't imagine his skin without it.

'Banjo told me that the other person who has this tattoo is your lost brother.'

Arlo blinked slowly. 'That's right.'

'How was he lost?'

'I don't want to talk about it.'

'Can you tell me more about how you know my dad, then?'

'No, I can't tell you that, either.'

It felt like a slap. So there was something to tell, after all? Arlo *did* know his father . . .

'Why don't you want me to know?'

Arlo stood and leant against the wall, one leg crossed over the other, arms folded.

'There are some things you need to find out on your own.'

'But if you told me, it'd be quicker.'

Arlo laughed then, a hacking sound that made Cam's mouth curl up.

'You're right. But I'm still not going to tell you. And you shouldn't tell Byron Vos anything about your dad, either. Let people find things out for themselves – it's a good rule to live by. Especially if you're going to get involved in something as dangerous as the truth.' He paused, trapping Cam in his gaze.

'Truth. You said *truth*. Do you know something about it?'

'I know that it can't be told to be believed.'

Cam grunted with frustration. Arlo's eyes glistened and a corner of his mouth lifted with amusement. 'Fill your head with questions,' he advised. 'Because if you don't, someone else will fill it with lies. Understand?'

Cam didn't but he nodded, caught up in Arlo's curious contradictions. He had a warm manner but cold eyes; he was open about the past but he held things back; he spoke straight, but his sentences were riddles. And he was secretive and alone and somehow involved with everyone. With all the people he had tattooed. With Banjo, Petra, Cam, his dad.

Who exactly *was* Arlo? Did he know the truth, or didn't he?

And if the truth was dangerous like Arlo said, is that why Dad had never come home?

Chapter 11

The Truth About the Truth

Cam heard his mother get up, and he scrambled out of bed. The rising sun barely touched the dark sky, so he lit an oil lamp and placed tea on the table. His news would make everything better.

She shuffled downstairs with heavy footsteps and a cascade of yawns.

'Cam?' She blinked. 'Why are you up?'

'Sit, Mumma. I have some news.'

Cam pushed a cup of tea towards her. She wrapped her hands around it and sat, looking at him with curiosity.

'You won't believe it, Mumma. News of my talk in the square reached Byron Vos, and yesterday I went up to Fort Eden. You went to bed so early last night. I would have told you before . . .'

Her eyes widened and she tried to talk, but her words came out in a cough. She slammed the cup back down on the table and shook her head furiously.

'You don't need to be scared any more,' Cam said.

'No . . . No.' Her hand curled into a fist.

'It's alright,' Cam soothed. 'Everything is going to be fine. We're just planning Day of the Whale together. He's friendly, Mumma. He likes me.'

She stopped shaking and took a big breath. She reached across the table imploringly. 'Then you stay close to him,' she commanded. 'Stay close. Be good. A good Cetacea boy. No loose talk. You let him speak. You do as he says.'

'Of course I –'

They were interrupted by a hard rap on the door. It was ajar to let in the breeze, and Cam could see two pairs of legs through the gap. His mother shot him a worried look. A second later, the door swung open. The faces of the men on the doorstep were barely visible in the gloomy dawn light.

'Cam Solomon, could you come with us, please.' It wasn't a question. Cam's mother whimpered. 'Nothing to worry about, Mrs Solomon. Mr Vos would just like your son's company this morning for a dawn walk. He likes his dawn walks.'

'I'll be out in a minute,' Cam told the men. He closed the door a little and then wrapped his arms around his mother's neck. 'It's fine. Byron just wants to see me.'

'B-but they're Watchers,' she whispered. 'Don't say anything.'

'Watchers? What are Watchers?'

'Watchers,' she repeated. She gripped his arm. 'Be

good, Cam. Remember what I said. Stay close.'

Cam kissed her goodbye and tried to hold back the tears; her episodes were getting worse. He should probably talk to the herbalist again.

He accompanied the men down the street to where their horses were tethered, and they rode up the track to Fort Eden in the dim light, the peaks of the Higher Ranges looming in the distance, like vast gatekeepers of the sea beyond. He envied the men whose job it was to guard the dangerous cliff edges. Just imagine their view, looking down on the ocean! They probably saw whales from up there. They probably told Byron when Big Blue was coming.

On the lawn of Fort Eden, Byron was waiting, ghostly in his white linens. 'Morning, Cam! Not too early for you, I hope?'

'I was already up,' Cam said.

'Of course you were. You're the kind of boy to make the most of a day, aren't you?'

'Yes, I think so.'

'Good, good. I thought we could go for a sunrise walk.'

Leaving the horses and the house behind, they trekked on foot up through the gum forests east of Fort Eden. Byron weaved through the eucalyptus trees and Cam followed behind. It was quiet, apart from the shrieks of waking birds and the snap of dry leaves under their feet.

'Where are we going, Byron?'

Byron stopped. 'Do we *need* to be going somewhere? Do you require there to be a destination? Is it not enough that we are just walking?'

Cam felt caught off-guard. Being with Byron was easy, but at the same time it felt hard, especially when he was trying to not say or do anything wrong. 'Yes, of course. Just wondering, that's all.'

'And I've been wondering about you, Cam. So yes, perhaps now would be a good time to stop and have a little chat.'

They had reached a clearing, where spindly old gums had snapped and fallen over, creating natural benches. Byron sat on one and beckoned Cam to sit next to him. He took Cam's hand and poured into it a sprinkling of seeds.

'Hold your palm flat, like this. And stay still.'

Seconds later, parakeets arrived, fluttering above them, wings beating their hair. Cam tried not to flinch as their cold claws grabbed at his fingers and perched along his arm.

'So, Cam Solomon, son of David. Is there anything you should tell me?'

'What do you mean?'

'I'll let you think about it.'

Cam's mind flitted like a falling leaf; the flurry of wings and beaks was making it hard to concentrate. Byron Vos knew something. But *what*? In his daily life, there was only Eden Place and the kelp barns and he'd been good all his life . . . apart from the food he and Banjo had taken – but that would have been dealt with by the community advisors. Byron had to be talking about something more serious.

Then he remembered: the sea wall. But how would Byron have known about that? It had just been the three of them. They hadn't met anyone on the way – there had been no one in the farm fields or down at Terra Beach or . . . Wait. Matteo had been spying on them at Eden Place. Perhaps he had been following them all along.

'Cam? Are you hiding something from me?'

If he told Byron about the beach, he might lose his chance. He could deny it. Say it wasn't him. Matteo was mistaken.

'Cam, nothing is ever as bad as it seems,' Byron prompted. 'Whatever it is, you can put it down to being human. Humans make mistakes all the time. We're seventy-three per cent water and one hundred per cent mistake.' The man flicked his hand, sending a king parrot squawking into the treetops, and crossed his arms over his knees. 'What makes a human exceptional, however, is when he admits his mistakes.'

He gazed with patient anticipation at Cam.

He knew. He definitely knew. There was no point in lying. And if he admitted it, it might force Byron to tell his secrets, too.

Cam composed himself. 'I climbed the beach wall. I saw the sea.'

Byron's eyebrows raised in slow motion. 'Oh, I see . . .' He sucked in his cheeks and tutted. 'Is that it?'

'I ate some bread from a windowsill in the canteen quarter.'

Byron chuckled. 'Anything else? May as well get it all out now, so we can begin our friendship on clean, untroubled ground.'

Cam shook his head and looked up at the whale-talker. 'No, that's it.'

Byron sighed with disappointment. 'Why did you do it – why did you go to the sea wall?'

He hadn't asked Cam what he had seen, only why he did it. What should Cam say?

Arlo had said not to, but a truth for a truth . . .

'I think Big Blue has a secret, so I went to the beach and called out a message to the whales and asked them. That's all I did. I didn't even go on the sand, I promise.'

Byron's eyes widened and a smile came and went. He blinked several times. Cam wondered if he'd said something wrong.

'A secret? In the name of Cetacea's paradise land, what put that idea into your head?'

Cam brushed the seeds on to the ground so the birds would leave him alone. He could feel Byron's green eyes boring into him. It was time. Time to be bold.

'My father put that idea in my head. Byron, *is* there a

truth? Do you know what it is?'

Byron knotted his brow and thought for a while. Eventually, he said, 'Yes, Cam, I do.'

He knew!

'Is it . . . big?'

'It's incredible.'

'What is it?'

Byron blinked and put his finger against his lips and said nothing. But Cam wasn't going to be put off. He'd given something, now he wanted something back.

'Did you find it out when you were a scientist?'

Byron scoffed. 'No, no, no. Science taught me nothing.'

'But all your work on whales?'

The whale expert pulled his hair from its ponytail and shook out his mane. 'I was a scientist when I didn't know better, Cam. The day Cetacea was born, I gave all my research back to the whales. My books and papers are at the bottom of the sea, where they belong.'

'But why?'

'Knowledge comes at a cost. It makes us feel like gods, and it makes us forget that there are still plenty of things we *don't* know. We concentrate on the wrong things. That's how species are wiped off the face of the Earth.'

'So how did you find out about the truth?'

'Lots of questions, Cam,' Byron said flatly.

'But how will I find it?'

Cam thought he saw a flash of irritation cross Byron's face, but when he looked again, the whale-talker was smiling.

'The truth is like a sea anemone.' Byron opened out his hand and wiggled his fingers, then snapped them back into a fist. 'Make a wrong move . . . and it vanishes.'

Why did adults only ever tell riddles? His dad, Byron and Arlo. Even Mumma. Cam's annoyance made his skin itch and he raked his nails across his neck, pulling on his tunic by accident.

'What's that on your chest? A painting?' Byron drew back the cloth and looked closer. His eyes widened. His breath caught in his throat with a little rasp and his eyes looked up into Cam's, glistening like emeralds. 'What a beautiful thing. Who did it – not you, surely?'

Arlo's words rushed into his head like a wave. *That's between you and me.*

'Who did this marvellous picture, Cam?' Byron insisted.

'A tattooist.'

'Name?'

Cam realised he couldn't get round it. He couldn't say no to Byron Vos. 'Arlo Fox.'

Byron mouthed Arlo's name, as if he were trying to find a match in his memory. A face to go with it. 'Did this Arlo person design it just for you?'

'No. His brother had one the same.'

'His *brother*? Ah.' Byron stared at the tattoo once more,

and Cam thought he saw a bloom of red in his cheeks. 'It suits you, Cam. A bold symbol to show your passion. Now, I think you should come back to Fort Eden with me.'

'Really?'

'Yes. This honesty session has been good for us, I think. It's brought us closer. And we really need to get on and organise Day of the Whale, and perhaps we can also try to work out where your father went. I'd like to know, too. Would you like that?'

Cam felt queasy. He'd broken a Birth of Cetacea law – thought he'd lost all chance of getting close to Big Blue – and now, suddenly, he was closer than ever before. It was behind smoked glass. He could make out the shape of it; he just needed to break through.

They walked back through the forest with hands full of seeds, arms outstretched and lined with greedy parrots.

'Have you noticed how they trust you when you give them what they want, Cam?' Byron turned. 'For all they know, the seeds could be poisoned.' He flapped his arms gently and the parrots clung on. 'Silly parrots.'

When they reached Fort Eden, Byron told Cam to wait by the lake while he fetched something from inside.

Cooled by the waterfall's spray, Cam felt alive yet dreamlike, buzzing from the dawn walk and mesmerised by the gardens – tucked between the gum hills, Fort Eden was like a secret: a pocket of utopia hidden inside a paradise island.

Hardly anyone got to see it, and yet here he was.

Byron returned and crouched in front of Cam with his hands cupped in front of him. He opened them slowly like a yawning clam to reveal a necklace – a string of small, thick grey discs that shone syrupy in the sun. Byron held it up and as it twisted in the light, shots of colour swam across the surface of each piece like a broken rainbow.

'What is it?'

'This,' Byron said, 'is your pass into the grounds.' He placed the necklace over Cam's head, and it sat cool against his neck. 'Welcome to our happy family. Now, if you just wait on the terrace, Dana will come out and give you a job to do.'

'Won't I be working with you?' Cam said.

'Yes, of course. Just not *alongside* me. Fort Eden is a community. Help yourself to some breakfast.' He waved his hand towards a low table on the terrace, where there were baskets of bread and fruits. 'See you later, Cam Solomon.'

CHAPTER 12

Milo's Pantry

Cam sat at the table and ate a pastry and a banana, and wished his mother could be here to see that everything was OK. Perhaps he should tell Byron about her fear – he might be able to put her mind at rest.

A few minutes later, Dana ran from the house, her russet hair tumbling around her shoulders and her peach dress flicking in the breeze. She looked caught up in thoughts, but when she saw Cam an efficient smile zipped across her face.

'Morning, Cam. He made you start early, I see. Follow me.'

Inside Fort Eden it was cool and still, as he had imagined. The stone walls were smooth and huge lights made with glass beads poured from the high ceilings like waterfalls. Dana led Cam into a large room where the walls were covered with tapestries – every one of them a whale, woven with a million threads. There were sculptures, too. One of a whale tail, set on a plinth, carved in polished white stone. A chandelier scattered blue light across the floor like sunny ripples on a reef.

'This is the Whale Hall,' Dana explained. 'Take a seat.'

Cam sat on a white sofa and watched the brittle woman as she retrieved a pencil and paper from a bag slung over her shoulder. Her expression was still. It looked like something close to numb – a look that his mother had when she was neither living nor fretting. Just existing.

'So, I'll be planning Day of the Whale. Would you like to tell me what you expect from the event?'

She refused to make eye contact. She reminded Cam of a sulky child.

'I think it has to be a proper celebration,' he said as Petra burst into his mind, dancing around the crater. 'Music, singing, dancing, feasting.'

Dana wrote the words down and he frantically searched for something else to say. He might have made up the festival on the spur of the moment, but it had to seem like something he'd given a lot of thought to.

'And we should probably pray to the whales.' Something he'd heard people say: *pray to the whales it rains this month*.

Dana looked up sharply. '*Pray* to the whales?' she repeated flatly.

Cam blushed and shrugged. 'Or we could *think* about the whales.'

'Think about the whales.' She wrote it down, with a sigh.

Cam felt so foolish. 'Does that sound silly?'

Her face softened. 'Byron shouldn't be putting this kind of pressure on you.'

'No, it's fine, really,' Cam protested. 'It's as important as whale work, he said.'

She bit her lip and Cam wondered if she knew about the truth. Had Byron shared it with her? Should he try to find out?

'He says that love for the whales is dying,' Cam said. 'Do you think he's right?'

'Oh, I don't know. My . . . boss . . . worries, that's all.'

'Does Byron tell you everything about the whales?'

She shifted position a little. 'We should get on with the planning, Cam.'

'Were you there when Byron started talking to the whales? At the start, I mean, when he created Cetacea and made the laws? What was it like in the beginning?'

'The beginning?' Dana started coughing, but Cam could see it was put on. She was buying herself time to think. 'Just how I imagined it,' she said, eventually. 'It was a blank canvas. A perfect place to build a perfect society.' Quite suddenly, she stood up and tucked the pencil and paper away in her bag. 'You'll be working in the kitchen today.'

Cam traipsed behind Dana, confused by her manner. Hot and cold. Things he said that made Byron happy had the opposite effect on his assistant. Perhaps it was better if he kept his mouth shut and his eyes open.

The kitchen was a vast room with small doors that led to pantries and laundries, outside yards and kitchen gardens. There were big ovens. Floor to ceiling cupboards held a hundred jars of leaves, twigs and powders. A long wooden table cut through the middle, overflowing with herb pots, chopping boards, knife racks and vegetable baskets. There was so much to take in, Cam didn't notice the man cooking at the grill until flames leapt across the kitchen, followed by a cuss. The cook was short and wiry. Through the steam, Cam could only see his lower arms – thin and brown, with sinews that twisted like twine as he shook pans on the stove top.

'That's Milo,' Dana whispered. 'I'll introduce you in moment. Sit here.' She pulled out a stool from under the table and Cam wriggled on to it. On the other side of the table, the chef continued to move quickly along the stoves, dodging flames, dashing to the spice racks and back again. The pans smoked clouds of delicious smells, sweet and savoury all at once.

Dana placed a cloth bag filled with bright green pods on the table. 'Milo, the peas, yes?' she called.

Milo finally turned to look at his visitor. He had a small, ratty face, with drawn cheeks and a blank stare. Dana set down the bag of peas and fetched two large enamel bowls.

'One bowl for the peas, the other for the pods. When

you're finished, Milo will tell you what to do next.'

Milo gave her a nod and a wink, and turned back to his pans. Dana left, leaving Cam feeling very uncomfortable. At the kelp barn he knew the routine, and Mr Freedman was always chatty. Milo muttered under his breath and didn't even look up to say hello. Cam's hands shook as he picked up the first pea pod. Perhaps Milo was just bad at starting conversations.

'Are you cooking for Byron?'

'Yes. I am cooking for Byron,' Milo replied, without turning.

'Looks like hard work.'

'It is.'

'I won't talk any more if you don't want me to.'

Milo rolled his sleeves up, exposing a large black mark on his forearm. A burn or a birthmark, maybe. He placed his fisted hands on the table and leant forward on his knuckles, his coal-black eyes drilling into Cam's.

'Look, kid, it's nothing personal. Today's just not a good day. I've had ten menu changes and it isn't even lunchtime.'

'Urgh!' Cam said, hoping disgust would be the correct response.

Milo suddenly grinned, showing wonky teeth. 'Mr King is very picky, that's all.'

'Byron's just like us. I'm sure he'll love whatever you cook him.'

The man laughed. It was a sound that crackled, as

if he had burning logs in the back of his throat. 'You're funny. What are you even doing here, kid?'

'Planning a festival to celebrate the whales.'

'Is that right?' The chef smirked.

'What activities would you like to see at a festival?'

Milo shook his head. 'The only activity I want to see is you shelling those peas. And when you've done those, you can wash up.' He pointed with a skinny finger to a tub piled with pans. Cam didn't mind. He was just happy that Milo didn't look as if he wanted to kill him any more. The cook was a strange character; he looked old, but he sliced carrots so fast you couldn't even see the blade, and his eyes were sharp. He was nothing like the oldies his mother worked with in the Food Quality barns.

Cam washed up, listening to the rumble of kitchen life, peppered with Milo's outbursts – they were directed at the stray flame that licked the chef's hand, or the knife that nicked his thumb. Sometimes they were muttered at the ceiling, accompanied by rolling eyes and a shake of the head. Cam settled into the drama; it was almost a relief after the stillness and perfection of Byron, where he had to be careful of every word he said.

After Cam had finished washing the pans, Milo tossed him a bread roll with instructions to help himself to stuff in the pantry for lunch. The small room had floor-to-ceiling shelves with more jars, covered bowls, cloth parcels and something under a glass dome that looked squidgy and pink.

'You alright in there?' Milo shouted over the rattling of pans.

'Yes, I just don't know what things are.'

Milo came in, wiping his hands on his apron, and pointed out items quick and fast – 'Chutney, pickles, cheese, lettuce, cold beef' – then walked out again. There were things that Cam had never heard of. He reached for the thing called 'cold beef'.

'No, wait!' Milo hurried in again, shaking his head at his own mistake. 'Not that one.' He took the beef and marched with it back to the kitchen. 'Anything else is fine.'

'What was wrong with it?'

Milo rolled his eyes. 'Don't ask too many questions.'

Cam ate a bread roll in silence, then Milo told him to go and find something else to do. Cam didn't hesitate. This was the perfect chance to look around.

He wandered through the spacious halls on the ground floor and, when there was no sign of Dana or Byron, he ventured up the stairs. On the upper floor, there were corridors and tucked-away rooms. Bedrooms and bathrooms and cupboards. Behind one door was a room filled with storage boxes. There were papers pinned to the walls. *Photos*. Mostly of a woman with a round face and kind eyes. In some pictures the woman was cuddling a little girl with red hair. In the centre of them all was a large framed picture of a child's drawing.

Cam stepped into the room for a closer look. The

drawing was of an island with trees, birds and animals, and happy-looking people working in fields. There were rooftops and forests and mountains and beaches, lakes and paths. Arrows and labels explained what everyone was doing, what everything was for, which fields held which crops. So much tiny detail. At the bottom was a shaky signature: *For Mum. Our Perfect Paradise, Dana, 10.*

Cam heard the shuffle of soft shoes and turned to see Dana in the doorway.

'Milo was supposed to keep you in the kitchen. Did you get lost?'

'I was trying to find you.'

'Well, no harm done.' Her tone was snappy. 'Byron's at the lake taking a dip. He'd like to see you.'

Nobody had said he couldn't explore, but Cam felt as if he'd been caught out. He followed Dana in silence down the stairs, looking at her thick red hair and wondering if she'd lost her mother in the floods, and, if so, how she'd got to Cetacea. He didn't want to ask her now, not when she was in such a mood.

They walked through the hallway and out on to the back terrace. Without a word, Dana left him there.

Cam watched as Byron slid, smooth as a seal, through the waters of the lake. Should he try and ask about the truth again, or would it vanish like the sea anemone?

'Are you coming in or not?'

He'd been spotted. 'Hi, Byron!'

'The water's lovely,' Byron hollered. 'Good for purifying the body!'

Cam ran down to the water's edge, slipped off his shirt and lowered himself in. His toes touched silty mud on the bottom, and when the water hit his chest, it took his breath away. So cold. So gloriously cold. He paddled towards Byron, who was floating with a serene expression on his face.

'I was worried I might not be able to see you again today,' Byron said. 'But how fortunate – I have you to myself for a while. So, what did you do this morning? Tell me.'

'I helped Milo in the k-kitchen,' Cam said, his teeth chattering with cold.

'A real character, isn't he?'

Cam was pleased he'd said that. 'Yes – he says funny things. He called you a king.'

'Oh!' Byron laughed. 'A king! Ha ha! Let me tell you something about Milo. He's harmless, really, but he's old and a bit . . .' Byron tapped his head. 'I gave him a job because I felt sorry for him, and he's a good cook. But don't take too much notice of what he says.'

'I saw some –' Cam was about to ask about the beef in the pantry, but he didn't want to get Milo into trouble. 'I saw some beautiful sculptures in the house. The whale tail was my favourite.'

'I knew it wouldn't take long to get the conversation back to whales.'

'Have you spoken with Big Blue today?'

'Too many questions, Cam. Too many questions.'

Byron swam past Cam to the edge of the lake, and in one swift movement he'd pulled himself on to the grass bank, slipped on a shirt and wrapped a towel around his legs. Cam clambered out after him, less gracefully, taking weed and mud with him.

'You confuse me, Cam. On the one hand you are blessed with understanding, and on the other you are cursed with curiosity. If you want to learn, you have to listen.'

Cam felt hot prickles of humiliation creep up his neck. He didn't know what he'd done wrong. 'I'm sorry.'

'I like you a lot, Cam, so I'm going to give you a chance. Because I get curious too, sometimes. It's human nature to be curious. But it's also human nature to be selfish, destructive and violent. It's all linked.'

'You don't want me to ask questions?'

'You're a quick learner. That's right. You have to reject the questions your mind creates. Understand?'

'We have to reject questions because it leads us to damage the Earth?'

'Precisely. Now, I want to talk about your father. I said I'd help you, and I will. I've spoken to the men who investigated his disappearance when it happened – they say they interviewed all your father's friends at the time. But now we have reason to believe that he had . . . *another* group of friends. Friends that betrayed him. Do you know who they might be?'

Cam shook his head.

'Someone must know *something*. Will you think about it?'

Cam nodded.

'Think very hard. We must find out who these people are. No one should go missing on Cetacea. And certainly not the father of one of my favourite people. Now, why don't you head home? There's a basket of perfume bottles by the front door, made with our very own frangipani flowers – take one for your mother as a present.'

Byron sat down then lay back on the grass. He drummed his fingers on his stomach, staring at the whale tattoo as Cam pulled on his shirt.

'Cam? If you can show me you are a true friend of Cetacea, I will tell you the truth. I promise you this.'

'You will?'

'Do as the whales say and don't question their leadership. Show me your absolute loyalty. And then . . . the truth will be yours.'

Chapter 13

Lawbreakers

Cam made it back to the town just before mealtime, carrying a gift of perfume for his mother. She had finished her early shift and was playing solitaire. At the sight of him in the doorway, she leapt to her feet and gave him a hug so tight, it squeezed the air from him.

'OK? Everything OK?' she asked urgently, shaking him for answers.

'Yes. Yes, everything's fine. I don't know what you were so worried about.'

She stood back. Her face relaxed and her eyes softened – although she scowled at the bottle of perfume and waved it away, saying she didn't want that muck in the house. Knowing her moods leapt like crickets, Cam decided not say anything about searching for Big Blue's truth, or how Byron was going to help him find out what had happened to his dad. It was better to keep the grief monster at bay.

They ate at Eden Place together – banana curry

with flatbreads and mango juice. She was chatty and talked about the good crops; there were hardly any bad vegetables in the Food Quality barn – a few wasps, a couple of wrigglers, that's all. For the first time in ages she seemed at ease, as though Cam's acceptance to Fort Eden had thrown a ring of light around their tiny family. Cam felt it too. Everyone on Cetacea was supposed to be equal, but he couldn't help feeling that perhaps he was a little bit special.

After mealtime, his mother returned home to play cards with Gelda, their neighbour, and Cam circled the runners, looking for Banjo. He was bursting to tell his friends everything – how things had gone better than he had ever anticipated, how close he was now to finding the truth.

Cam waited and waited, watching the people of Cetacea eating then leaving, until there was no one left in the square but him and a man, who skulked in the shadows. He wore brown linen. Perhaps he was an artist. Or trouble, his mother would say. Perhaps he was hoping to steal leftovers. The canteen managers barked at him to go away – they had clearing up to do – and the man slunk, empty-handed into the alleys. Cam set off for the secret caves. He couldn't break the rules any more. Not one. Absolute loyalty to the whales and Byron. So he avoided the canteen district and instead wove his way through the residential streets.

As he rounded a corner, he caught sight of two figures

who quickly turned off into a passageway further along. Cam stopped and listened. No talking, no footsteps. But they were definitely there. It gave his skin icy prickles, and he remembered Byron's talk of the group of friends who might have betrayed his father. Were they the same people as the Watchers? Perhaps it wasn't gibberish, after all.

More likely it was Matteo and Dean playing tricks. But whoever it was, he couldn't risk bringing anyone to Petra's hideout, not even a nosy wombat, so he ran through the alleys as fast as his legs would take him, zigzagging and backtracking, making sure he wasn't being followed. After one final check, he sprinted across the scrubland into the cover of the forest.

The air was still, woody and warm, filled with the chatter of lorikeets, which skittered between the trees like rainbow darts. It reminded him of feeding the parrots at dawn. Dawn! He yawned, realising how long he had been up. He was shaken awake by a thudding on the forest floor behind him. He turned, his heart in his throat. Banjo, again!

Cam laughed as his friend leapt through the jungle of roots and shoots like a woodland animal. He was carrying a large sack in his arms, and tears were streaming down his face.

'Are you OK, Banj?'

'Yeah, sore eyes, that's all. And I got no break today. No meal.'

'Why not?'

'They caught me daydreaming. Got the strap, too.' He turned to show Cam the welt across the back of his knees. 'All day, no break, no food. I'm dying. Did you bring food?'

'Sorry, no. What have you got in the bag?'

'I'll show you when we get to the caves. Hope Petra's got some leftovers. Urgh, I'm so hungry, I could eat the bum of a passing wallaby.'

'The bum of a passing wallaby?' Cam burst out laughing.

'Yeah, why not?' Banjo grinned. 'My ancestors ate the bums of passing wallabies. Maybe not the bums, though. Maybe just the meaty tails.'

Cam laughed thinly. His friend was talking of ancestors *and* eating animals, which was definitely against the law . . . He'd been forgiven once, but there was too much at stake now.

'Can we talk about something else?' he said, abruptly.

'You alright, Cam?' Banjo said.

'Yeah, fine. Come on, let's see if Petra's got any food for you.' Cam smiled, glad to have moved the conversation forward.

When they got to the outcrop, they called in unison. 'Coo-ee! Coo-ee!'

And Petra's reply came. 'Come on up, y'old dogs!'

Instead of descending into the gloomy caves, they sat outside in the crater amid the rose-gold shafts of the evening sun. Petra had some fruits that Arlo had delivered earlier and she watched with mock disgust as Banjo tucked into them, letting the juice pour down his face.

'You'd think *he* was the one living all alone!' she chided. 'You're supposed to bring *me* things, remember? I'm the hobo with no home. Come on, then, what y'got? Give me your gifts!' She held out her hands.

'I forgot food,' Cam admitted. 'But I do have something for you.' He pulled the little perfume bottle from his shoulder bag, the one his mother had rejected.

Petra took it and yanked out the cork. 'Perfume! Are you saying I stink, Cam?'

Cam blushed. 'No, of course not. I –'

'Only joking, y'idiot. Mmm. Frangipanis are my favourite. Where did you get it?'

Cam smiled and waited until they were both leaning in with interest. 'Fort Eden.'

Petra and Banjo gasped at the same time, their mouths and eyes stretched as wide as they could go.

'Go on,' Petra said. 'Tell us.'

Cam loved the excitement. He couldn't wait to see their faces, but he noticed Banjo tapping the heavy sack he'd carried all the way there.

'No, let's do Banjo's news first,' he said.

'Alright, show us, Banjo.' Petra clapped her hands with glee.

Without a word, Banjo tipped the sack upside down. Heavy blocks tumbled on to the ground.

'B-books?' Petra gasped. 'For me?'

'For all of us, but actually, these are mainly for Cam,' Banjo said, smiling warmly at his friend. 'Arlo told me to give you a message. He said he's sorry if he annoyed you, and that everyone needs to start somewhere. He hopes this helps you on your way. Oh, and he still hasn't found any indigo ink.'

'What are they?' Cam felt instantly anxious. 'Books of what?'

'He wouldn't tell me. He said we'd find out for ourselves.'

'Typical Arlo,' Petra said, rolling her eyes, although it was with affection.

'We have to look after them. Properly. Keep them hidden in the caves,' Banjo added. 'Arlo made me promise. They're precious.'

Petra pulled one book towards her and stroked its cover. 'They're not burned.'

'Cam, you're going to go wild.' Banjo handed him a thick book with a blue cover and white writing.

Whales and Migration by Byron Vos. Cam dropped it like a hot stone.

'What's the matter?'

'These are Byron's science books!'

'I know they're Byron's science books. The most famous whale scientist the world has ever known. Everything you want to find out about Big Blue and the whales – it'll be in these books.'

'Where did Arlo get them?'

'He didn't say.'

'But Byron just told me he gave all his books back to the whales. They should be at the bottom of the sea. They shouldn't be here.'

'They don't look as if they've ever seen the sea – or any water, come to that. Pages are smooth, see? Look at this – a picture of whale gut.' Banjo held it up and Cam looked away. 'I thought you'd be pleased.'

'Let me see,' Petra said, snatching it. 'That is *terrible*. Look at all the plastic inside it.'

'It's the dirty past.' Cam stood up. 'Don't look. You mustn't look.'

'You're being so weird,' Petra snapped. 'It's really ruining the mood.'

'What's up, Cam?' Banjo tugged his tunic.

'Byron told me that the more we know, the more we destroy things. We made a promise to the whales to change our ways. That's the law. We should respect it.'

Petra blinked at him as if he was mad. 'I don't think I like this side of you.'

'Steady, P,' Banjo said. 'Cam's just being cautious. Come on, Cam, don't tell us this doesn't excite you.' But Banjo's smile faded as Cam's expression darkened.

'The laws. We have to stick to the laws.'

Petra was on her feet. 'You're being dopey. Stop and think a minute. Knowing about whales – properly knowing – doesn't mean we'll destroy them. We'll *understand* them. Besides, we can't destroy whales, can we, because we're stuck behind a massive wall. So what's the problem?'

Cam gripped his hair and turned in circles. 'Byron said he's going to tell me the truth. But not until he can trust me. I have to prove that I respect the whales a hundred per cent.'

'Byron's going to tell you the truth, just like that?' Petra laughed caustically. Cam's cheeks burned and he looked away. She began to pace like a caged cat. 'This is real knowledge. It's all you've dreamed of.'

'And whales are a symbol of communication and knowledge,' Banjo argued. 'They'd *want* us to know.'

Cam thought his head might explode. 'But Byron said they *don't* want us to know. Knowledge in the wrong hands is what got the planet into this trouble. He's going to help me. He really is. He's on my side. I told him about the beach, and he forgave me. He actually *forgave* me. But I've promised not to do any of that again. I have –'

'You told him about the *beach*?' Petra interrupted. Her voice was pure fury. 'So he knows about us?'

'I only told him about me.'

'It was *our* secret!' she yelled.

Cam shook his head, as if he didn't understand. 'I just said: he doesn't know about *you*!' he shouted back at her.

'That's not what *secrets that bind* mean. It was ours. *Ours*.'

'Whatever. What's done is done. But I don't want to

look at these books and I don't want you to look at them, either. You might ruin everything for me.'

'So this is all about you, then,' Banjo said softly.

'And the whales,' Cam replied. 'It'll make them angry.'

'Well, excuse me for not taking y'word for it, but *I'd* rather find that out for myself,' Petra said. 'Or have you forgotten what you said after the beach? About the things Byron's hiding from us?' She began to climb the outcrop behind them, tugging herself violently up the steepest parts, frustration in her every movement. She leapt from a high ledge and landed at Cam's feet, making him recoil.

'This island, with its systems and rules . . . it's killing me. Expanding my mind is all I have. I have read every scrap of unburned paper I've found, each one a million times, looking for something I missed, something extra to feed my brain. And now you're telling me I can't read these books?'

'It's wrong,' Cam repeated sullenly.

'So, it's OK for you to be up at Fort Eden having new experiences – *you* get to do all that mind-expanding stuff while me and Banjo sit here like good, obedient Cetacea islanders, waiting to die of boredom. Is that it?'

Cam looked desperately at Banjo, but he was avoiding Cam's eye.

'You don't understand. Byron is helping me find out what happened to Dad, and he's going to tell me about

Big Blue. He promised. But he thinks these books no longer exist and if he finds out . . . Arlo could get into trouble.' Cam looked at Petra imploringly. 'Destroy them, please. *Please.* I'm so close to the truth.'

'If you don't know what the truth is, how can you possibly know when you're close to it?'

'I just know, alright? Anyway, this is *my* mission and *my* promise to *my* dad. Suddenly you two are acting like you own the expedition. I knew I shouldn't have told you. I knew I'd be better off sorting this out on my own.'

There was a silence that buzzed. Cam felt bold and full of purpose – the way he always felt when he was on the brink of something new. Only, the power felt somehow dangerous and out of control.

Banjo collected the books in a pile and squatted over them, protectively. 'These books are going nowhere. And if you think hanging around us is going to bring you bad luck, then I suppose you'd better leave.'

The words hit Cam in the chest like a sack of potatoes. It was happening. For real, this time. He was losing friends he thought he'd have forever. He looked at them one more time. Petra's wide face, now pinched with anger. Banjo's big smile packed away behind tightly closed lips.

Cam turned and walked away, following the track around the outcrop down into the gully. His chest burned but his head was strangely cool – perhaps getting to the truth was always meant to be a lonely path. Perhaps that was why there was only one whale-talker. Byron Vos, all alone on the hill.

Suddenly, Cam saw he had company. Blocking the path was a Big Red. It stood on its haunches, strong and lean, nearly two metres tall, regarding him with a steady gaze as if it was reading his thoughts. It reminded him of something. Or someone.

It was too dangerous to approach so Cam changed direction, turning and walking uphill into the trees, a safe distance from the path. He continued west towards the town and the setting sun. Picking an unbeaten route through the bush was time-consuming, and the light was dropping quickly. Brambles caught in his hair and sticks rolled under his feet. The cracking of his footsteps on the undergrowth set him on edge and sent his head spinning. He half hoped that Banjo might be following him, but he pushed that thought away. His time with Banjo and Petra was done. They were breaking Birth of Cetacea laws like matchsticks. He'd never find the truth with them by his side.

He couldn't let anything get in his way.

By the time he reached the outskirts of the town, the sky was plummy with apricot edges, just light enough to make out shapes. And ahead of him was the outline of another kangaroo – or was it the same one? Cam couldn't tell. However, he now knew exactly who it reminded him of: a large, steady presence, unreadable, appearing out of nowhere, standing in his way.

Arlo.

Arlo had planted the idea about going to the beach; he'd talked about secrets; he'd lured Cam into telling him about his father; he'd somehow stolen Byron's science books. What was he up to? *Let people find things out for themselves.*

Cam clenched his jaw. He was going to find out, alright.

His feet marched him on, past the kangaroo, which leapt aside, and through the town. He didn't know what he'd say to the devious tattooist when he got there. He just hoped the right words would come.

Evening had swept away the vibrancy of the art district, revealing a different side to it: colourful and noisy by day, moody and quiet by night. Cam crept past doorways, catching wafts of smoke and whispered conversations, beginning to understand his mother's feelings about the place. Troublemakers.

When he turned into Arlo's street, the light behind the curtain in the tattooist's window glowed, drawing him like a moth. Cam tiptoed closer. Closer.

Behind him, footsteps rang out on the stone. He backed up against a wall in the shadows and watched the stranger stop at Arlo's door. The man looked left and right and knocked. The door opened a fraction and he slipped inside.

Cam ran over to Arlo's house and flattened himself against the wall to the right of the doorway. The man hadn't shut the door behind him properly and there was a gap along the hinge, thin as an arrow slit. Cam pressed his eye to it and peeked into the little living room. It was full of people, talking in low tones. He could see Arlo's legs, extended from his chair, his long ink-stained fingers tapping his knees. Cam turned his head and placed his ear against the gap, trying to pull something from the hum of conversation. He began to sort the different voices, picking out words, then full sentences.

'Does he know?'

'How much have you told him?'

'Is he close?'

'What do we do when he finds out?'

'Are we ready to act?'

'What about the dangers?'

'Did someone leave the door open?'

Cam quickly reversed back into the shadows and held his breath. A man came to the door and peered out into the street. Then he heard the door click shut and the block of Arlo's home-made lock fall into place. It felt like the sting of the strap. He hadn't wanted it to be true. He'd wanted to be wrong about Arlo, but sometimes you had to see things to believe them.

Arlo was betraying him. Not just Arlo. Others.

Byron's words came to him. *But now we have reason to believe that he had another group of friends. Friends that betrayed him. Do you know who they might be?*

Cam stumbled back out of the art district, tears

pouring down his face. Arlo. Arlo, who had marked him with his brother's tattoo. Why?

He ran back through Eden Place. It was eerily quiet. Usually there was someone hanging around the square, unable to sleep in the heat. But tonight there were only brown snakes – venomous, slithering like omens. They came closer and closer, sidewinding towards him. He remembered being told in kindergarten that snakes were more scared of people than people were of them, so he stamped his feet, forcing them to recoil and hide. Then he went to the fountain and splashed his face with water and went home.

Chapter 14

Everywhere, Snakes

Cam saw him too late. He was standing in the shade of a palm tree at the start of the path that led up to the Ranges. Calm, unreadable, powerful. Blocking his way like Big Red.

Cam's heart thumped against his ribs. Now was a chance to challenge him, as he'd intended to do the night before. But Arlo spoke first.

'I know you were outside my house last night.'

Cam swallowed hard. 'How?'

'A friend of mine smelled frangipani petal perfume. And there's only one place where that comes from. Also, I have a mirror positioned on my windowsill so I can see who's at my door.' Arlo smiled sadly. 'I suspect you overheard things that might have confused you. I'll explain everything later, if you'll let me.'

'I understood every word.'

Arlo nodded. 'I'm sure you think you did.'

'I speak English, you know.'

Arlo laughed and nodded. 'Tell me, when you look at the screen in the square, do you see the whole sea?'

'No, just the Cetacea Sea.'

'And that's just a small part of the world's oceans. You can't understand the whole of the planet's ecosystem by looking at a tiny piece of it . . . and you can't understand a full story by hearing just a sentence.'

'Stop talking in riddles. Why are you trying to stop me getting to the truth?'

Arlo looked genuinely startled. 'I'm not.'

'I heard you say it.'

'Think again.'

Cam hesitated. No, perhaps he hadn't heard those words exactly.

'Tell me what you did to my father, then,' Cam challenged.

Arlo stared at him and shook his head. 'I didn't do anything to your father.'

'I'll find out, you know. I'll find out what part you played in this.'

'I hope you do. You're headed up to Fort Eden now, are you?'

'Yes.'

'Have you told him about your father's last words?'

Cam bit his lip. 'No.'

Arlo stared without blinking, absorbing Cam's lie. 'Well, that's your information to share, I guess, although I've warned you.'

'He said he's going to show me the truth. That's more than you've done.'

Arlo closed his eyes and breathed in slowly. In and out like bellows. 'The truth about Big Blue and the truth about what happened to your father are not the same thing. But they *are* connected. And it's important that you don't rush to find one without thinking of the other. You must discover them at the same time.'

'I don't understand.'

Arlo crouched down, his fingers searching for something on the ground. When he got up again, he was holding two sticks in one hand, positioned like the chopsticks they used when the canteen served noodles.

'These sticks represent two separate truths. One is what happened to your father, the other is the whale truth.' He clicked the ends of the sticks together on the palm of his other hand, where he'd rested a small stone. 'The sticks can only grab the stone when they come together. If I concentrate on just one,' – he let a twig fall – 'then the other is useless.'

'What's the stone?'

'It's everything, Cam. *Everything*.'

'And you'll explain it all to me later?'

'If you ask the right questions.' Arlo put his finger against his lips. 'And don't tell that man on the hill about me. Stay close but don't tell him anything.'

Cam looked down at his feet. Had he told Byron

about Arlo? Yes, but only his name. Only that he'd given him the tattoo.

When he looked up, Arlo had gone.

The path ahead was clear – a brown dusty road leading straight to the Lower Ranges. Cam began the trek up, crunching Arlo's words over and over in his mind. Arlo was trying to fox him with riddles again, but he wasn't going to fall for all that mysterious talk any more – not like Banjo and Petra. It was almost funny when he thought of it like that. He would go back and listen to Arlo's ridiculous words, not because he believed they would explain anything, but just in case he let something slip – like a clue to how he knew his father or how the tattooist and his troublemaker friends betrayed him.

He was so deep in thought that the sudden sight of Fort Eden knocked his questions clean away. He lifted his necklace for the men in white to see, and walked through the gates and across the grass to the courtyard to wait for Dana.

The large paved area had seating and a low table with baskets of fruit and bread. Cam sat on a sofa, nibbling at a sugar bun and watched the men circling the gardens. He wondered what their purpose was. When he'd eaten three sugar buns and there had still been no sign of Dana, he decided to walk round to the back. Perhaps Byron was taking a morning swim. But when he found the lakeside garden empty, he headed inside, to the kitchen. Maybe he was expected to shell more peas.

He was relieved to finally find someone at home. Milo was tidying his workspace, wiping down the areas where he'd chopped carrots and onions, scooping the peel into a bucket. His movements were even more exaggerated than usual. Jerk, mutter, fling, stamp. When he saw Cam, he thrust the scraps bucket into his hands.

'Go and chuck this in the chicken coop, boy.' He pointed to a small door on the other side of the kitchen. 'Through the herb garden, down the steps and you'll see it. Open the wire door, empty it and shut it again quick before the chooks escape.'

Cam followed the gravel path to the coop, which was on the edge of the gum forest. A giant cage holding a clutch of bronze birds. He did as he was told and, although he didn't let birds escape, he brought back bad news. One of the hens was on its back, legs in the air.

'Right.' Milo didn't seem bothered. 'I'll make something of her this afternoon.'

'What do you mean?'

Milo froze, then wiped his hands on his sleeves. 'Forget about it.'

'Why?'

'Look, there's a lot you don't know.'

'Like beef,' Cam tested. He saw Milo blink. 'Don't worry, I don't want to know. Curiosity is the curse of humans.'

Milo sucked his teeth and stared at Cam for a long time before he shook his head and turned away. Cam hoped he hadn't upset him, but he didn't worry about it too much. Byron had said he was a bit loopy. He washed up for Milo, and chopped some herbs, and when Milo told him to get lost, he helped himself to a bread roll and some cheese and took his lunch out to the terrace overlooking the lake.

Footsteps rang out on the stone pathway and he looked up to see Dana carrying a stack of papers. She was dressed strangely – wearing a tight dress and funny, pointed shoes that she had trouble walking in. Her heel caught and she tripped. Her papers dropped around her.

'Dana! Can I help?'

When she looked up, her expression was blank. It was as if she didn't recognise him. She quickly hooked up a smile but it was a bit too late. Cam realised, then, that she wasn't expecting him. They'd forgotten he was coming.

'What are those papers?'

'Just, er, preparations for Day of the Whale, Cam. There's a lot to organise. Now, why don't you go home.' Her voice was firm.

'OK, Dana. I'll see you tomorrow.'

'Maybe not tomorrow, Cam.'

'I need to talk to Byron about something. About my father.'

Dana hesitated. 'Byron's been having trouble getting into the right frame of mind. For the whales. Whatever message you have, I think it can wait.'

'Is it my fault?'

'No, no.' Her forehead creased. She seemed to fumble for words. 'Nothing is your fault, Cam. We'll see you really soon, OK? Go back through the kitchen and out by the gum forest.'

'Why?'

'Because that's the way I'd like you to leave.'

Don't ask questions, Cam reminded himself, although they rapped on his brain like bony knuckles.

Rain started falling as he made his way back down the hill. Rain. It had been weeks. Weeks with occasional grey clouds that dangled tantalisingly above them before evaporating in the sun. But out of nowhere, a bank of cloud had swept over on a high sky breeze, bringing with it a gentle pitter-patter, heavier than a drizzle but lighter than a shower. He heard the whoops from the town long before he could see the people, but he knew everyone would be out of their barns, tongues sticking out to grab the drops, which somehow tasted a million times better than the fountain water. When the rains came, everyone was allowed to stop work, just long enough to get soaked.

When he reached the final stretch of the path, he could see right down into Eden Place. It was half full. The other half of Cetacea would be at Terra Beach, no doubt, watching the patterns on the water and rain-bathing on the white sands. His mother, if she was still well, would be sitting outside their house with Gelda, swishing her bare toes across the slippery paving stones.

He would go there right away and sit alongside her.

But a figure was waiting for him at the end of the path, curled in a ball, hugging his knees.

'Banjo? What are you doing here?'

The boy unfurled and got to his feet. His blond mop was flattened, his long arms hung by his side. His face should have been rain-happy but it hung like wet washing. Tears wiggled down his face in rivulets, collecting at the corners of his mouth.

'She's gone, Cam,' he cried.

'Who?'

'Petra.'

'Where?'

'Don't know.'

Cam hesitated. He didn't know what he was supposed to do.

'So? Are you going to help me find her?' Banjo looked at him, exasperated. 'Either she's been found out or she's run away – because of *you*.'

'Why me?'

'Because Petra believed the three of us were bound by our secrets. The beach was holding us together, remember? Now, she doesn't trust you not to tell anyone about her.'

Cam was stunned. 'But . . . I wouldn't. I didn't.'

'She doesn't know that. Neither do I. You've changed. You're a different person to the one we made friends with.'

'I didn't tell anyone about her, I swear. I swear on the

whales. And I only told Byron about the beach because he already knew.'

'How did he know?'

'Matteo must have told him.'

'Matteo didn't know anything about it.'

'How do you know that?'

'Because I asked him, of course. I went to tell him to leave you alone because you're my mate and I'd kick his bum if he bothered you ever again. But he didn't know anything about that night. He only followed us from the garment district.'

'Oh.' Cam frowned in confusion.

'So you'll help me find Petra?'

'I can't, Banjo. I just can't. You don't understand.'

Banjo shoved him so hard, it took him by surprise. 'When things get difficult you turn your back, just like that! You're no different to Matteo, are you? You're made for each other.'

As Banjo strode away, Cam thought he looked small – his shoulders hung loosely from his frame – and he sensed loneliness. Because, without him or Petra, Banjo was alone. Petra was alone, too. Cam felt a wave of sadness at how the three of them had been torn apart. But he should have known it wasn't going to be easy by the way his father tightly gripped his arm before he left. *Follow Big Blue. Find the truth.* Cam had thought it was a simple instruction, but now he realised his dad had said it as if there was everything to lose.

Everything.

Arlo.

Arlo could help find Petra. This mess was partly his fault – he had stolen Byron's books. Cam thought of her, running into Shepherds' Country, soaking wet, afraid and alone. The bush was hard and hostile, miles from town and the canteen. Her life would be in danger. Yes, he would tell Arlo to help. And he could do all his explaining at the same time.

Cam ran through the crowds and into the art district, where the rain had taken people by surprise. Paintings rained pigments on to the streets and artists were frantically trying to save their work. As usual, Arlo's home shared nothing of the colour or the activity. His door was firmly closed. Cam rapped on it hard. But there was no answer, no twitch of the curtain.

'Arlo, I want to speak to you!' he shouted, pressing his mouth against the wood. 'Arlo!'

'He's gone.' Arlo's neighbour was stacking bowls outside her house. She was elderly – she had white hair in waves down to her waist, wrinkles like ravines, and blue eyes so bright they jumped. 'He left earlier. Worried someone would reveal his identity, no doubt.' She stared at Cam pointedly. 'Help me load these on to my wheelbarrow, will you? I'm taking them to the square to give out to whoever'll have them.'

Cam obliged, stacking the bowls carefully. They were perfectly round and washed with a pretty aquamarine glaze. 'There's nothing wrong with them. Why are you giving them away?'

'Got my reasons. You're that Cam Solomon, aren't you?'

Cam blushed. Of course – she must have seen him on the stage. He nodded.

'Take one, Cam Solomon,' she insisted. 'Give it to your mother. Be sure she looks at it.'

'Thank you. Do you know when Arlo will be back?'

She sucked in her cheeks and stepped close. 'He told me he won't be back until it's over.' She grabbed Cam's wrist, hard. 'Everything you need to know is right here.' She nodded at Arlo's door. 'All the pieces of the puzzle. Look, boy. *Look*.'

She returned to stacking her pottery, and Cam realised that he was shaking like a leaf. She was just a confused, crazy old woman, but her words were so strange – they were like splinters in his skin. *Everything you need to know is right here.* He looked at Arlo's door, sealed tight, the window blacked out by a curtain. When he looked back the old lady's eyes were on him again.

'Remember to give the bowl to your mother,' she said.

He nodded, turned and ran. He wanted to be away from there. His mother was right – the art district was unpredictable. It spoke a different language and its people were strange. And what identity did Arlo Fox fear being revealed? His part in his father's betrayal?

The intensity of the art district dissolved when he reached Eden Place. Despite the rain, the canteen crew had set up for late meal and the square was filling quickly. No one minded the damp. The space was a kaleidoscope of colour and hands, legs, heads; it was hard to see where one person ended and the next began. Cam filed up and down the runners, keeping an eye out for Arlo, and for a place to sit.

He spotted the blond hair and yellow tunic. Banjo. And next to him – *Matteo*? They were deep in discussion, wearing grown-up expressions. Seeing them together was like a slap on sunburn. Cam didn't understand. Friends and enemies, slithering from side to side like snakes.

He sat down in the nearest place he could find, next to a man so old his hair was wispy and his arms were like sticks. Cam reached forward and filled a banana leaf with curry, topped with rice, and then he made one for the man, to spare him the effort. When he turned to offer it, the old man had gone. In his place was a younger one with light brown hair. Cam noticed a mark on his wrist as he reached for a flatbread. He would have thought nothing of it if he hadn't already seen something similar. On Arlo. On Drake. And now he could see clearly that it wasn't a tick or a wave. It was the letter 'V'.

V was for Venom. Vicious. Villain.

Now, everywhere he looked he thought he could see eyes, watching him. A woman three runners down, a man further along. Another standing nearby, apparently looking for a seat. Were these the Watchers? Were the Watchers related to the V symbol?

Head spinning, Cam grabbed his aquamarine bowl and left the square, hurrying down the side streets, cutting through alleyways. At the back of his mind was an image of sharks. He and his dad used to watch them on the screen, lurking, circling the reef. *Wouldn't want to get hunted by one of them. Snap!* his dad would say, followed by a quick tickle to dispel the fear.

There was nothing to dispel it now. He ran home and shut the door.

'Leave it open, love. We need the breeze.'

His mother's voice was light. He didn't want to scare her, so he opened it halfway then sat at the back of the room.

'Why are you sitting down here?' His mother crouched by his side. 'Everything OK?'

'It will be,' Cam said, trying a smile. 'Just a friends thing, that's all. Here, this is for you.'

'That's a beautiful bowl.'

'A lady gave it to me. She said to show it to you. You have to look at it.'

'I'll put it somewhere safe. And how about Fort Eden? You're staying close to Byron, right? Being a good Cetacea boy?'

'Of course.'

'So what do you do up there?'

Cam would tell her about the truth when he was

closer to it. For now, it was best to stick to the other things. He told her about the characters at Fort Eden. The men in white linen who looked like silly corellas. Dana, who looked like fire but froze like ice. And Milo, who resembled a beady-eyed quoll. He told her about the dead chicken too, and how the mad old chef wanted to make something of it. *Make* something! As if he was going to pluck the feathers for a headdress or turn the beak into a clothes peg.

'Can't beat chicken soup,' his mother murmured, licking her lips. She stopped, horrified, when she realised what she'd said out loud. 'It's what we used to do before our diets became plant-based,' she whispered. 'A hot chook on a Sunday with potatoes and gravy. My sister always stole the wishbone. Used every bit of it. Chicken soup when we were sick.'

Cam recoiled. Eating an animal, with its skin and blood and bones! Was that what Milo meant? No one in their right mind would do that, now. Eating flesh was part of the dirty past. *We do not eat animals – all creatures are equal.*

'Best not to talk about it, Mumma,' Cam said, carefully, trying not to sound fearful.

She nodded and drifted into the storeroom to look for a place to set her new bowl.

Aaaargh!

Her scream was followed by the crack and smash of pottery hitting the stone floor.

‘Mumma? Mumma, what is it?’

She wailed again and ran upstairs, sobbing uncontrollably. Cam’s heart flew into a canter. Her fear. Something had triggered it. But what? He peered into the storeroom, expecting to see an intruder, but the room was empty. Nothing out of place apart from the mess of pottery shards on the floor. That beautiful bowl. He gathered the pieces together, stacking the larger ones in the palm of his hand, turning them over to look at what was left of the beautiful glaze, which sat like a layer of ice on the warm terracotta clay.

The largest piece was the flat bottom section of the bowl. Etched into it was the potter’s name in an arc, *Rosemary Kerrich*.

And the letter V.

Chapter 15
Questions, Questions, Questions

Cam woke late. From the noises that filtered down the lanes, he knew that early meal was already under way. His mother was still in bed. She groaned when he tried to turn her over. A tear leaked from her eye. They'd both had bad dreams.

'You must get up and eat, Mumma.' He rested a hand on her damp cheek. 'I'll be back as soon as I can.'

Eden Place was buzzing. It was a cloudy day, with light drizzle. Two days in a row! This kind of weather didn't happen often; the sun either baked the ground until it cracked, or it poured as if all the oceans had been sucked up into the sky. Drizzle was fun. The canteen teams smiled as they ran between runners with their breakfast baskets, trying not to skid on the slippery stone.

Cam would have liked to eat to quell his queasy stomach, but there was no time.

He was going to Fort Eden.

Dana had asked him not to. But something big was

about to happen. He felt close to discovering a truth, a fact – he didn't know what exactly – but forces were trying to trip him up. Secret symbols, whispered messages, riddles everywhere he turned. Questions grabbed at him like brambles. He had to talk to Byron. Byron had a way of making worries evaporate like wet footprints in the sun. And Cam had information to give him. The gang responsible for his father's disappearance. V. Why else would Arlo be on the run? Why else would his mother have reacted the way she did?

As he ran up into the Lower Ranges, the drizzle became a downpour. The raindrops were warm and big, and red-clay rivers ran down the hillside and splashed up his legs. Everything was soaked through with rust-coloured stains.

Outside the gates of Fort Eden, he stopped and caught his breath. Up here in the hills there was a strong wind. It made the palms thrash, and the white-clothed guards shivered beneath them, their linen uniforms glued to their skin. Cam lifted his necklace and they nodded him through, shoulders hunched beneath their ears. The mood was strange. It was the weather, perhaps.

Cam headed to the kitchen for a warm drink. Milo arrived at the same time through the herb garden door, walking in jerky movements like a nervous rat, swinging a bag. His hair dripped with rain.

'Argh. You made me jump, boy.' His face cracked into a jagged smile and he shook his head with amusement. 'I can see why he keeps you around. Keeps him on his toes. Here, pass me that knife – and don't touch the blade unless you want a finger taking off.'

'What are you cooking?' Cam asked, peering into the bag the chef had slung on the table. There was something fluffy inside. Milo stuck his hand in, dragged out a limp creature and slammed it on the worktop. 'A rabbit! What for?' Cam was horrified.

'Rabbit stew.'

Milo looked at Cam's face, contorted with confusion, and laughed wheezily. 'No point in hiding it now, is there? You caught me, red-handed. The truth is,' he said with mock secrecy, 'he's not exactly a vegetarian.'

'What's a vegetarian?'

Milo whistled through his teeth and shook his head.

'Oh! It's someone who eats vegetables, I get it. But if the whales say we can't eat animals, why would he do that?'

'Did the whales say that?' Milo asked, his face a picture of innocence.

'Yes,' Cam said, hurriedly. 'At least, I think so. But if they didn't, why would Byron tell us all that eating animals is bad, Milo?'

Milo paused. 'If you were allowed to eat animals, you'd be off catching them, wouldn't you?'

'I suppose some people might if they were hungry . . .'

Milo raised his eyebrows and pursed his lips. 'I'm not saying any more.'

'Is beef an animal, too?'

'Questions, questions, questions.'

Cam blushed crimson. 'I'm sorry. I'm very sorry.'

'I was joking. You're a kid. You're supposed to ask questions. Ask me what you should do now.'

'What shall I do now?'

'Get out of my kitchen and let me work. King will want this fellow and his fluffy friends all slow-cooked and tender, so I've got to get them in the oven.'

Cam looked again at the poor rabbit, splayed out on the worktop. 'Where is everyone?'

'He's probably taken his guests fishing. When it rains is the best time.'

'Fishing? Here, on the island?'

'Doubt it. He's probably gone out for the big fish – and he does love an excuse to exercise the speedboat.' He looked at Cam and sighed. 'It's a boat that speeds. Right, unless you want to help me rip the fuzz off that rabbit, get lost.'

Cam grimaced and backed out of the kitchen to the sound of Milo's chuckle. He felt sick at the thought of animal flesh, and also at discovering another layer of things he didn't understand – Byron acting like a king, eating animals, taking fish from the sea, and driving a fast boat on top of the whales' world.

In Cam's head, Byron's voice said, *Reject the questions your mind creates.*

Arlo's replied, *Fill your head with questions. If you don't, someone else will fill it with lies.*

The riddles! Hunting for the truth was so much easier at the start, when the thought of finding it was just a dream.

Cam went to the Whale Hall for comfort. A fire crackled in the fireplace and a large rug was rolled out in front of it, white and soft. Cam wandered around the room. He stroked the huge whale-tail sculpture and stared at the beautiful tapestries. A large mirror above the fireplace reflected everything back at him, making the room look twice the size. On either side of the fireplace was an alcove with panelled walls, each holding a large painting of a whale. But he caught sight of something shiny. Door handles. Not alcoves, but secret doors.

Cam tried the right-hand panel; it opened.

He found himself in a narrow stone-floored corridor that ran behind the fireplace wall of the Whale Room to join the kitchen pantry on the left. On his right was another room, the door of which was ajar.

I'm not curious, I'm just looking for Byron, he told himself.

The room was vast, mirroring the kitchen on the opposite side, but this one had carpet, sofas and cupboards. It was so different to anything Cam had seen before; it took his breath away. There were miniature Eden Screens, shiny equipment with buttons and glass doors. A cupboard with lots of holes, each one holding a bottle. He pulled one out to look. Its label said *Vos Winery*. On the sideboard stood photos in silver frames.

Photos – memories of the dirty past! Byron kept photos! Cam's hand shook as he turned a frame towards him. Inside it was a picture of a man with dark hair holding a prize of some kind. In another, the same man was leaning out of a metal box, grinning. There were other people, too. Old people. Enormous houses and fancy boats. Who were these people and things? Were they all lost in the floods? And why were they here? Everything from the Long Ago had been destroyed at the Birth of Cetacea. Hadn't it?

It was as if this room had escaped the Great Silence altogether.

Instead of being silent, it shouted things from the past – technology, photos, wine – but Cam didn't understand that language. Petra might, he thought. Petra would try. She would try to expand her mind and her understanding.

On the far wall was a giant map in a gold frame. Gridlines chopped the huge page into big squares. There were island shapes, meticulously detailed, with peaks and beaches and labels in perfect, regular print. Enormous islands at the top called France, Spain, Norway, Sweden. America. Russia. And at the bottom there was a line – much fainter than the others – in a wide raggedy shape, like a slice of rustic loaf. *Australia*. Inside the fragile border of Australia sat Cetacea. But there were other islands too. Woollemi, Flinders, Moffat. None of them were big, but they were definitely there, claiming their part of the old country with just as much land as Cetacea, if not more.

If this map was true, then Cetacea wasn't alone in the Southern Oceans.

Impossible. Perhaps they were sunken volcanoes or underwater trenches. If there was more land, they'd know. They'd have been told.

And what about the Northern Hemisphere? They had learned that there were a few scraps of land left, where people struggled on with the old ways and nature rotted around them; they'd be dead before the next generation grew up. Not like Cetacea, saved by the whales. But on this map, these landmasses had strong borders, and they were enormous. Russia a million times the size of Cetacea.

Cam shook his head. This must be an old map, drawn before the third floods. He walked away before his brain filled in the gaps with made-up guesses and nonsense, but at the door he turned back and gazed again at the room.

'You did admit you were only human,' Cam thought aloud. 'Perhaps you planned to tell me about all this when you told me the truth.'

He was pulled back to the map, and he stood in front of it and stared again at the little blob of Cetacea. The grid-like districts and chunks of pastures had always made Cetacea feel square, but on this map the island had a bigger, wilder shape. They had been taught that beyond the Higher Ranges there was nothing but a deadly drop into the sea – that's why men were said to be up there, guarding the edge, although no one ever had the energy to climb that long and that high after a day's work, especially in their thin shoes. But this map showed land north of the mountains. Lots and lots of it.

An old map. Olden times. Had to be.

Fill your head with questions.

If it was an old map, drawn up before the third floods, then why would there be a marker for Eden Place? Cam traced his fingers along the mystery coastline. The sea wiggled against the land and carved out scoops and protrusions. They all had their own names, like Squid Bay, Shark Point, King's Landing. The latter, a curious strip of land in the far north-west, pointed out to sea like a thin finger.

King's Landing.

Cam traced a line from King's Landing to the south-west coast where he, Banjo and Petra had been standing when they saw the lights. *This* was what they'd seen from the sea wall. Land, north of the Higher Ranges. His heart began to thump. There *was* more land.

And if everything else about this map was correct, then Cetacea was double the size. Cam thought of Petra, who craved more space to explore, breathe and live, and his stomach churned at the memory of that dazzling night.

He needed fresh air. He needed to get out.

He found his way out to the back garden and stood by the lake. Raindrops drummed on the lily pads and the waterfall behind thundered. It was like kettle drums and xylophones, so loud it drowned out the shrieking parrots in the gum forests. Not so loud that it drowned out the questions, which hit Cam's head like a storm of nails, some burying themselves deeper than others. The hidden land, the Great Silence, eating meat.

Do as the whales say. Show me your absolute loyalty. And the truth will be yours.

What if it was all a test?

That might explain it. Yes, perhaps it was all a test.

Cam had to clear his head, and there was one place he could always do that. In water. He shed his clothes and slipped into the freezing lake. He swam lengths, hoping that it would freeze his brain and cool his curiosity. But the voices were louder than ever.

Byron's came like a chime. *Absolute loyalty.*

But other voices chimed in too. Arlo, Petra, Banjo. His dad.

Fill your head with questions. If you don't, someone else will fill it with lies.

Expanding my mind is all I have.

Whales are a symbol of communication and knowledge.

Rebuild an intelligent society.

Follow Big Blue. Find the truth.

When the cold reached his bones, Cam dragged himself out, frustrated with the stubbornness of his own mind. If Byron didn't get back soon, he thought he might burst.

He slipped off his shoes at the door and padded through Fort Eden, his bare feet leaving damp prints on the stone. He needed food and warmth, even if it meant smelling rabbit cooking in the oven.

In the kitchen, Milo's head was shrouded in a cloud of steam. He was muttering loudly, occasionally shouting at the ceiling. He seemed particularly annoyed today. Cam decided not to bother him, or he'd risk catching a saucepan lid across the cheek. Carefully, he lifted a bun from a basket of breads on the sideboard and crawled on hands and knees, bun in mouth, through the little pantry door and into the secret stone corridor behind.

Ahead of him was the strange room with the shiny things and the map. But the door was now shut and there were voices coming from within. He could make out Byron's rich tones – not soothing and dreamlike, but bold and round, words coming out strong, like thwacks from a bat and ball. Cam peered through a hole where a knot in the wood had been pushed through. He saw people. Strange people, wearing clothing so tight, a wisp of air wouldn't get to their skin. On their feet were hard, shiny shoes.

Cam chewed his bread and watched with interest. Who dressed like that?

Who were they?

Stop it, stop it, stop asking questions.

Then Byron came into view, and Cam's heart leapt into his throat. Byron was dressed in the same dark, tight clothes, with a shiny green ribbon around his neck. Cam had never seen him wear anything but a floaty cloth tunic, soft and cool as cobwebs. All these clothes were tight, like the seed-pods of a bottlebrush tree – totally wrong for Cetacea's climate. As wrong as Arlo's door, which was closed against the breeze, as if he was hiding something.

Cam listened.

'With fifty barns working at full capacity, we can clean and prepare a hundred tons a day. It can be bought raw for burning – as you can see, kelp burns two and a half times slower than wood and is therefore extremely efficient – or we can sell you top-grade biofuel, which we process in our plants in the north. It'll run your homes, your electricity, your boats, your cars. We soon expect to produce a lot more. With investment, of course.'

'And where do you grow such huge amounts of kelp?' It was a man holding a flat screen in his lap.

'The sea, of course. Because the sea has no limits.' Byron put on a dazzling smile, which dropped when he looked at the door. He paused, then smiled again. 'Now, are we going to make a deal before lunch?'

Cam noticed his dripping clothes had made a puddle that was creeping under the door. If he didn't move that instant, he'd be caught. He ran as fast as he could, damp feet slapping against the stone, back into the kitchen. He ignored Milo's sarcastic comments and the stomach-turning smell of rabbit stew and dashed out into the kitchen garden, then round to the front. He hit the path that wound down through the Ranges, trying not to stub his bare feet or slip on the sodden clay. He ran and ran. And he didn't know why.

Yes, he did. He did know why.

This wasn't a test. It was one big lie.

Petra was right. If everyone on Cetacea was supposed to be equal, then something was very wrong with Byron Vos.

He heard the bustle of the town. A friendly, welcome noise. It pulled him faster. He yearned to be in the crowds, anonymous, hidden. He was nearly there. But a thundering of hooves reached his ear – like another storm, rolling down from the Ranges. Men were shouting his name.

'Cam Solomon. Stop.'

He turned to see three horses, ridden by men that Cam had never seen before. They weren't the ones in white linen that strolled the gardens. These ones wore brown.

'Who are you?' Cam asked, panting.

'Come with us.'

'Who are you?' he asked again.

'You're not in any trouble, Cam.'

One man reached down and pulled Cam up behind him. Cam wrapped his hands round the man's waist and stared glumly at his giant neck as they began to ride back up the hill. He saw tattoos – lines, blue as veins, twisted beneath the man's collar to make a picture. Rope. A sail. Some kind of boat. Cam didn't care. His head was sore and his heart sat like a lead ball above his stomach.

He didn't know what he'd just seen or what was about to happen. His existence felt like a snake-filled desert.

The horses walked back up the Ranges, cutting across the bush north of Eden Place as if they didn't want to be seen by the orchard workers who worked the fields on either side of the main track. Cam's rider slowed so the two in front went ahead. Cam sensed danger. He didn't want to face Byron, but he didn't want to be left alone with this man, either.

'Where are you taking me?' he asked.

'Back up the hill.' The man's voice dropped to a gravelly whisper. 'You'll be fine.'

'Why should I believe you?'

'My name is Greg. And on the mark of Veritas – you can trust me.'

The rider reached behind him and rested his hand on Cam's knee for a moment. Just long enough for Cam to see that he had a small inky V on the base of his thumb. Cam felt a trickle of fear. There wasn't a lot he understood, but he understood his mother's reaction to the bowl. V meant something bad. But if V was bad, why would this man show him as if it was something reassuring? He wished that something made sense.

'I couldn't trust you any more than I could lift you,' Cam growled.

'Well, you'd better start building some muscle, then.' The man chuckled, and Cam's mind twisted once again with the never-ending puzzle. But now he knew V was for Veritas. Whatever that meant.

'What's Veritas?'

'Keep your voice down,' the man hissed. And he said no more.

They joined the dirt path back up to Fort Eden, where Byron was waiting on the lawn, mindlessly picking the proud strelitzia flowers and dropping them at his feet. He was back in his cool linens. His smile was unnaturally wide.

'Where did you find him?' Cam heard Byron whisper to the front rider.

'We got him before he reached town.'

Byron helped Cam down and pulled him into a tight, perfumed hug. When he was released, the others had vanished and it was just the two of them again, in paradise. The rain had stopped and the palms and parrots were once again fluttering above their heads.

'Look, kiddo. I think you overheard some things that might have confused you.'

Now, where have I heard that before? Cam thought. Defiantly, he crossed his arms over his chest. Byron tugged him towards Fort Eden but Cam refused to budge.

'Cam, please,' Byron pleaded. 'Come inside and I'll tell you everything.'

'I want to ask questions. I want to be curious.'

'You can be. It's about time you knew the full story anyway. But you have to come inside.'

Cam was annoyed that everything had strings attached – strings that had to be tugged on and unlocked, like Arlo's door device. He suddenly felt overcome with exhaustion.

'Why? Why should I trust you?'

'Because someone needs to take over Cetacea one day. And that someone is you.'

Chapter 16

Growing Kelp

Cam, freshly showered and dressed in new linens, sat in front of the fire, his toes buried in the soft rug and his hands wrapped around a warm mug.

'Try it,' Byron said. He sat opposite him, cross-legged. 'It's a taste you might have to get used to. But when you do . . . yum!'

Cam sipped the sweet, thick liquid and wrinkled his nose. 'What is it?'

'Chocolate.'

'Tastes like wood.'

'More of a seed. We don't grow chocolate on Cetacea. Cacao trees need rain – far more than we get here.'

'Where do they grow then?'

'Papua.'

'Where?'

'It's another island, Cam. North of here. You see, Cetacea isn't alone in the region.' Byron stared at him intensely, waiting for his shock and confusion. But Cam had seen the map. The knowledge that there was a wider world had now settled in his mind like a stone on the bottom of a riverbed.

'Go on,' Cam said, dipping back into his chocolate.

'You heard me talking about the kelp to those people, and I need to explain that first. From there it will all be easier to understand. When the old country flooded, it created a shallow shelf beneath the waters, perfect for growing kelp. We grow tons and tons of it. It grows easily, but when you add nutrients, a plant can grow your height in a single day.'

'What nutrients?' Cam said, thinking of the Old World chemicals. Dirty. Wrong.

Byron smiled. 'You're going to find this funny, Cam. We use wee. Nothing on Cetacea is wasted. All your urine is collected and the seaweed loves it. And kelp is a miracle – it can be eaten, used as a fertiliser for crops and it can be burned as fuel, all without hurting the environment. We are doing our bit to supply the few islands left out there with as much kelp as they need. It stops them burning wood and oil. We – you and I – are going to clean up the entire world.'

'But you told us that cleaning kelp is for the whales. You lied.'

Byron thought a while. 'Yes and no. The kelp has to be clean before it's processed to make fuel. Ultimately, we *are* doing it for the whales. If we can persuade everyone else to use our clean fuel, the planet will get better and the whales will be happy.'

'They said that? The whales said that?'

'Yes, they said that.'

Cam wasn't swept along like he had been before. He felt like a sea anemone; he mistrusted sudden movement. And all this was very sudden. Byron was watching him closely. His face was open and kind; it was as if sharing his secrets had set him free. But how many secrets did he have?

'What about the land beyond the Higher Ranges in the north?' Cam prompted. 'I saw your map.'

'It's where the processing plants are, that's all. There's nothing but processing plants and homes for the workers. All hidden from view, so it doesn't spoil paradise.'

He made us believe in paradise, alright. Arlo's words floated back to him.

Arlo.

'And what about finding my father?'

Byron placed his hands, one on top of the other, over this heart. 'It's all I think about.'

'I discovered the group that betrayed him.' Cam stopped himself. He wasn't sure any more. He didn't know the full picture. But perhaps Byron's reaction would help him work it out? 'I can take you to them now.'

'I understand your hurry, but we mustn't rush in or they'll scurry away like beetles into the cracks. A raid takes careful planning.' He tapped the tips of his fingers together. 'But why don't we discuss the other matter connected to your father – the truth?'

'You'll tell me?'

'I won't. But Big Blue will. He's here, in Cetacea waters. He wants to meet you.'

What?

Byron smiled. 'This is a once in a lifetime experience, Cam. You'll take it, won't you?'

Cam's armour of caution and questions fell away. Like a flash flood that instantly refreshes the town's drinking wells, he felt himself refill with the sense of awe he'd carried for years. It bubbled inside him. Yes, at the end of the day, everything he had searched for came down to this: his father's wish. It was more important than kelp and tattoos and animal flesh. The truth was what everything had been for.

'Really? *Really?*'

Byron sprawled back on the carpet, laughter bursting from his chest.

'But I don't know whale-talk.'

'One day you will. We'll start your lessons soon. We can't have a leader of Cetacea who can't talk to the whales. But for now he just wants to meet you. He'll speak through me and you can ask him any questions you like. You can ask him *anything*.'

The door opened and Dana entered. 'What are you two talking about?' she asked cautiously.

'I'm going to meet Big Blue,' Cam said. 'And, Dana,

I had an idea for the festival. I think everyone, like me, dreams of speaking to whales. So we could have a whale message box, where people write down a message and then Byron can read them to Big Blue.'

'The boy's a genius!' Byron exclaimed, clapping with delight.

'It's a lovely idea,' Dana said, although her voice said otherwise. 'But what –'

'Enough!' Byron boomed. 'You can discuss the party later. Right now, we've got other things to talk about.' Byron reached over and ruffled Cam's hair affectionately. 'I'm teaching Cam Solomon a lesson.'

He locked eyes with his assistant. Cam thought he saw the flash of the jealous child in her again. Perhaps she'd been hoping to inherit the governance of Cetacea. And instead, it was all going to a thirteen-year-old boy. That did seem strange, come to think of it, but Cam didn't have time to ponder it, as Byron grabbed his hand and pulled him to his feet. He dragged a footstool in front of the fireplace and lifted Cam on to it, so they were both looking into the huge mirror. Side by side.

'It's so nice to have a young face around Fort Eden again, isn't it, Dana?'

Byron turned to look at the woman directly, but Cam could see her reflection in the mirror, and she wasn't smiling. She wasn't happy at all. Cam focused on himself. He had never seen himself so clearly before. There was no reflective glass this shiny and clear down in the town.

Through a gap in his top he saw his tattoo – unfinished, but still beautiful. A perfect image of the creature he was destined to meet. One of a kind.

No, it wasn't one of a kind.

Arlo's brother had one. A small detail that still niggled him.

'Cam, we're going. Right now.'

Dana stepped forwards. 'Dad –'

'Now!' he boomed.

'Now?' Cam blinked.

'This very moment.'

Everything went silent. The house, the air, the noise in Cam's head. It dropped to a pure, still hum, as if the entire world was waiting for what came next. Without a word, Byron took his hand and led him past Dana, who stood dazed as a deer, out of Fort Eden to the stables. She said *Dad*, Cam remembered. *Dad*. But Byron was a whirlwind and Cam couldn't find a moment's peace to think.

'What do you think, kiddo? Isn't she a beauty?'

Propped in the middle of the stable barn was a shiny silver machine with two fat wheels and a heart of pipes and twisted metal. Byron patted a black solid cushion on top.

'What is it?' Cam said, alarmed.

'It's like a little horse. Hop up.'

Cam carefully swung his leg over the seat, heart beating wildly. What was happening? Byron sat on the front seat and looked over his shoulder.

'Sit still, lean into the motion and hold on tight.'

Cam yelped as the machine suddenly vibrated beneath him like a noise box and he wrapped his arms round Byron's middle just as it started to move. So slowly at first that Cam didn't know how it stayed upright. But Byron did something to make it pick up speed, and they cruised round the front of the gardens and past the men on the lawn. Some in white, three others in brown. One of them, Greg.

Greg's face was scrunched, furrows buried deep in his forehead. He followed Cam with his eyes and then began to run to the stables.

'Byron, that man –' Cam began.

'Whatever it is, we'll talk about it later,' Byron shouted over his shoulder. 'We can't be late.'

They took a right turn round the hillside and headed north, following the wide contours of the Lower Ranges on a track that looped across the hills, before zigzagging, steeper and steeper, towards the peaks.

The Higher Ranges sliced across Cetacea from east to west like a steep, jagged wall, insurmountable. Impossible to climb, even with the energy of twenty farm labourers. A machine would surely be unable to take on the sheer gradient and the wilderness it supported – trees as thick as stone walls and bushes like balls of wire. But Byron's machine found a path through the rocks and turned into a cave, cut into the mountain. Cam's stomach flipped as they entered darkness.

'Hold tight. Don't wriggle. I have to keep a straight line. Can't see a thing, and we're going right through rock.'

Byron twisted the handlebars. The engine roared like a dragon. The darkness closed in around them: there was nothing but black and the deafening boom, which seemed to go on forever. Cam thought of the Long Ago and how this was the Far Ahead. The noise and the speed – he wasn't ready for them. He closed his eyes and hoped it would end soon.

When he opened them again, a pinhole of light had appeared. It expanded, bigger and bigger, until it was a huge blinding white circle of daylight. With an extra burst of speed they were through it, blinking in the sunshine on the north side of the mountain. The secret half of Cetacea. Byron skidded the machine to a stop and put his foot down to hold it upright.

'There are the processing plants for kelp biofuel, villages for workers. Right down there. Can you see them? And the boats to bring the kelp down the coast to the district. In the middle of the night, of course.'

'And the sand? What do you do with that?'

'Take the particles out. What use is titanium and gold to the whales?'

Byron took the machine gently down the mountainside. Cam's stomach lurched as the wheels slewed on the loose stones. When the ground finally levelled out, Cam was awash with relief. They passed little houses, with square lakes as blue as Terra Beach, machines in the driveways. Fields with chickens and peculiar, large animals that *moo*-ed as they drove past. Cam laughed at them. But he'd ask what they were later; his mind was flooded with wonder at the sight of the sea in the distance.

The journey was over – the *whole* journey, the machine ride and the questions about Byron and the following of Big Blue. After years and so many fears, Cam would be standing right next to the truth. Or swimming?

'Will I be in the water?'

'Of course, Cam.'

In the water. Alongside a giant.

'What do I do when Big Blue swims up to me?'

'Nothing, kiddo. Just float by his side. Let him get the feel of you. You have to let him connect with you. You can swim, can't you?'

'Yes.'

'Good. Because we'll be going deep. Whales can't come too close to the shore, for obvious reasons.'

'The shallow shelf of Australia – I mean, the Old World?'

'That's right. The shallow shelf of the Old World.' Byron grinned. 'You're an intelligent boy. You can't imagine how happy I am right now.'

'Ready to rebuild an intelligent society!' Cam said, thinking it sounded good.

'What you do with Cetacea is up to you now.'

Cam smiled. The old whale-talker and the new whale-talker: they slotted together like the land and the sea. There had been moments of unease, but there was often turbulence along a coastline. It was the natural way of things. He hugged Byron's middle tighter as the machine picked up speed and shot across the land and on to roads that had solid black surfaces, smooth as nut butter. They were heading north-west, towards the pointed headland. King's Landing.

Chapter 17
The Deep Sea

The machine stopped. Cam slid off and stretched his legs, marvelling at how just days ago they had considered falling stars and spaceships. It was just a strip of land. Secret land surrounded by boats. So many boats, big and small, moored to jetties that jutted from the headland like teeth on a comb. They bobbed and rocked on the thick green water.

Byron said it was algae, and they grew it on purpose to absorb the contamination from the boats; it was collected and used as fertiliser. But no more questions, he added. It was time. He strode down King's Landing and stopped next to a boat the size of the stage in Eden Place, white with a pointed nose. He patted it.

'Come on, then!'

Cam noticed the boat was called *Juggler-45*, which was a strange name, he thought. Onboard, there were sofas and cupboards full of drinks. It was better equipped than any house Cam had seen. He gawped as Byron skipped from one side of the deck to the other, flicking switches and pulling open storage boxes. It was like a floating home. But smooth and shiny, the way he imagined spaceships to be.

Byron pulled out a box containing masks, tubes and flat, floppy shoes.

'Find a mask that fits your face so you can see properly. And a pair of flippers. For your feet.' He looked at Cam's expression. 'They help you swim faster, like a fish.'

Cam peered at the flat rubber fins. 'No, fish have vertical tails. These are horizontal with a vertical swish, like a whale tail.'

'Yeah, something like that.'

Cam sorted through the flippers. 'This boat has everything!'

'It certainly does,' Byron said. 'Have you found a mask yet? That one, there. Yes, that one. Looks your size. Now, sit down and hold on. We're going to go fast.' Byron grinned. Not the slow, sleepy smile that took forever. This was a flash. Boyish. Excited.

Byron turned a key on the dashboard, pulled a lever and turned the boat's steering wheel. *Juggler-45* chuntered away from its mooring. Cam's body vibrated with the boat's purr. It was like the silver machine but bigger. Like he was sitting on top of a beast. Byron pointed the boat out to sea.

'What's that rumbling?'

'It's the engine. And you're about to feel what it does. Ready?'

The boat shot forward, squealing then groaning as it hit the waves, bouncing on the surface like an unripe mango. Cam was thrown against the hard seats. He was terrified. His hair whipped his face and the rushing wind stole the cries from his mouth. Byron, standing at the wheel and protected by a curved screen, looked like a proud horse.

The deep green of the algae water became a lighter, murky green as they headed out to sea. Kelp. The flat ribbons waved beneath the surface as far as Cam could see – in even rows, straight lines – and the boat drove down the spaces between them. This wasn't like the tumble-jumble forests they'd been shown on the screen; it was planted like a crop, like sunflowers or corn. Cam had lived with the colour and feel of kelp his whole life, but the sight of it like this made him queasy. How long until they got to the bright blue sea?

A gaping distance grew between them and Cetacea. Eventually, the kelp rows stopped. Then the island was gone from sight. They were beyond the shallow shelf, out in the deep. Where the whales swam.

Byron turned around to look behind them. 'Dammit!'

He was staring at something. Cam turned to see another boat following their wake. A man was standing at the wheel, waving an arm. He could see the darkness of his mouth, shouting. Was it Greg with the Veritas mark?

Byron grabbed a pair of binoculars hanging from a hook on the control panel. He brought them to his eyes and growled. 'Who is it?' He thrust the binoculars at Cam. 'Do you recognise him?'

Cam put the circles against his eyes. An image leapt through the glass.

'It's Arlo!' he shouted. 'Arlo Fox. The tattooist.'

'He's trying to stop us,' Byron shouted. 'He's trying to stop you meeting Big Blue. Take the wheel. Keep the lever pushed up.'

Byron let go before Cam could get hold of the controls and the boat swerved, lurching to a violent stop. The motion threw Byron on to the deck, but he didn't seem worried about that. He opened a panel in the boat's side and pulled out a small metal object, checked it over and stood up. He spread his legs, found his balance, and pointed the metal object at their pursuer.

The metal thing banged once, twice. The sound cracked the air with a metallic ring, like a wheelbarrow falling down steps.

Bang, bang.

Behind them, the chasing boat swerved and stopped. Arlo was still standing, waving, shouting. His mouth said, 'Cam, Cam!'

Byron leapt back to the controls and thrust *Juggler-45* forward.

'What was that metal thing?' Cam asked.

'A gun. I put a hole in his boat. On the way back, I'll make sure I put a hole in him too, don't you worry. He won't be bothering you again.'

Cam didn't understand. 'Why's he trying to stop me meeting Big Blue?'

Byron's face was wild. 'Because he's a whale-hater. A whale killed his brother.'

'But why?'

'Questions, Cam!' Byron shouted. 'Too many questions!'

Cam thought about Arlo's face in the strange glasses. Whales had killed his brother? He felt uncertain and sad as he watched the other boat shrink into the distance. *Juggler* roared on. Byron looked over at Cam and winked.

'Nothing's going to stop you now,' he said. 'Ready?'

Was he ready? His brain and his heart were fighting. Everything spun around him.

'I said, are you ready?' Byron repeated.

Yes, this was it. Big Blue. *Follow Big Blue. Find the truth*. He had to be ready.

'I am!'

'Good.'

Byron cut the engine. The boat came to a stop, bobbing and tilting on the small waves. Everything was silent, apart from the slap of the water against the hull. Cam had a flashback of being on the pontoon with Banjo. He ached for it now – just a taster of friendship before he took the biggest leap of his life.

'Cam?' Byron held the prayer position, wrists together, pressed against his chest.

Cam's hands shook as he raised them in a whale tail.

'You wouldn't give up what you believed in. That's what brought you to this moment, here, now. Mask on, flippers on.'

Cam slipped on the flippers and securely fastened his mask so that no water could get in. Byron opened a door at the back of the boat. Cam, shivering with fear and anticipation under the baking sun, gave a brave thumbs-up and leapt through it, splashing into the sea. He turned and clung to the boat's ladder, looking for encouragement from Byron.

'Swim out,' the man said. 'He won't come close to the boat.'

Cam pushed himself off, gasping as he felt his legs dangle in deep nothingness. He trod water a while, looking up at the whale-talker. 'Aren't you coming, too?'

Byron shook his head.

'But how will you translate for me?'

'You'll understand everything.'

But how? His mind crashed with confusion. Arlo, the boat, the gun, Big Blue.

Cam ducked his head under and peered around. He had expected bright blue water, teeming with fish. But there was only an occasional sliver of silver, flitting through an endless murky sea. He could barely see five metres in front of him.

'Where are the colourful fish?'

Byron looked down patiently. 'In the reefs, the shallows. You're out deep now. It's a whole different picture. And Cam.' Byron closed the little door at the back of the boat and leant on it. 'You're about to find out what happened to your father.'

'What?' Cam felt winded.

'The answer you're looking for is down there. Go, before it's too late.'

Cam took a deep breath and went under, using his arms to propel him further down. Three metres under, he stopped and tried to calm his heart and hold his breath. He looked around the vast expanse of gloomy nothingness, waiting. Waiting. Searching the depths.

Graaaaar.

There was a sudden roar, and huge bubbles raced towards him. Cam curled into a protective ball, not knowing if he'd be hit by a large fish or pierced by the teeth of something bigger. A giant wave of frothing bubbles hit his skin with the force of a summer storm, the air bouncing and rolling over him, then fading away until there was nothing left of the tornado but a stream of tiny bubbles disappearing into the distance. Panicking, he fought his way up to the surface.

Juggler-45 was speeding back towards Cetacea.

Byron had abandoned him.

Arlo hadn't been trying to stop *him*. He'd been trying to stop Byron. And now Byron was going back to kill him. Arlo would get away, though. Arlo was invincible.

But he, Cam, was not. Despair lodged in his chest as he looked around at the endlessness of filthy water.

No land in sight. Nothing to cling to. He trod water, remembering Petra's words. *Life is like a desert. Every way you look, nothing but the same view.* He understood now. For her, life was like this: an expanse with no history, no future. He, too, was lost and drifting.

He swam face down, propelling himself with his flippers and searching the depths for creatures that might kill him or save him. But the visibility was so poor, murkier than a barrel of dirty kelp water. There were no shoals, no turtles, nothing he'd expected to see in the Cetacea Sea. Just lonesome fish with sad mouths, cruising the emptiness as if they had nowhere to go. After a while, Cam became one of them; he no longer flinched at their sudden flashes of metallic grey. He drifted. Minutes became hours. His back began to blister under the relentless sun, and the salt stung his lips. He paddled on, his head dizzy with doom and heat. If the whales had wanted to save him, they would have.

You're about to find out what happened to your father.

This was where he'd ended up. Ended.

Cam couldn't cry. His throat was too dry. Instead, the pain stuck in his chest.

Was there anything worth living for now?

He wondered if he should let himself drown, just get it over with, but his body seemed to hold on to hope even when he had no energy left, and he floated, drifted on. Three, four hours. Then he saw a slick shape gliding below him. Another. And another. Bigger than any fish.

They had vertical tails with a horizontal swish.

Not whales. *Sharks.*

Cam was too tired to fight. He thought of his mother, and pain throbbed through him like the afterburn of a paper-wasp sting. He couldn't save himself – or her. He'd lost everything. A dark fog drew over his eyes and he felt himself give up breath and hope. He sank down and down, seeing, a second before he passed out, a large, dark shape in the distance.

A torpedo. With grooves at its throat.

Big Blue?

Chapter 18

The Woven Dream

Cam's eyelids fluttered open. His eyelashes were brittle with salt. The hard daylight hurt his eyes and he turned to shield himself from the glare.

'Cover his face, quickly.'

A shadow fell over him and cold water splashed across his chest and down his legs. He moaned. His tongue was thick and swollen.

'You're safe, Cam.' A woman's voice.

Cam tried to sit up, but his head was spinning. He turned to one side to vomit. Someone dribbled fresh water on to his lips. There were several voices now. Cam rolled his eyes and saw the sky dipping into the sea, over and over. He was on a boat.

'Arlo?'

A face loomed over him. A face he knew.

'M–M–'

'Don't try to speak.' Matteo propped Cam's head on his thigh, and trickled more water into his mouth.

Cam fell into little sleeps, his mind forcing him awake with flashbacks. *Big Blue. What happened? What happened?* A headache pounded his skull like a trapped animal.

The journey seemed endless. When they finally pulled into the shelter of rocks in the late afternoon, Cam was able to sit up and look around. That's when he saw Greg. His shirt was off, and a tattoo of a sailing ship covered the width of his giant back. He was with another, shorter man, with muscles as big as possums. And next to him was a young woman who seemed to be watching Cam closely. On her wrist was a tiny V.

'Matteo?'

'Hi, Cam.'

'Why . . . what . . . happened?'

'It's a long story.'

'Who are these people?'

'I'll tell you later. Right now, we have to be quiet.'

The boat rocked wildly as the wash rolled against the land and back out to sea again. Greg got out and waded in the water, which reached up to his knees, and tugged the nose of the boat until it was wedged solidly between the rocks. He helped the others on to the shore – first the young woman, then Matteo and the muscle man. Cam was last. His legs wobbled as he stood, but Greg lifted him gently and placed him on the beach. He wiggled his toes in the sand, willing the strength to return to his limbs.

'Sit on this rock a minute. Put these on.' The woman handed Cam a bag containing fresh clothes.

He winced as the dry material brushed against his burned skin. She poured fresh water from a bottle on to his feet, which were rubbed sore from the flippers. She applied cream and bandaged them before easing them gently into oversized cloth shoes. The smaller man crouched at his side.

'I'm Keith, Matteo's dad. And I'm sorry for everything, Cam. I really am.'

'Explain later,' Greg said. 'There's no time now.'

Cam noticed the V on Keith's wrist, but his mind grazed over it as quickly as his eyes. Nothing made sense. And he was too dizzy to care. He looked back at the boat. Its hull was wide and lined with strakes – ridges that scored the length of the vessel. Grooves. It had never been a whale. It had been a rescue.

They moved slowly, carefully, in single file up the beach.

'Where are we?' Cam whispered to Matteo.

'We're behind the sea wall, east.'

There were rolls of wire here too, but both men had cutters in their pockets. They set about twisting the fencing until the wires snapped, then they yanked apart sections and ushered everyone through. They did the same for the next fence, and the next, until they were standing at the base of a sea wall. Greg whistled. A whistle returned from the other side, then a ladder flew over the top and crashed at their feet. One by one they helped each other over – a man on the other side, helping them land in the soft compost. Greg carried Cam over his shoulder all the way, like a precious bundle.

The evening light was flickering through the orange trees, casting dancing shadows on the ground. It would cover their movement as they made their way across the field. Matteo helped Cam, giving him a shoulder to lean on as they picked their way through the brittle stalks towards a harvesting barn. Once inside it, they sat at the far end, where a high window brought in a square of late evening sun and they could see each other's faces. The woman searched the room and brought over a melon – overripe but OK to eat. She smashed it with her fist and handed out the pieces. The first piece was for Cam. He sank his teeth in and sucked the sweet water.

'We need to go back and hide the boat,' Greg said. Keith nodded and patted Cam's knee.

'You'll be safe here for a few hours.'

'Where's Arlo?' Cam asked, but they all looked down at the floor. No one spoke. *Arlo. Oh, Arlo.* Cam's heart cracked like a dry leaf.

Matteo's father gave him a sorry smile. 'You're safe. That's the important thing.'

The young woman handed him a pouch. 'Inside are some crackers. Just nibble them to get your energy back. There are fresh dressings and a pot of chamomile oil in there too. Rub it into your skin every hour and don't scratch, even if you're desperate to. You're burned. If the skin blisters, it needs to heal on its own. There's an irrigation pump outside the barn. Drink as much water as you can before you move on. But sip, don't gulp.' She smiled efficiently and followed the men out.

That left Matteo. The boys sat together in silence, watching the golden sun disappear. With the evening came a violet sky and a cool breeze. Cam shivered. Sunburn and shock. He opened his mouth, then closed it again in case the torrent of questions tore him apart on its way out. Instead, he stared at his poor feet. The bandages had rolled down and the skin beneath them was peeling like bark.

Matteo rummaged in the pouch the young woman had given Cam and pulled out the fresh bandages. He gently took Cam's feet, unwinding the old ones and reapplying oil. Cam winced at the pain. Matteo looked up at him through his floppy fringe.

'Y'alright, Cam?'

Cam searched Matteo's face in the dim light. 'Why are you helping me?'

Matteo carefully wound the new bandages round each foot. 'Our dads were in this together, you know. This Veritas thing.'

'Veritas,' Cam repeated, too tired to even ask what it was.

'They tried to bring Byron down for years. But Byron had Watchers, people who live among us, making sure we do as we're told. One of them caught on to your dad. Someone they thought was a friend snitched for a basket of fruit. After that, Veritas didn't know who they could trust and the Watchers multiplied. You can sometimes tell who they are, by the way they stare or appear from nowhere and stand there doing nothing. My dad got freaked out. He told me stories about you being a liar, and he said a bunch of bad things about you so I'd keep away. He was just trying to protect me so we wouldn't get caught. But I believed him. I shouldn't have, Cam. I should've gone with my gut.'

'Our dads were in Veritas? But they were never friends.'

'Veritas members stayed apart so if one got caught, they wouldn't all get caught. They didn't even all know each other – only Arlo knew them all. After your dad – you know – he gave them the V mark so they could recognise each other and pass along information.'

Cam thought. 'If Veritas is a group, why was Arlo out there all alone?'

'His part was to distract Byron so we could rescue you. He called a Veritas meeting a few nights ago. Ordered everyone to keep an eye on you and get ready for something. The word got out somehow.'

Cam remembered the old woman and the pottery bowls she had handed out. All etched with a telltale V. She was spreading the word. It was a signal to stand by.

'Mum . . .' It hit him. All this time, she had been

frightened that Cam would join Veritas, like his dad, not that he'd be harmed by it. 'She's going to be worried sick.'

'Dad will get a message to her that you're safe. Don't worry.'

'And the truth? What's the big truth? That Byron's a liar?'

'I think there's more to it than that, but I don't know.' Matteo sighed. 'Dad says we've done our bit. We can't get involved any more.'

'But we can't stop now,' Cam said, his lips cracking.

Matteo's face dropped. 'I don't think Dad'll let me see you again – not until things have settled down. But you've got some good friends looking out for you.'

'Banjo and Petra? They're not my friends.'

'That's not what I hear. When I first saw you guys together, I got a bit jealous, y'know? Acted like a total frill.' Matteo put his hands either side of his neck and wiggled his fingers, like an angry frill-necked lizard. Cam laughed, wincing in pain. 'But until I can be your friend again, I'm glad you've got them. Before I go, I've got to teach you a song. Banjo said.'

'A song?'

'Yep. Listen and learn – fast.'

Cornfield on the right,
Three steps, then left.
Wiggle like a snake till you meet the rock ahead.

Climb up the rock,
Move right along the ridge.
Wait at the tree that's broken like a bridge.

Cam whispered it again and again through his swollen lips. Matteo nodded.

'That's it. As soon as the sun drops, you have to move. Don't fall asleep. Early in the morning, harvesters will be back to get the rest of the melons and you don't want to get caught. Head north. Sing the song. When you get to the end of it, make the call. Get that – Banjo said make the call. Bye, Cam.'

Matteo slipped out of the barn, and Cam was left with silence and the memory of floating in a dirty sea, blistered as a scorpionfish, and in his head, the noise of a million questions. If the sea was still rotting, then what had they been working for all this time? He lay down, too tired to think any more. Sleep pulled at him so fast, he felt as if he was being sucked out into the universe. Into a dream.

He swam through the night sky. The air was silky and warm. He lay on his back and looked up at the infinite space above – a canopy dusted with planets and stars that fell into patterns, moving and morphing, creating a shape he knew. Not solid. Like knowing something without seeing it. The starry whale pulled pieces of his story from his weary mind, twisting the strands, building a wavy tale that he knew in his heart to be true, beneath a whale tattoo.

Cam sat up, disorientated. Matteo? No, Matteo had gone. The light in the barn was inky. The sun was low and the moon was already climbing. He had to go. What had Matteo said? *Head north*. He scrambled to his sore feet, went outside to the pump, where he took a sip of water, then began to hobble across the melon field, gasping as his burned skin twisted with each movement. He kept the distant glow of the sun on his left and headed towards the hills.

Wait. The song. He had to sing the song.

Cornfield on the right,
Three steps, then left.
Wiggle like a snake till you meet the rock ahead.
Climb up the rock,
Move right along the ridge.
Wait at the tree that's broken like a bridge.

At the end of the melon patch he saw the swaying ears of corn. Three steps.

To the left was a rough track through the field opposite. He followed it, noticing how it wiggled like a snake through the dry crops, then ascended gradually into the hills. Below and to the right, he could see dim lights, like glow-worms, from the town's oil lamps. He thought of bed, comfort, Mumma. He had to keep going.

He limped along, wondering if he would make it. But then the path stopped. In front of him a tall rock rose into the sky like a giant sentry. He'd managed the first part. If he took the journey bit by bit, he'd make the rest.

He felt for handholds, grimacing as pain pulsed through his swollen fingers. But there were ledges to rest on and crevices to get his feet and hands into. He wrapped the remaining bandages round his fingers to protect them, and slowly he worked his way up the rock face, the cool night air singing across his sore neck, halfway between agony and ecstasy. He stopped to gulp the air when the memories of Arlo and his father overwhelmed him, which they did, time after time, like a lapping tide. Then he pushed on.

At the top, he rested and looked out at the dark lumps and bumps of Cetacea. An entire island of people fooled by a wide smile and a pair of green eyes and years of suffocating lies. Wait until things settle down, Matteo said.

Not going to happen, Cam thought, willing his complaining legs to stand again.

He sang the song again, turning right and walking carefully along the ridge, which had been cut into the side of the hill. There was a huge drop to the ground on his left and he placed his feet carefully, feeling them shake with tiredness. Then, ahead, he saw a ghost gum, its bright white bark luminous in the moonlight. It had been sliced by lightning: half of it still pointed at the sky, while the other half had fallen to one side. It lay across a deep crevasse in the rocky hill, forming a bridge to the other side.

He had come to the end of the song. He had arrived.

Matteo had said, *make the call.* But what call? He looked up and saw the five stars, and beyond that the trillions of twinkling crystals. Ah, *that* call. He smiled and cupped his mouth with his hands.

'Coo-ee. Coo-ee.'

Although hoarse, his voice carved the silence, sounding as natural to the bush as the sound of any nocturnal animal. And like a boomerang, it came right back.

'Coo-ee. Coo-ee.'

On the other side of the gum bridge, two silhouettes emerged, moonlight brushing their hair. The friends who would always come when you called.

Chapter 19

The Shepherd's Hut

Shepherds' Country covered the upper east side of Cetacea, stretching from the farms right up to the Higher Ranges. It was an untamed mountainous bushland filled with camouflaged snakes, funnel-web spiders and dry undergrowth that sliced at your legs. They said if you were in Shepherds' Country and you weren't a shepherd, you'd soon be dead on the herbalist's table.

But that's where they were going.

The bush wasn't asleep. There were the rustles of nocturnal rodents; nightjars creaked at the moon; and there was a twanging that repeated, over and over, like a plucked guitar string.

'Listen. Pling, pling. Hear that?' Banjo said, patting his chest. 'It's the banjo frog.'

'That's what you're named after? Hilarious!' Petra laughed.

'I quite like it,' Banjo said with a shrug.

'Me, too, Banj. It suits you.' Cam's body was wracked

with exhaustion and his mind was sore, but his funny friend gave him strength. The three of them together felt like safety.

As the path got steeper, the effort took away their breath. Loose stones rolled underfoot, making every step perilous. Cam struggled, but Banjo walked behind him all the way, ready to catch him. Petra was up ahead. She had no map, but she said she knew where to go, even in the dark, and they all agreed she could navigate the bush better than anyone, even though Banjo tried to argue that it was in his blood.

'Not far. Just up there.' Petra pointed. 'That's where the shepherd's hut is.'

'And what's at the shepherd's hut?' Cam asked.

'Home.'

Twenty minutes later they were standing outside a wooden shack raised on legs with a corrugated iron roof and a small veranda. Petra motioned for them to wait. She went inside and a minute later came to the doorway and beckoned them in.

She'd lit a candle. Its flickering glow spread a homely warmth. There was bread and fruit on the table, cushions and blankets on the floor, a water drum filled with fresh water. Where from? It didn't matter. It was a safe place.

They sat and ate. The feeling of food hitting his sore stomach made Cam wince at first, but after a while it began to feel good. He noticed that Banjo and Petra were staring at him edgily, as if they were too nervous to speak. He put down his bread and looked at them.

'So, do you want to hear what happened?'

'Only if you're ready,' Banjo said.

'Absolutely yes, tell us now!' Petra demanded.

Cam told them the full story: about Byron's business meetings, the secret land north of the Ranges, and the string of lights they'd seen – a mooring place for Byron's boats. And he told them how Veritas had been ready for something; how they'd planned an operation, knowing that Byron would take Cam out to sea; how Greg sent the alarm when he saw Byron and Cam on the silver machine, heading north. And finally, Cam explained Arlo's role. No, his *sacrifice*.

They were shocked. They didn't know. How could they? They'd received word from Matteo to wait in Shepherds' Country for Cam *and* Arlo, expecting them to arrive together, tired and hungry, but alive.

Why did it have to happen? Why Arlo, who had protected them?

They didn't have the answers, only tears. And they lay in a pile on the cushions and cried themselves to sleep.

When sunrise turned the shack into an oven, they woke, stretching and achy, their eyes crusty. By night the hut was a hideaway cabin, mysterious with candlelight. By day, it was nothing more than four walls and basic furniture. Just a place for a shepherd to eat his meal out of the sun. Shepherds were too far away from town and too basted in solitude to cope with mealtimes in the square. It was an untamed lifestyle that suited Petra.

She leapt up and began to rifle through the cupboards.

'Aha!' She emerged with a tin can and held it up. It had a picture of peaches on the front. 'See this? There were a few of these in the cupboards when I got here. Not so many now, though.' She rubbed her tummy. 'From the Long Ago, I reckon. Tastes alright.' She stabbed the top of it with a knife and poured the syrup on to her tongue. She passed the tin to Banjo.

'Whose place is this?' Cam asked.

'A friend of Arlo's.'

There was a silence at the sound of his name. Banjo leapt up and flung open the door.

'He wanted you to see another day, so let's go see it.'

Standing outside the wooden hut, they were shocked wide awake by the searing white sun and the nose-tickling scent of eucalyptus. Cam hadn't realised just how high they'd climbed. The hut was on a flat terrace of the hill. Just a few steps in front of them, bushes and rocks tumbled down into the gum-tree sea. At eye-level, flocks of black cockatoos trailed across the sky. Petra pointed out a furry grey animal, tucked between two branches of a nearby gum.

'See that? It's a koala bear. There's hardly any left, Arlo said. Maybe fifty.'

'Yeah, I've seen them,' Banjo said, stretching out his

back. 'Well, maybe not *seen* them. I've definitely heard of them, though. Wiradjuri country, this is. Neighbouring land of my forefathers.'

'You can't claim everything, Banjo.' Petra laughed. 'Next you'll be telling me your great-great-great-great-grandmother's spirit is in that rock over there.'

'Yeah, that's her.' He flashed his cheeky smile.

'Follow me! I've got a surprise for you.' Petra took off back towards the hut, but skirted it and climbed a small steep path up the hill behind.

They scrambled up after her, holding on to rocks and using tree trunks to pull themselves up, Cam crying out as his skin stretched and itched.

'This had better be worth it!' Banjo panted for effect. 'It's OK, Cam, I've got you.'

After a few minutes' climb, the ground evened out, the scrub turned to coarse grass, and the air fizzed with the sound of popping bubbles and running water. Cutting through the hard ground was a mountain river that collected in a wide, clear pool before cascading down the other side of the hill. It called to their dusty skin and dry mouths.

'Fresh water.' Petra wafted a hand in front of her nose. 'And you two need it!'

Petra and Banjo plunged right in, leaping back out like flying fish.

'Come on, Cam! Come on!' Banjo shouted.

But Cam couldn't run. His body felt broken. Instead,

he slid slowly into the river, letting the water edge up his sunburned body. It was so cold it made his teeth chatter, but it was instant relief and he rolled like a crocodile, over and over, until every part of him had been soothed. Then he swam back to the shallows and sat on the stones, scrubbing the sea salt from his hair and gargling water to wash out his mouth.

He looked down at the whale tattoo on his wet chest – glistening like it was alive – and remembered his dream. Just pictures in the night, confused and wild, but they had left a mark. A message. It felt as if his brain was busy shedding complications like seed husks to get at the core – he knew beneath the drama there was a story they hadn't yet found.

He looked at his friends playing in the water, easy like it was the start of a new day, but the old day wasn't over. It was far from over.

'Hey, what happens now?' he called.

Petra pulled herself alongside him. Banjo advanced towards them, swinging his arms, sweeping the water up into the air and making it fall like a shower on their heads.

'The plan is that you and me live in the shepherd's hut and Veritas brings us food and we live happily ever after,' Petra said. 'Banjo will visit. So will your mum.'

'That's it?' Cam asked.

'It's not so bad, right?' Petra said with an encouraging smile.

Cam got to his feet. 'No. It doesn't just end there. We need to get Byron.'

'Veritas said they'll deal with it.'

'When? How?'

'I don't know. One day. They need time to plan.'

Cam scowled. 'No more time. It has to be now. Arlo didn't die just to keep us safe. He died because he wanted me to discover something. Just like Dad did. Both of them meant that it's time the truth was known.'

'But we know the truth now,' Petra insisted. 'Byron was selling kelp, not planting it. And he tried to kill you because you found out.'

Cam shook his head. 'There's more to it than that. Kelp is clean fuel. There has to be something else we're not seeing. Besides, Dad said to follow Big Blue. He could have said follow kelp, or Byron Vos.'

'But you said that Byron needs to be stopped,' Petra said.

'If we stop him before we know the whole picture, then we'll only know half the story. And it's up to us to find it.' He remembered Arlo's chopsticks. If they only chased just one truth, everything would be lost.

'But Matteo's dad said it's too dangerous now and –'

'If we keep hiding behind excuses, the truth will get buried, don't you see? Just like before – people forget, get old, or settle for an easy life. If Veritas is giving up, that means we are the last chance Cetacea has.'

'To do what?' Petra said.

'To know *everything*. To be able to talk about the past. To be free to leave, Petra.'

'What do you want to do then?' Banjo asked. 'Force Veritas to tell us what's going on?'

Cam thought. 'They won't tell us. They'll just treat us like children. We have to find out on our own. Arlo kept his house locked. There has to be a reason why. I'm guessing there's something in there that will tell us.'

'I've been in there loads of times,' Banjo said. 'There's just a load of random stuff.'

Cam remembered Rosemary Kerrich. 'The old woman next door to Arlo said, *"Everything you need to know is right here. All the pieces of the puzzle."* I think she was guiding me, or maybe it was even a message from Arlo. So let's find the puzzle pieces. Let's put them together and see what the picture is. Not tomorrow. Now. We have to start now.'

Banjo sighed. 'I can't. I'm already in big trouble for staying out.'

Cam whipped off his Fort Eden necklace. 'Wear that. Tell them you've been working with Byron Vos. You won't get the strap then. And where are the books Arlo gave you – the ones he told you to keep safe?'

'They're in the caves.'

'I didn't destroy them, sorry,' Banjo said, grinning.

They looked at each other, remembering the words that had passed between them, each with the sting of a fire ant.

'Alright, alright,' Cam said, holding up his hand. 'I was stupid and I'm sorry.'

'Nah, can't blame you,' Banjo said. 'Byron tricked you, that's all.'

'Arlo said that the truth can't be told. But I let Byron tell me everything.'

'You'd spent years looking, Cam,' Petra said softly. 'Can't blame you for wanting things to be easy.'

There was a moment of softness. But there was also work to do. Cam clapped his hands for attention. 'Petra, you know the caves better than anyone. Go and bring back the books and anything else you think might help. Banjo and I will head to Arlo's.'

'I don't want us to split up,' Petra said. 'Not after everything that's happened. It doesn't feel right, y'know?'

'We'll be back later,' Cam said. 'I promise.'

'We're a people now. Whale Mob,' Banjo said. He looked at their confused faces. 'It means we're people who belong together. In the language of my ancestors.'

'Whale Mob,' Cam and Petra agreed.

They dried off and headed back down the hill, passing the shepherd's hut and continuing along the track that led to the ghost gum bridge. They walked silently, listening out for shepherds but seeing only sheep, which clung to the hillside like dust-clouds snagged on gorse. The steep paths and rising heat made them dizzy. The crickets chirped over and over; the only noise for miles, it seemed. Banjo, Petra and Cam trekked on, heads mulling over what had happened and what was to come.

A shuddering noise shook them out of their trance. The sound of rocks tumbling. Hooves. The drumming came closer and closer. The sound of ten, maybe fifteen horses. Cam scrambled to a low outcrop and the others followed, hearts thumping. The dust billowed and the ground shook. As the shapes formed in the morning haze, they expected the worst – Byron and his men.

Petra bent the branch of boronia bush to hide her face and peered over the top of the rock, then suddenly stood up, letting the branch twang back. Banjo tried to pull her back down, and she batted his hand away.

'It's OK. Look!' she shouted over the roar. 'They're brumbies.'

Cam and Banjo got to their feet. Their hair was whipped by the stampeding of the wild chestnut horses, which galloped across the landscape in front of them, somehow navigating the steep paths and the rocks that crumbled beneath their pounding hooves. They were like tumbling conkers, running without rules. Cam looked sideways at Petra. The wind lifted her dark mane and she held her head high, eyes sparkling. He understood now. That's what she was. Untamed, born to be free. A brumby.

When the band of brumbies had passed, they continued with Petra leading, leaping and skidding down the rocks as if she'd been given extra horsepower. Along the path, over the ghost gum, across the ridge. At the top of the sentry rock she stopped and flattened her hand, telling them to stay low.

Below them, workers in red tunics toiled in the fields.

The three would stand out a mile in their non-district rags, and they couldn't risk getting caught. Cam motioned for them to carry on west along the ridge, which wound through forest on the other side of the rock. They'd have to descend at a different point.

An hour later, Petra stopped. 'I think I know where we are. The caves are right down there. If you two continue straight on, you'll hit the scrub north of Eden Place. Be careful. Don't be seen. See ya later, mob.'

Petra hopped down into the thicket, heading towards her old underground home, and Cam and Banjo walked on. The air was cool and echoey. Whipbirds whistled in the canopy and lyre birds copied their song, mixing it with kookaburra calls and parakeet shrieks. But it wasn't long before the forest music was drowned out by the din and clatter of the canteen setting up for mid meal down in the town. When the trees thinned to scrub, the back of the enormous Eden Screen reared up on their left-hand side. It blocked the view, but at least they knew exactly where they were.

'Banj, we can't go in together. It's too dangerous. There may be Watchers.'

As he said it, he shivered. All this time, they were being watched. Controlled. So Byron could live like a king. And the people in the north of the island, too, with their private swimming lakes and boats. Workers and Watchers, living like mini-kings. No wonder they were loyal to Byron. He took a big breath, suddenly overcome with emotion. How could he have thought it was Arlo doing wrong? *How*? He blinked away the tears and pulled himself together.

'Banjo, if anyone could be a Watcher then we'll have to suspect everyone. But I'm the only one that will raise an alarm, so you go first and find empty streets to guide me through. At the end of each street, whistle if it's clear. Just once. Twice if there's danger. If we get separated, then I'll see you back at the shepherd's hut.'

Banjo looked as if he might cry.

'Everything is going to be fine. We just have to be careful.'

They scrambled down into the scrubland directly behind the square. Banjo went on ahead while Cam hid behind a bush and waited for his call. He looked at the back of the giant screen above him, smooth and black as space; he heard the sound of water and knew that on the other side of it, facing Eden Place, the image of the bubbling reef that was always sunny, night and day, was beaming across the square.

All this time, the fake underwater dream world had been a distraction. While people worked hard to clean up the planet, Byron was allowing nature to rot around him.

A long sharp whistle. Cam peeked out from behind

the bush. Banjo was several metres away. He smiled and disappeared down the road leading west. With the pit covered in runners and canteen crews, and probably Watchers too, they'd have to take the long way round to the art district. Every time the way ahead was clear, the whistle came and Cam scuttled to the next corner, peering round it carefully to see which way Banjo was going. Playing hide and seek, they crossed Cetacea's maze of residential streets, eventually entering the narrower lanes with their colourful banners and clay-dust smells.

Banjo whistled. A single long note with a whip. *All clear.*

Cam scurried across the road to Arlo's door and ran his fingers along the top. He found the hidden loop of string and quickly yanked it, feeling the lock lift on the inside. He looked left then right and went inside, closing the door behind him.

Arlo's little room. Its rows of inks and needles, papers and posters were all in place, frozen in time. Peaceful as it had always been, but this time with an air of sadness, as if the house ached for its owner. Cam clenched his jaw to stop the tears. The best thing he could do for Arlo now was to keep his head and finish the job.

He opened the curtains a little to let in the light and noticed a mirror on the windowsill, propped up to face the door. All this time, Arlo had been watching for the Watchers . . . Cam gazed around the room, looking for anything that might help him unlock the full story. He found Arlo's jute shopping bag and began to stuff it. The picture of Big Blue. The logbook too, with all its secrets. What else, what else?

On the desk he found some kind of chart. It was a large, hand-drawn map of Cetacea. *All* of Cetacea – with the headland in the north-west. And north of that, in the middle of the ocean, Arlo had drawn a red cross and a dotted line from the cross that looped up and round the top of the island, travelling right down to the bottom of the east coast. It was the route of his rescue boat. There was a message scrawled at the bottom.

> V. My guess is that he'll take Cam north-west – I estimate it's 4,000 miles from there to the next island in Old Indonesia, so Cam wouldn't be able to swim to land and it's unlikely he'd come across any other boats. On a full tank of fuel, he'll be able to go 30 miles before turning back. I have a V good friend who's prepared a boat for me at the landing. There's one waiting for you by the rocks, east of the kelp district. On Greg's command, I'll chase Byron so he comes back for me. That leaves you free to find Cam and return to the east. And you *must find Cam*.
> Arlo

'Thank you, Arlo.' Cam stroked the signature. 'I'll rescue the truth. I promise.' He rolled up the map, put it in the bag and turned, hunting for anything else that might fit into the puzzle. He looked up and spotted on the very top of the highest shelf a book, hiding behind the inks. He dragged a chair over, clambered on top and flicked the corner of it. It tumbled down into his hands. Dusty. He wiped the surface.

Whale Communication by Byron Vos.

Then came the whistle. Two sharp sounds. Danger. There was no time to look now. No time. He dropped the book into the shopping bag and looked up to see shadows flickering in the mirror on the windowsill. People outside. Carefully, silently, he slotted the wooden block back into the lock before retreating into the shadows beneath the desk. There was a knock. Then a shove. The sound of wood splintering. Voices murmuring. The old lady next door shouting. Then silence.

Cam waited for his heart to steady before crawling back to the window. He peered up at the mirror. The people had gone.

If Arlo was dead, what did they want?

Cam looked inside the bag at the book he'd just placed there. Perhaps Byron wanted this back. That meant the truth was bigger than kelp. Cam knew it. The truth was worth killing for, and the Watchers would return.

Cam took another quick look around the room. From his position, crouched on the floor, he saw that the seat of Arlo's chair wasn't flat. The corner was lifted a little. Just a small triangle that stood proud of the wooden frame.

Cam grabbed a pencil and prised it upwards. Inside was a secret compartment, and inside that was a paper folder. It *had* to be important, Cam thought. He quickly pushed it into the bag and left Arlo's house. As he did so, he bumped straight into the old lady from the next door.

She stood there, her blue eyes dancing with excitement. She had a bowl in her hands.

'They'll be back soon with something to break the door down,' she said, handing him a glazed bowl. 'Arlo asked me to make this for you. The secret's baked in. Go.'

'Thank you, Rosemary.' Cam put it in the bag.

Banjo's whistle came from the next alley. *All clear.* It was time to get back to the shepherd's hut.

Chapter 20
The Jigsaw

'What are we looking for here?' Petra asked. She stood on a chair then stepped up on to the table, tiptoeing between the books and papers like a wading bird.

'Answers, of course,' Banjo said, trying to tickle her feet.

'But we don't know what the questions are.'

'So we start asking them,' Cam said. 'Like, why did Byron try to kill me?'

'Because he wanted to stop you finding the truth,' Petra said.

'Exactly. So what is the truth?'

Petra leapt off the table. 'He made everyone work for him so he could get rich.'

'He made us work so much!' Banjo moaned. 'All day long.'

'Yes, and why? So people would be too tired to ask questions or explore the island. Too tired to *think*. But there's more to it than that.' Cam closed his eyes. 'Think about it. *Follow Big Blue.* What's Big Blue got to do with it? I haven't found Big Blue yet.'

'How can you, y'idiot? He's out there in the ocean!' Petra sighed. She flicked open the book Cam had brought back from Arlo's. 'Hey, what's that?'

On the inside flap of the dust jacket was a photo of two men, one dark, one blond, standing on a boat. Underneath, a caption.

Byron Vos and his brother Arlo aboard the research vessel.

They stopped and stared. At the book. At each other. What?

'Byron and Arlo are *brothers*!' Cam whispered.

'No way!' Banjo squealed. 'Why didn't he say?'

'Probably because we didn't ask,' Petra said, tutting. 'Typical.'

'No, no, no . . . that's just crazy.' Cam ran his eyes all over the image.

He peered closely at the dark-haired man. He had long hair, but it was unmistakably Arlo. There were the grey eyes, the cheekbones. His face was fleshier and he wore a wide smile: happier days. The other man looked kind of like Byron – blond hair, green eyes. But there was something in the shape of his face or his expression that wasn't right. Cam couldn't work out what it was. The man looked somehow softer, less intense.

'So let's ask some questions,' Petra said. 'And boy, are there questions!'

'If they're brothers, why wasn't Arlo living up at Fort Eden with Byron?' Banjo said.

'Good start,' Petra said, patting his shoulder.

Cam shook his head. He didn't know. Confused, he stared again at the photo of the blond man. There was no mystery to him – he was relaxed, with a smile like sunshine and a tattoo on his arm. *Of course.* Cam looked more closely at the blue whale tattoo on his chest, just below his collarbone. A realisation settled and a pain clamped onto his heart like a snake bite.

'Oh no . . .'

'What is it?' Banjo and Petra said at once.

Cam touched his tattooed chest and his eyes watered. He nodded his head at the picture. 'If *this* is Byron Vos, then the man at Fort Eden is *not* Byron Vos. He's an imposter.'

It felt as if all the air had been sucked out of the shepherd's hut, making it hard to breathe. Petra and Banjo gulped like fish out of water. Even Cam was shocked by the words that had fallen from his mouth.

'Wh-what?' Petra said, glaring at Cam as if he'd said something offensive.

'This is Byron Vos, Arlo's brother, the whale expert,' Cam said, pointing to the photo in the book. 'But the man over there, up in Fort Eden, doesn't have my tattoo, and he doesn't have the right face. It's different somehow.'

'Maybe he had the tattoo removed,' Petra suggested. 'And faces change with age.'

Maybe. Maybe. But a memory returned to Cam, and he shook his head. 'He saw my tattoo. If he was Arlo's brother, then surely he would have told me that he used to have one just like it. Instead, it amused him. It was as if –'

'As if what, Cam?' Petra urged.

'I don't know. I can't put my finger on it. Let's try some more questions.'

'I've got a question,' Banjo said. 'Why did Arlo change his surname to Fox?'

Cam focused on the photo again, looking harder at the smaller details. The bright sea behind the boat. The boat itself. White and wide, with ropes and portholes. And there, in red writing on the prow, *The Rosella*.

The Rosella was a boat! But it had been disguised as a parrot on Arlo's arm.

Hiding things. Arlo kept his door locked. Hiding things.

'Arlo was *hiding* from Byron – or whoever is pretending to be Byron.'

'So that's the answer!' Petra said.

'No,' Cam said sharply. 'We're nowhere near finding out everything. Now we have even *more* questions to answer. What happened to the real Byron, and who is that man on the hill?'

'My brain hurts,' Petra cried, thumping the table. The table shook and the paper file spilled its contents like a deck of cards. Banjo started laughing at Petra's tantrum.

'You're like a baby sometimes, P!'

While his friends play-fought, Cam turned back to the book in his hands, feeling a strange connection with the man who wore that tattoo, and an overwhelming sadness at the loss of Arlo. Arlo, who had prodded him, annoyed him and infuriated him, but all the time had just been trying to get Cam to *think* and ask questions and find things out. To rebuild an intelligent society.

An awareness zipped through him like lightning. *Whale Communication*. It was here, in his hands. If he wanted to talk with Big Blue, then right here was the answer, written by the real whale expert. Arlo knew the truth, didn't he? Maybe because it was here all along – his brother's legacy. He opened the book at the last page and read the final paragraph.

Conclusion

My research has convinced me that whale language is complex and sophisticated. Their calls relay information about dangers, feeding grounds, locations and mates. But while we will certainly build a more detailed database of whale calls over time and possibly establish communications between us and them, fluent conversation will not be possible in my lifetime. We may share similar emotions, but not the same words. And while we will never understand the intricacies of their

talk, we could do well to live by their essential motivations of communication and wisdom.
Byron Vos

Cam let the book fall from his hands. He felt cold.

What do you think, Cam? Do you really think they're talking to us? His father had been asking him to think, to really think – not about whether whales were talking to humans, but if they could talk at all.

Dad. Veritas.

Banjo leapt to his side. 'What's the matter? Cam?'

'There's no such thing as whale-talk. We can't talk to whales any more than we can talk to cicadas or wombats. None of us, not anyone. Not the man at Fort Eden. Not even the real Byron Vos.'

'Then how can whales tell us what to do?' Banjo said.

'They can't. They never have.' Cam plunged his face into his hands.

'Then all of Cetacea is a lie. *All* of it.' Petra gasped.

'But . . . but . . .' Banjo rubbed his face.

He made us believe in paradise, alright.

'It was a trick, Banj. A trick. He made us believe he could talk to whales, but he was making it up. That's why he pretended to be Byron Vos, the world's greatest whale expert. How else could he convince people he could talk to the whales?'

'So, whale work was all a hoax,' Banjo said flatly. 'Oh, my tides!'

'And we haven't been living by what's good for the planet, only by what's good for that man,' Petra added. 'So what happened to Arlo's brother, the real Byron Vos?'

'I don't know. Let's keep looking. What else can we do? Let's look through all the papers in the file.'

'It's just strange bits of paper with columns of writing and photographs,' Petra said. 'I found some like this in the caves. Arlo said they were nuisance paper clippings.'

'*News*paper.' Banjo laughed. 'They used to make sheets of paper with all the new information in the world, and you could read them every day.'

'*King of the Hill*,' Petra read, plucking one from the pile. '*Liam King puts in bid for Blue Mountains and buys Thredbo and Victorian Alps*. What does that mean?'

'Mr King, Mr King . . .' Cam mused, remembering Milo's comment. Not such a fool after all. 'I think that's him –'

'Oooh, what's the bowl for?' Banjo interrupted, picking up the beautiful object.

'Arlo's neighbour gave it to me. She said there was a secret baked in it.'

'There are whales scratched into the glaze.'

'What are the whales doing?'

'Just swimming, I think.' Banjo bounced the bowl in his hands to feel the weight.

'Guys.' Petra's voice grabbed their attention.

She held up a large piece of paper. Deep creases distorted the picture, but they could see what it was. It was the same as the photo in the book. Two men on a boat called *The Rosella*. But beneath the photo in large letters were the words:

MISSING: BYRON VOS
06.04.87
LAST SEEN – BOTANY BAY MARINE SANCTUARY

Cam recognised the numbers. They were the ones tattooed beneath the parrot on Arlo's arm. A date.

'So the real Byron went missing and was never found.'

'And someone pretending to be him appeared a few months later,' Petra said.

'Liam King,' Cam said. 'If he's the man at Fort Eden, then Byron's disappearance has to have something to do with him.'

'Here's another nuisance cutting. *King named in world's richest list.*' She turned the paper so they could see a photo of the man leaning out of a metal machine – the very photo Cam had seen in the shiny office.

'That's him! It's him. So now we know for sure. He took Byron's identity and he probably killed him, too.'

'Oh, that's terrible!' Banjo blinked. 'Poor Arlo. Poor Byron.' He let the bowl slip through his fingers. It fell on to the wooden floor with a crack. 'Sorry! I'm so sorry.'

'It's OK, Banjo.' Cam picked it up and checked it for damage.

A white crack ran through the glaze from the top to the bare clay bottom, where the familiar words *Rosemary Kerrich* were etched. But the crack had exposed a secret – a slip of paper baked inside the terracotta clay. *The secret's baked in.* Cam raised the dish over his head then threw it on the floor with all his might.

'Are you *mad*?' Petra shrieked.

He dropped to his hands and knees. There, among the shards, was a small sealed envelope. On it were words. They said simply: *When you're ready.*

There was something huge about this moment. Arlo had said that Cam had to be ready for the truth. As if all his other discoveries had been a ladder leading to this revelation. Cam had climbed the ladder. He was dizzy with the speed at which he'd found himself at the top, but he was there, and he was as ready as he'd ever be.

He stepped outside and sat on the veranda, turning over the little envelope in his fingers. He looked up at the darkening sky. A day had gone without Arlo in it, and still, just like the stars that had begun to glimmer, that gentle man was trying to guide him. He took a big breath, broke the seal and pulled out a slip of paper. It was old and tattered, handwritten in shaky lettering. But it wasn't addressed to him.

Dear Arlo

They're gone.

All the research I submitted to the leaders of the

shrinking world – it was for nothing. You'd think after the first floods they'd have done something. And after the second floods, it would be impossible to ignore. But no. Even as the land beneath their feet crumbled, they couldn't give up their fishing and dredging; their miracle cures and oil extraction; their tourism and souvenirs. In the end, they couldn't give up their addiction to money.
I warned them it would happen, and now it has. Whales are extinct. Gone forever. And that probably won't even make the news.
Of course, there could be a few out there, hiding from us, waiting until we disappear.
We can dream. We can dream.
I wish I had happier news, dear brother.
Byron

Cam's heart thudded to a stop. There was a moment of numbness before rage began to boil at the base of his skull and spread across his neck. He had believed the whales were there all this time. He had put his hopes and dreams into something that could never be. And those beautiful creatures. Gone. *Gone.*

A cry left his lips. He pushed it out with all the force of his lungs. He wanted it to echo into the night, across the hills to the ocean. But it hit the low ceiling of the veranda and fell back in on him like a suffocating blanket of pain.

Banjo and Petra rushed out. Banjo wrapped his arms around Cam's neck and Petra took the letter from his hands and read it out aloud. An agonised groan burst from her as she reached the damning line. *Whales are extinct*. Banjo wailed.

'It's not fair,' Petra said, hiccupping. 'It's not fair.'

But Cam wasn't in the mood for misery. Anger was filling every cell in his body. Fury like he'd never felt. 'Arlo knew this all along. He could have told us!' he spat. 'He could have said something!'

'No, he couldn't.'

The soft voice came from the darkness beyond. Matteo stepped forward into the dim light of the shepherd's hut.

'You wouldn't have believed it,' he said softly. 'None of us would. After years of sermons and whale work, you'd think he was making it up. Or you'd have told someone and got him killed.'

'He should have risked it,' Cam said. 'He should have tried to persuade us.'

Banjo got to his feet. 'He's right, Cam. We can't blame Arlo. He tried the best he could. If you think of the story of Toorongong –'

Cam turned, his eyes blazing. 'But the whales are dead. So Toorongong is dead. You put a story in my head that doesn't make any sense.'

Banjo smiled patiently. 'Toorongong is Everywhen.'

'That's made-up stuff.'

'Cam, stop it.' Petra stood unusually still. 'I've done a lot of thinking, living on my own in my caves with only the past for company. And what I've learned is that everything lives on. Science, art, words. The creators disappear, but the creation lives on. Just like your dad and you. Just like the stories and wisdom of Banjo's ancestors. And the stars that burned out years ago, they're still up there, aren't they?'

Cam looked up at the star-shapes forming above them and burst into tears. There was something so solid and wise in the way they persisted. They'd seen a trillion tides come and go. No, it wasn't Arlo's fault. Cam knew he was just looking for someone to blame. He was bewildered. He was just so tired.

'I'm so sorry. Banjo, I'm sorry.'

'It's OK. You're just a bit cross, I reckon. Understandable.' Banjo smiled. 'And if you can't get angry around your friends – well. That's what we're here for.'

'Long live friendship!' Petra said with a whoosh of relief.

'Spread across Earth as we know it by Toorongong,' Cam said, nudging Banjo.

The three of them, snotty with tears, hugged on the veranda. Until they remembered that there were now four of them. Cam looked at Matteo, still standing at the bottom of the steps, waiting.

'How did you find us?'

'I sang the song, then followed the tracks. Wasn't that hard, to be honest.'

'But *what* are you doing here? I thought your dad said you couldn't get involved?'

Matteo climbed the steps to the veranda. 'If the adults want to sit back and forget about it all, that's their choice. But it's our future, right? And Byron and his men won't be expecting a fight from a bunch of kids.' He raised his eyebrows. 'What can I do to help?'

They woke in the morning hot and stuffy, but Petra had already been out to the river and returned with a bucket of fresh water, which they drank and splashed on their faces. The daylight had introduced a sense of normality, as if any moment they'd throw on their tunics and head down to the yards – Cam, Banjo and Matteo, all whale workers.

Whale work. The words hung above Cam's head like rocks on a string. He didn't dare look up and inspect them in case they fell and crushed his spirit.

They had worked through the night, going through everything in case they had missed any detail. They had found a box of old nails, and used them to pin pages to the wall – from books, newspaper cuttings, and a large piece of paper where they had connected all the dots and mapped out the truth. Or the many truths, as it turned out.

Matteo yawned and stretched. 'So what do we do now?'

'Where do we even begin?' Banjo said, shaking his head.

'We go through it again. To make sure we're not missing anything.' Cam walked to the wall and tapped the newspaper cutting with the headline *King of the Hill*. 'So this rich man, Liam King, bought the high land in Australia when the second floods came. He guessed that if more floods came there'd be chaos – no police, no law and order – and he could use that chaos to create his own kingdom and live in it however he liked. And he wanted obedient workers who would make him rich. But he had to make the people *want* to be servants so they wouldn't overthrow him. He had an idea so crazy, people believed it. He said that because humans destroyed the planet and caused the floods, it was time that another creature was allowed to rule. The whale.

'To convince people, he would have to be a whale expert, right? The most famous whale expert of all time, with years of research and prizes and stuff. He killed Byron Vos and stole his identity. Then the third floods came, just as he'd hoped. He renamed the island Cetacea, which is the scientific name for the whale family, and told anyone who arrived on the disaster boats looking for refuge that they would have to give up their old lives as payment – their possessions, their memories, their rights. To earn their right to live, they would have to work hard and do whatever the whales told them to do. Time passed. The new generation – that's us – didn't know any different. But there were some grown-ups who planned to take Liam King down. A secret group called

Veritas. Only, every time they tried, they were caught by Liam's men, the Watchers.

'The Watchers live nice lives in the north. They don't want us lot in the south getting above our station. That's why they do what Liam King tells them to. Including disappearing people who get too close to the truth.'

Petra leant over and held Cam's hand.

'My dad died trying to get the truth out. And he passed the duty to me.'

'Why didn't he just tell you, Cam?' Banjo said, chewing a lump of stale bread.

'Same reason that Arlo didn't, I guess. He wanted me to start using my brain. I remember he sometimes got annoyed when he asked questions and I just repeated the laws, or the kindergarten stories, or parts of the sermons. We were brainwashed. Unless we began to think, ask questions and use logic, we would never be able to see the truth, let alone be smart enough to do something about it.'

'It has to come from us. Change has to come from us.' Matteo nodded wisely.

'And what do we do now? He's a murderer. And the Watchers are out there and we don't even know how to recognise them. It's all so dangerous.' Banjo threw his bread across the room and began to pace angrily. 'What do we even tell people? They're all brainwashed still.'

'We're going to need help.'

'If not Veritas, then who?' Banjo said.

Cam watched the whale tattoo on his friend's back, rising and falling as he moved, diving through a dotty dream. The first whale. How everything started. Beginnings were simple. Beginnings were perfect.

In the beginning it was *perfect. Perfect society.*

Perfect Island.

'Someone who wants a perfect world with people and nature in harmony,' he mused.

'Nice.' Banjo nodded. 'Sounds a bit childish, though. Well, it does,' he added, seeing Petra's disapproving look.

Cam's eyes twinkled. 'You're right, Banjo. You're right. It is childish. It's a childish dream, but do you know whose childish dream Cetacea was? Dana's.'

'What?' Petra wrinkled her nose. 'She's his assistant. She's in this mess right up to her stupid red curls.'

'No. She's his *daughter.* She called him "Dad". I remember now. And I found a room full of Dana's memories of her mother. She must have died. And on the wall was a drawing Dana did when she was ten, of a perfect island just like this one. She called it Perfect Island.'

'She's still right in it up to her stupid red curls.'

'No – hear me out. *Paradise* was her idea, but not the rest of it. There was a really good truth in what Dana envisaged: a place that cared about the environment. Without a bit of truth, Liam King would never have managed to trick us. Because the Earth *did* need cleaning. Humans *did* destroy it. All that was fact. You need a bit of truth to grow a believable lie.'

'Yes, false directions,' Petra said. 'A bit of truth makes your head point one way so the lies can continue behind your back. All this time, we've been facing the wrong way. She's probably part of it.'

Cam shrugged. 'I might be wrong, but I really don't think so. She's miserable.'

'But even if she does help, he has all those guards,' Banjo said.

Cam thought a while. 'There are a few guards, and maybe there are lots of Watchers – but against the whole of Cetacea, they wouldn't be able to do much. Especially if we take them by surprise.'

'You mean, tell everyone *everything*?' Matteo whistled. 'Are they going to believe it?'

'Not if we tell them one by one. But if we tell them all at the same time . . .' Cam remembered his first attempt to talk about Day of the Whale. What a difference a crowd made. 'The power of a crowd. It has a force of its own.'

'But the whales are gone. What will we say about who rules Cetacea now?'

'Whales are a symbol of wisdom, aren't they? So we will be guided by wisdom.'

There was a silence as Cam's words sank in.

Banjo tapped his lips. 'You sure you're not descended from the Darkinjung people, my friend?'

Chapter 21
Dana's Paradise

They had a plan. Or part of a plan.

Matteo and Banjo headed back down the path towards the town and Cam and Petra went up, carrying a bag with evidence and Arlo's logbook, in case they might need to contact someone for help.

They enjoyed a dip in the river before taking the path that wound across the bottom half of Shepherds' County into the Lower Ranges, Petra going first to stamp down the undergrowth so it wouldn't scratch against Cam's sore body. They found a ridge path that wound westward, which gave them occasional views over small hills below them and Cetacea town in the distance. Eventually, Fort Eden appeared as a white speck against the base of the Higher Ranges, straight ahead.

They picked their way through the scrub with the goal in their sights, and within two hours found themselves standing on top of a flat rocky cliff, sliced in two by a fast-flowing river that came from further up the Ranges and tumbled over the edge into a lake below. Fort Eden. They splashed themselves with river water, washing away the scratches and prickles, and peered over the edge. Petra gasped. Cam held his finger to his lips.

There was a swimmer in the lake below. Red hair billowed out behind her like underwater smoke. She was alone.

'Are you sure about this?' Petra whispered.

'No, but she's our only chance.'

Cam sat on the edge of the waterfall rock. He squeezed one shoulder through the handles of the jute bag, so it sat tight across his torso, then flipped over on to his stomach, ready to descend. The pain of his burned skin vanished as his focus sharpened. One slip and it could all be over. The drop was deadly. Cam looked for handholds and footholds, every muscle working as he lowered himself down the rock face, step by step, ignoring the pain. When his feet finally touched the ground, he didn't know whether to laugh or cry. Petra leapt the last few metres and landed with a thud next to him. They looked behind them at the sheer, treacherous descent they'd just conquered.

'We must be crazy,' Petra said.

'Ready?'

Cam breathed in deeply. For a moment, he wondered if this was how his dad had felt before he confronted Liam King. Because that's what he'd done, Cam was certain; Mr Freedman had said he was last seen going up to the

Ranges. David Solomon must have tired of Veritas's plan to 'wait for the right time', Cam thought. Just like him.

Dana had finished her swim and was standing at the far end of the lake, drying her hair with a towel. She hadn't noticed them. Her face was still and her eyes were blank. It was if she had given up all feeling.

'Hi, Dana.'

She dropped her towel in shock, her lip trembling. 'B-but you're alive!' she stammered, blinking rapidly. 'Byron said there'd been an accident. He said you were . . . *dead*.' She rushed forward and wrapped her arms around Cam and rocked him side to side, like long-lost family. Petra pulled a face.

'Thought you said she was an ice queen,' she mumbled.

Cam pulled away. 'Is he here?'

'No, he's gone out. Spearfishing.'

'Good. We need to talk to you.'

Dana looked briefly at Petra, clearly unsure of the wild-looking girl, but nodded. 'Wait here. I'll get rid of the guards.'

For three minutes, Cam and Petra stood by the lake, wondering if at any moment they'd be ambushed. Trusting Dana was a risk. But then there was the sound of hooves moving away and Dana appeared again, and beckoned them inside.

She wanted to sit in the Whale Hall – the place guests were taken to admire Byron's connection with the whales – but Cam shook his head. It would be wrong to sit among that fakery when the villain's true personality was in that other room, the peculiar one with its screens and photographs and nonsensical items.

Byron's glitzy chamber took Petra by surprise. She looked up at the chandeliers, and then around at the white leather sofas and sliding glass cabinets, and whistled.

'All built on the pain of bloody kelp hands and sand-blinded eyes. It's not even *nice*.'

Cam shot her a look, warning her to be gentle with Dana, but it was too late. Dana's cheeks had already reddened. They all took a seat on the squishy sofas and looked at each other awkwardly.

'Tell me what happened, Cam.'

'Don't you know?'

'I have an idea,' she said miserably. 'But let me hear it.'

'Short story, he tried to drown me.'

Dana looked down at her fingernails and shook her head, like she had so much to say but no way to say it. Eventually, she looked him in the eye. 'You were too much for him, Cam. Too many questions. It became hard work, hiding all the lies all the time.'

'Why did he even let me into Fort Eden in the first place?'

'In the beginning, he thought it would be fun to have a besotted little boy hanging around.' Cam blushed, remembering how easily impressed he was. 'He didn't realise you were David's son. Then, when you revealed that information, he thought he might be able to use you to root out any other rebels in Cetacea. He had people follow you. But I had no idea he was going to . . . Not to a child . . .' She trailed off, tears welling.

'Luckily, Arlo had an idea,' Petra said. 'He's the one who saved Cam.'

'Who *are* you?' Dana looked quizzically at Cam's bedraggled friend. 'And who is Arlo?'

Cam jumped in before Petra said something insensitive. 'That's Petra, my friend. And Arlo was my friend, too. His brother was the real Byron Vos.'

Dana's mouth made an 'o' and her shoulders dropped. 'You know about that, too.'

Cam and Petra looked at each other. They wouldn't need the evidence in their bag after all. Dana's face was a confession. But now, it could go one of two ways – she could help or she could run. And they needed her on their side.

'I know that this paradise was your idea. I saw your picture on the wall in that room. The one you did for your mother. *Perfect Island*. Happy people looking after the planet.' Cam tried to warm her with a smile. 'The good things about Cetacea were your idea, weren't they?'

'That was so long ago, Cam. When I was like you – wanting everything to be perfect. But time moves, people change, they grow up. You realise that dreams can't make the leap to reality.'

'Is that what your dad told you?' Petra said. 'So when did you give up on paradise?'

Dana shrugged. A tear trickled down her cheek and she wiped it away. 'I don't know.'

'Tell me more about the picture,' Cam said.

Dana wiped her nose on her sleeve. 'I remember, after the second floods, a family approached our house asking for shelter and my father turned them away. We had a mansion with twenty bedrooms! So much room! They had a newborn baby and nowhere else to go. His guards pushed them back down the hill and on to the overcrowded boats. I was only nine at the time, but I knew it was wrong. So I started to draw a perfect world to help me block out the horrible things. I worked out how people on the island would live, how they would work together for good, not for greed, like my father and the terrible people he was friends with. I dedicated it to Mum. She died just before the third floods and Dad said, to honour her, he'd make my picture come true. Guilt, I suppose, because all his money couldn't save her. But he kept his word. And I believed in Cetacea. I helped decide what crops we'd grow, how we'd eat together, share everything. I thought I was helping Dad make paradise. I never wanted . . . I never wanted –'

'You never wanted people to be toilers,' Petra said flatly. 'Tied down by rules and punishments, forbidden to swim in the ocean.'

Cam saw the anger in Petra's face and squeezed her hand. But Dana seemed too lost in misery to notice Petra's aggressive tone.

'No.' Dana sniffed. 'And I promise you, I didn't even know the extent of my father's lies until I was in my twenties, and by then I was already trapped. He had guards follow me everywhere too, until he was sure my spirit had gone.' Dana began to pace the room. Cam kept his eyes trained on her, as if she might suddenly flee like a wild animal. She ran her hand slowly along the sideboards, knocking over her father's precious trinkets parading shamelessly on the shelves.

'Nothing is ever enough for him,' she said. 'He wants to be king of everything. He wants to buy the other islands, use their precious metals, sell off their rare plants. Everything is for sale.'

Petra and Cam froze, listening to her anger grow, watching Liam's trophies and souvenirs tumble to the floor. It looked as if Dana had chosen her side.

'Will you help us put a stop to it?' Cam said.

'And what will happen to me?'

'You can go back to who you were. You can remake Cetacea to be just like your dream.'

She smiled sadly. 'Real life is harder to fix.'

'If you tell the truth, you can reset everything.'

Dana pressed her fingers into her eyes, muttering. Petra looked at Cam worriedly. Liam could return any minute. Cam motioned for Petra to be still, but he saw by the stubborn line of her jaw that it wasn't going to be possible.

'Enough regret, Dana,' Petra said firmly. 'You can

either do something or you can do nothing, but whichever you choose, you'll make your mark on history. And no matter what the Birth of Cetacea's fake laws say, you cannot wipe out what's done. So you decide right here, right now: what will the past tell the future about *you*?'

Cam smiled. She was brilliant. Absolutely brilliant. Petra winked.

Dana stood like a rag doll but her large eyes glittered, as if a spark was returning. 'OK,' she whispered. 'I'll do it. Let's set Cetacea free. Tell me what to do.'

Cam and Petra exchanged a glance – it contained relief, surprise, exhilaration. It was happening.

'Show me all the secrets,' Cam said. 'How he does the sermons, the tricks. Everything must be out in the open. No surprises.'

'Quickly then, before he gets back.'

They went up the stairs. Dana led them to a room that was full of miniature Eden Screens and buttons and boxes. They looked like objects from space, completely at odds with the natural world. Liam had allowed some technology from the Long Ago – microphones, picture boxes and spotlights – to make communication easier: to project the whale-talker's face and voice and fantasy. But Cam had never seen how it all worked. Not the keyboards and circuits of wires that looked like tangles of worms.

Dana showed him how most of it worked, like the electric printer that spat paper and how to click and open files on a computer screen. One yellow folder on the 'desktop' was called 'Big Blue'. Cam looked at it, bewildered by the hard, unfeeling titles of the files inside: *Big Blue left-to-right sequence, Big Blue straight-to-camera sequence, Big Blue turning sequence.*

'These are just films – moving pictures, Cam. They were recorded many years ago. My father uses them to pretend that Big Blue exists. You can put filters and effects on top, see?' Dana opened a video and pressed buttons that made bubbles appear, then seaweed, then sunlight. 'He can make infinite new films from one old recording.'

'So Big Blue's sermons only happened when he could be bothered to make a new film?' Of course, he thought. Whales were extinct. How else would King do it?

Dana pressed her lips together. 'I'm so sorry.'

Cam straightened. 'We're going to make our own moving picture sequence – but we don't have much time.' Cam got Arlo's logbook from his shoulder bag and turned to pages he'd earmarked. 'If I give you the names of some people, can you get your guards to fetch them?'

'Of course. I'll make up reasons. Who have you got?'

Cam read. '*Cara Chadwick, Herbalist, tattoo of a peach.*' He looked up and grinned. '*Reeva Duprey, information technology manager, tattoo of words: Carpe Diem*. And we need Milo, too. He's here, in the book, you know – *Milo Takis, chef, tattoo of Crete.*'

Dana hit her forehead with the heel of her wrist. 'The tattoo is of Crete! Of course! The Greek island, his lost homeland. I never knew what that mark on his arm was, and with his temper, I was always too afraid to ask.'

'Me too,' Cam said, and they laughed. 'What's the story with him? Why is he loyal to your father?'

'Milo's been with our family since before I was born. My father saved him from a flood. Don't think for a moment he was being kind – he'd just lost a cook and needed another. Milo's remained loyal because of it. But he's seen how my father behaves. He doesn't like him at all.'

'But he'd do anything for *you*?' Cam asked carefully.

'Yes, I think he would.'

Cam smiled. 'All he'd have to do is cook a very big, sleepy meal.'

'To give us enough time to prepare.' Dana nodded, catching on.

'Prepare to deliver the absolute truth?' Petra fixed Cam with a look that was a cross between exhilarated and petrified.

'Prepare for Day of the Whale.' Cam turned to Dana. 'When the full story comes out – the whole thing, not just the kelp and the sand and the whales, but who you actually are – it's going to be hard for you.'

'I know.' She reached for their hands and squeezed them tight. 'But it's time to begin again.'

Chapter 22

The Day of the Whale

Eden Place was buzzing. The raised seating with the best views had been taken early, and the floor space was packed from north to south. Bunting, dripping from strings across the square, fluttered above the chatter below, and children waved paper flags on sticks.

Everyone was there. People leant out of windows and clung to scaffolding and squished together in the pit, with babies stacked on shoulders. Work was cancelled, apart from the caterers, who had been promised an extra holiday. In the twenty-five years of Cetacea's existence, there had never been such a day.

Hard labour was what kept the place ticking over, producing crops and mending old mistakes. But for one day, for the first time ever, they would all be together. Because of the whales. Those who hadn't thought much of the ocean masters began to say thank you; they shouted it and waved their hand-drawn banners. Day of the Whale was working.

When as much of Cetacea as possible had crammed into the square, a small group of musicians walked on to the stage and positioned themselves below the giant screen. They picked up their instruments and began to play. Eden Place hushed as the violins' vibrations pulled apart the air before cellos took over, with their low chords and mysterious melodies. Behind the musicians, the Eden Screen came to life. A vision of the sea. The crowd waited with their hearts in their mouths.

Cam watched it all from the computer room in Fort Eden, next to Reeva, the computer expert from the Long Ago recruited from Arlo's logbook. They had little screens and monitors, microphones and soundboards. Reeva said they had everything they needed to make a broadcast. After all, that was just what Liam King had done all this time.

Liam King was locked in his lounge on the other side of the house, drugged by a large breakfast prepared by Milo Takis, containing a sleep-inducing tincture of corkwood extract made by Dr Cara Chadwick. Dana had sent the guards to deal with a reported break-in at a kelp plant in the north. Dana, Banjo, Petra and Matteo were down at the square, ready to help with the story and the crowd's reactions. The Watchers would probably be there, too. They were about to get a shock.

Clicking on the computer folder, Cam opened up Big Blue and sent him to the Eden Screen. For the people watching, it would be like any other sermon.

Big Blue sailed closer. Larger than life. Making every human feel like an ant.

But there was no whale call from the noise box, no Byron's voice to greet them. Just silence. Cam played with the buttons he'd been shown, sending the whale zipping into reverse, retreating the exact way he had come. Then forward again. Then the special effects. Bubbles, jellyfish, reef fish. Other whales. On top of each other. Confusion.

Cam didn't need to be in Eden Square to imagine how it was going down. The people would be silent, stunned.

Then Cam made the picture vanish altogether.

Through the monitor he watched Dana walk on to the stage in a floaty cream dress, her red hair cascading around her shoulders, her blue eyes nervous.

'Hello, everyone. I'd like you to meet Cam!' She turned, waving to the screen behind her.

Reeva adjusted a webcam on top of the computer screen and gave Cam a thumbs-up. The red light went on. Down in the square, where the imposter's face usually blinked on to the Eden Screen, Cam looked out instead. A hundred or more times his true size. His freckles big as tureen lids, his blue eyes as large as cartwheels.

Cam leant into his little microphone. 'Hi, Dana.'

What the hell was going on? The crowd murmured, but quietly – they didn't want to miss a thing.

Dana continued. 'Day of the Whale celebrates our

island's relationship with whales. Before we go any further, we want to take you on a tour of the island's history. Just so you get the full picture. Cam Solomon, go ahead.' Dana clapped her hands and the crowd hushed.

Reeva showed Cam which file to click. Cam's webcam switched off and he projected the picture made by young Dana on to the Eden Screen. Cam started at the beginning.

'When our paradise island was first dreamed up, it was a place where everyone worked together to create a better world. And it started out that way. Even those who didn't believe in the master whales at first, soon grew used to the idea. Everyone was happy to work fourteen-hour days for the planet. But we worked so hard, we never had the time to ask if that was actually what we were doing. We were too sick or too tired even to explore our environment . . .

'And why was that? Because the man you know as Byron Vos didn't want us to. We have been working until we drop for two reasons – to stop us asking questions, and to make him rich. We've been sorting sand to extract precious metals from it, not to clean it. And our forbidden beaches and shallows aren't kept free for marine life. They're all kelp farms to produce fuel that he sells to other islands!'

Cam nodded to Reeva, who quickly found the next file. The screen flicked to footage of underwater kelp. Not a lush kelp forest, but rows of sickly brown-green ribbons waving in a putrid sea.

'As far as the eye can see, Cetacea is surrounded by kelp farms. Fertilised with nitrates to grow fast. Nitrates. So much, that it's caused a plague of algae. Cetacea's waters are not what we see on the Eden Screen. There are no pretty fish or turtles. Cetacea is at the centre of a marine dead zone.'

On the monitor, Cam saw that everyone in Eden Place was on their feet, booing and shouting and yelling: 'It's a lie! It's a lie!'

'Quickly, Reeva. The processing plants.'

Reeva broadcast footage showing parts of the island that people had never seen before. A pointed headland lined with speedboats. Cars and trucks. A building with a sign outside: *Cetacea Fuel Depot.* The inside of the factories, the smelted gold, the liquid kelp oil. In the background towered the north face of Higher Ranges, proving it was happening on the very same island, just hidden from view.

'This is from a video presentation Vos made for buyers and investors from other islands around us. Because we are not alone in the Southern Ocean, like he told us. We have neighbours.'

There was silence as it all sank in. Cam nodded. *Now.* Reeva lined up the next image.

A photograph of two men, standing on board a boat named *The Rosella*. Cam felt his voice crack as he began.

'This is a photo of Byron Vos and his brother, who

some of you know as Arlo Fox, the tattooist. Many of you have told him your secrets. His home was a place where you could talk about the Long Ago. But now it's time we talked about Arlo's past. Dana?'

Down at Eden Square, Dana stepped on to the stage and tapped the microphone. 'Everyone, I'd like to introduce myself. I am the only daughter of a man called Liam King.'

Eden Place was eerily still. Even the breeze dropped, leaving the bunting hanging like old rags.

'Just before the third floods, my father bought the Australian High Lands – the area of the old country we now call Cetacea. He knew they were high enough to survive more floods, when they came. And he had an idea. To start a new kind of society.

'He chartered a boat ride to a marine sanctuary with Arlo's brother, Byron Vos. He pretended he was going to donate money to save the oceans. Instead, miles out to sea, he drowned Byron Vos and stole his identity. He dyed his hair blond and he wore green lenses to hide his true eye colour. He did everything he could to make you all think *he* was the world-renowned whale scientist. But my father is not an expert in anything apart from greed and murder. He murdered Byron Vos, Arlo Fox, David Solomon . . . and he almost murdered Cam.'

Cam clicked on the next slide. A picture of Liam as he was, and Liam dressed as Byron Vos.

The people stared at the images, magnified on the

screen, noticing for the first time the dark roots at the base of the sandy-blond hair. The unnatural green of his eyes. Side by side, the evidence was unmistakable.

Even from up in the Ranges, Cam could feel the strangeness in the air down in Eden Place. As if the square full of people wasn't pinned down to reality. Like it might float away. It buzzed with the hum of a thousand working brains. The seconds dragged.

Cam looked at the monitor, at Banjo, Matteo and Petra. They looked worried. They felt it too. It was like the calm before a storm. Like the start of the floods – waves you couldn't see, but you knew were coming. You knew that they would soon rush in and drown everything in chaos.

A man in the crowd stood up and shook his fist. 'We'll give him to Big Blue. The whales will see justice done. They'll decide on his punishment.' A roar of agreement followed.

The tsunami was coming.

Throw him to the whales! Throw him to the whales! Throw him to the whales!

Dana looked around desperately. The people didn't get it. They had been brainwashed for too long. 'Cam!' she called. 'Cam!'

Reeva switched on Cam's webcam and he leant forward into his microphone, to make his voice as big as possible.

'Everyone, please listen. LISTEN!'

The noise died down.

'There is no whale communication, there is no whale justice. We can't speak with whales. We never could. Whales are extinct.'

It had been a mistake. Cam knew it the moment he said it. It was too much, too soon.

A second wave hit. The cacophony that filled Eden Place was made from heartbreak, confusion, anger.

No whales? When? How? What's the boy saying?

'Veritas!' Cam shouted, hoping his voice would boom through the noise boxes and reach the ears it needed to. 'Veritas, it's now or never. Stand up!'

He watched the crowds. *Please, please, please,* he begged. They were getting out of control. A woman clambered on stage and grabbed the microphone, turning to Dana, jabbing an accusing finger at her.

'Where is he? Where is he?'

Dana tried to calm her down, but the woman was wild.

'And what about you?' she screamed. 'If you're his daughter, you should be punished, too!'

The crowd roared in agreement. Cam tore at his hair as he watched Banjo, Matteo and Petra try to shield Dana. Three children against an angry horde. He hadn't thought about this – about what the truth might unleash. He knew that grief could strike one person down, but when there were thousands . . . it made them vengeful.

The first people had reached the stage. Hands tried

to grab at Dana. The children could no longer hide their fear. This was a mob, and not in the way that Banjo meant. The people of Cetacea didn't feel like family now. There was no way they could hold them back. This wasn't supposed to happen!

And then, a crowd of people leapt on to the stage and formed a chain: a barrier of protection in front of Dana and his friends. Cam recognised Greg and Keith. And Drake. But there were fifty more besides. *Veritas.* Their faces looked uncertain but their bodies were as strong as a sea wall. But how long could the wall hold? A minute? Two?

Cam found something on the computer that might help. He clicked.

The noise boxes suddenly filled with sound. A blast so loud, it forced the front rows back from the stage and made everyone fall silent. It was the summoning call. Years and years of it had moulded their behaviour; it had made them immediately obedient. The people stood there, confused, as if they expected Byron Vos to appear and congratulate them on a hard day's work.

Instead, Cam smiled from the screen again. He held up Dana's childish picture in its frame. 'If we want to look for the truth, we have to go back to the beginning. The beginning of us, in this place, saved from the floods, is thanks to Dana. Dana is the mother of Cetacea,' he declared. 'She dreamed of this island. Her father stole her dream and broke it. And *that* is the truth we must hold on to.'

The crowd mumbled. There were yells. But it was calmer now. A queasy sea rather than a stormy ocean. It was sometimes hard to swallow the truth and not let it burn your insides. Cam knew that better than anyone.

'Finding the truth has been difficult, and accepting it has been even harder. But today is a new beginning, and we can't let the extinction of the whales be for nothing. They don't rule us, but they leave us with a lesson – communication and wisdom are everything. And we will celebrate them. Today is and will always be Day of the Whale.'

Members of the crowd who had stood up to fight, sat down one by one. A breeze picked up, flicking the bunting. Children began to wave their flags, slowly.

'On this day, every year, we should share stories of the Long Ago and the times ahead. We will study and learn. We will create a well of memories, and we'll go back as far as we can remember, so that we can learn from cultures and people that have gone before. And our stories of the past will create a map so we never get lost and never forget who we are, and we will never forget those who have gone.

'Arlo Fox once said to me, "Fill your head with questions. Because if you don't, someone else will fill it with lies." So we will ask questions. We will be curious. We will protect our environment. We will return to the beginning, to Dana's dream of paradise. We will swim in the sea, work the land, share responsibilities and have fun. We will live. And we should always and forever use this day to remember who we are.'

There was only a split-second of silence – a second that crackled with energy – before every person in Eden Place was on their feet.

Day of the Whale! Day of the Whale!

Wisdom rules!

'Are we done?' Reeva asked. 'Can I go down and celebrate?'

Cam nodded and grinned. 'I think we did it, Reeva. Thanks for your help.'

She planted a kiss on his head and ran. Cam turned back to the monitor, noticing how shaken Dana looked. Shaken but relieved. The members of Veritas stayed standing, just in case, but there wasn't a single person in Eden Square who wasn't whooping or hugging or dancing or laughing, as if the most brilliant future had risen from the most terrible news. Maybe some were getting swept up by the crowd and didn't understand, but in time they would.

People waved at him and Cam waved back, trying not to think about how big he looked on the massive screen.

Then there came a crash. Cam peered at the monitor. It hadn't come from the town.

The crash came again.

It was in the house, in Fort Eden.

'Cam Solomon!' a voice roared.

It was Liam King.

Chapter 23
Ceremony

They hadn't thought about this part either – about what to do with a man who has just lost everything. What they'd do once he'd recovered from the sleeping potion. It was supposed to last longer than this. And Liam had clearly found a way out of his room. Things had gone very wrong.

Reeva had left. The house staff were down at the square. Dana had sent the guards on a decoy trip to the north. Cam was alone at Fort Eden, apart from Milo. *Where was Milo?*

He had no time to think. If he stayed in the little computer room, he'd be trapped.

He tiptoed along the upstairs corridor towards the other end of the house, while Liam raged like a bull in the lower hallway. There was the thud of falling sculptures. Crashes and smashes as vases and chandeliers shattered on the stone floor. Then the scuff of soft leather shoes on the stone steps. He was coming.

Cam quickly slipped into a room lined with books and flattened himself against the wall.

'Come out here, boy!' Liam growled, ascending the steps with loud grunts.

Cam heard him fling open the doors one by one, his cries of frustration getting louder, angrier, twisting into howls of rage. And then came a different sound – a wail that ripped through the air. It was followed by a yawning silence.

Cam tried to control his breathing. What should he do? He should run, he should definitely run. But why was there no sound? What if Liam was sick or had fallen? He couldn't just leave him. He was Dana's father. He'd check. A little peek. If he was careful.

He tiptoed back to the control room he'd come from and saw Liam standing there, his shoulders slumped. He was looking at the screen, seeing what was happening down in Eden Place – watching his daughter on stage with Drake, waving at the crowd, with Banjo, Matteo and Petra dancing round them. Members of Veritas. Flags were flying. People were laughing. Catering teams were ushering people aside, bringing in runners and tureens. Day of the Whale was under way. And it was out of his control.

Cam saw his own reflection in the computer screen's surface. Too late.

Liam spun round and their eyes met. He roared. '*You!*'

Cam could feel the hatred radiating from him. He

backed out of the room and ran along the corridor and down the steps towards the Whale Room, skidding on a fallen tapestry in the hallway. It pushed out behind him, slippery as seaweed, and he fell on his front. The stone floor slapped the breath from his chest. He was paralysed. Just for a second, but a second was too long. Liam took his chance and pounced. Cam felt a tight grip around his ankle and the ground slid beneath him as Liam yanked him backwards across the floor. He reached out but there was nothing in reach, apart from the broken glass of the chandelier.

Cam closed his hand around a handful then flipped on to his back – his leg twisting painfully under him – and threw the glass at his assailant's face. In shock, Liam let go, and in that split-second Cam was on his feet again, running for the kitchen. The door to the herb garden and chicken coops would be a way out. But Liam was fast, and Cam found himself standing on the other side of the long kitchen table in a face-off. They edged one way then the other, neither daring to make the break. Between them was the bottle of corkwood sedative. Liam picked it up, read the label and threw it against the wall, roaring again.

'Milo poisons me, my own daughter betrays me!' he yelled. 'How do you think that feels, hey? Where's the bloody loyalty?'

'I was loyal,' Cam said shakily, bouncing on his feet, ready to bolt. 'I stayed loyal to you and Big Blue. Right up until the moment you tried to kill me.'

Liam rolled his eyes as if that was an inconvenient detail. 'I should have tied a rock to you, just like I did to your father. Ploof!' Liam mimed dropping a stone. 'Oh well, you missed your chance to die gracefully, kiddo.' He grabbed a kitchen knife and hissed.

Cam remembered the snakes. 'I think you're more scared of me than I am of you.'

'I'm not scared of you. I'm angry. You lost me *everything*.'

'It wasn't yours to begin with. You took it. You turned it into an evil game.'

'And you liked it, you little worm. You liked every minute of being the chosen one.'

'I still *am* the chosen one. Chosen to communicate the truth. Chosen by someone a million times better than the man you are. *Arlo Vos*.'

Without warning, Liam vaulted over the table, but he caught his backside on the edge and fell to the floor.

Cam ran. His heart was pounding so fast he couldn't catch his breath, but his feet took him through the door and outside to the west side of the property with its gardens, chickens and gum-tree forest. He grabbed gravel stones on the way – a small cluster in each hand – and bolted into the cover of the trees. Liam's footsteps came fast, skidding on the gravel then crunching on the dry gum leaves, cursing as the gum nuts dug into the soft soles of his shoes.

Holding his breath, Cam only moved under the cover of a chicken's shriek or Liam's crunching steps.

'Where are you?' the murderer sang mockingly. 'Big Blue wants to talk to you!'

He was getting close. Cam took a stone and threw it as far as he could. It fell metres away, with a crunch on the parched leaves. Liam's footsteps stopped. Cam kept throwing the stones, hoping Liam would think he was running. But even if Cam could run, where would he go? Liam was blocking his way back down the Ranges. With the thick crunchy forest on his left, the only other direction immediately available was the back garden. If he could make it across the lake lawn and round to the other side of the building, he could circle past the stables and back to the front of Fort Eden, then head down the Ranges towards town.

But as soon as he started to run, twigs snapped underfoot and parrots in the trees above him screeched, crying out his position. He heard Liam shout. Too late to change direction now. He had to keep going.

Cam bolted back through the gums and on to the soft grass, the house to his right and the lake straight ahead. Behind him, Liam was closing in. Seconds away. Cam panicked. Even if he did make it to the path down the Ranges, Liam had that silver machine. He'd never make it.

He had to hide. But where?

Cam looked at the water. *He'd have to be stupid to hide in a lake.*

Precisely.

He quickly slipped in, trying not to squeal at the temperature, and ducked his head under. He didn't know how long he could hold his breath – his starving lungs would force him up for air in seconds. He had to calm down. *Calm down.* But calming down was hard when you were being hunted. He knew the feeling, that ice-cold fear. He had felt it the last time he'd been in water. With sharks. He remembered the thudding chest and the claustrophobic panic. And he remembered the instant calm when he thought he saw Big Blue.

Instant calm. Cam closed his eyes and imagined swimming alongside the beast. But it wasn't Big Blue he pictured now, it was Toorongong. Gentle, kind, warm. Unsolid, the creature wrapped itself around him and held him until his breathing slowed, and he stopped thinking of lungs and air and life. Instead, he thought of the beautiful whales with their grooves and wise, wrinkled eyes, the vast downturned mouths and the funny blowholes for breathing. Even the best creatures on Earth couldn't hold their breath forever. *We can learn from the past.*

Cam made a tight fist and placed it thumb-first against his mouth. Then he tipped his head back and pushed his face towards the light. He let his fist break the surface of the water and breathed out old air through the tight gap, breathing in again quickly to replenish it. It was only tiny sips of air, but the relief of having oxygen drove away his panic. He continued to breathe through his blowhole and watch the distorted picture of the sky play on the water's surface.

Then a shadow appeared above him – a figure that cut and twisted through the water's curved lens. Cam moved carefully beneath the pond weeds to hide the shape of his fist. All he could see was a featureless circle of face inspecting the water for bubbles and ripples. After a few seconds the figure moved along. But he wasn't safe yet.

Suddenly, something wrapped around his neck. Trailing pond weed. Long and straggly, swaddling his face. Startled, Cam's fist slipped below the surface and he breathed in lake water. It ripped through his lungs and he burst to the surface, his eyes squeezed tight shut against the pain in his chest. He couldn't open his eyes, couldn't see what was coming for him, but he heard shouting. Felt hands pulling at him, dragging him out.

Liam had got him. He was going to die. A slap stung between his shoulder blades. Water shot out of his mouth like a jet, and he turned, blinking, to see a knife. He shut his eyes and screamed, ready for the end. But nothing happened. When he opened them again, it wasn't Liam he saw.

Milo laid him gently on the grass and stepped over him, his kitchen knife raised, his eyes fixed on something ahead.

'Stop, King. It's over.'

'Daddy, stop!'

Cam struggled up on to his elbows. Dana, Banjo, Petra. They stood close to him protectively but their eyes were on Liam, who was trapped against the rock face. He turned and began to climb.

'Stop. I'm warning you.' Milo's words bounced off the rock, unheeded. The chef, looking like a martial arts fighter, lined up his knife with the distant figure, pulled his arm back and threw.

The knife somersaulted the distance of the lake, spinning towards Liam, hitting blade-first and finding a home deep between the muscles in his calf.

Liam wailed.

'Give in!' Milo shouted. 'For God's sake, man.'

But Liam turned, his face twisted with hate. He bent down and pulled the knife out and chucked it aside. Blood gushed from the wound down his leg and dripped on to the ground below. They watched, astounded, as he fumbled with handholds, his feet sliding on the wet ledges, panting and grunting as he clambered up the treacherous rock. His shirt caught and ripped on a snag and his feet slipped out from beneath him, leaving him hanging by his fingertips. But he was fit, his upper body lean and lithe, and he swung his legs up, grabbed a safe hold and corrected his position. He made it to the top and didn't stop, disappearing over the edge to the other side without turning back.

'Dad! Dad!' Dana's voice lost its power.

'Where will he go?' Petra asked.

'I don't know.'

They stared at the top of the rock, unable to speak, until Milo's firm hands steered them away. Liam King was no doubt headed for his speedboat. There was nothing more they could do.

Inside, Milo made hot chocolate for everyone and they sat amid the destruction of the Whale Room, feeling awkward and out of place on the soft sofas. Milo was apologetic. With a kitchen full of knives, he should have been able to protect Cam from the start. He didn't know what had gone wrong – perhaps he misunderstood the doctor's dosage, or it just wasn't strong enough; but Liam had woken too soon and escaped out of his office window. When Milo had gone to check out the ruckus in the chicken coop, Liam had hit him over the head with a rock, then rolled him down the gum-covered hills and left him unconscious in a crevasse.

'Lucky you came round in time,' Cam said. 'Thank you, Milo.'

'I couldn't let you die – not after I've got used to having you under my feet.'

They could have stayed there all day, nursing their wounds and sleeping off the ordeal. But it didn't feel right being at Fort Eden. It was a fortress of lies. Their place was down in the town, being part of Day of the Whale, celebrating the truth with Matteo and Veritas and all the people whose eyes had just been opened to the truth.

They took the horses down the path from the Ranges, slowly, Cam riding with Dana, and Banjo, Petra and Milo squashed on to a steed. They took their time, looking at the fruit groves either side of the track. Lemons, limes, peaches. And then came vineyards, the grape fields where Cetacea's dead were buried in neat rows.

Dana stopped and motioned for Milo to halt. 'I think it's right that we reveal the last truth of Cetacea.' She didn't blink, but her lip quivered. 'Many adults died when Cetacea was established, but it wasn't because of illness or accident. They talked about the past. Some openly rejected the idea of whale-talk. They didn't believe any of it. If you ever wondered why my father managed to get away with such a big lie, it's because he and his men made sure that anyone who questioned him disappeared, one by one, or were too weak and frightened to stand up to him. Eventually, the protests stopped and people accepted. It was better than perishing in the floods. I'm so sorry.'

In stunned silence, the kids stared across the grapevines where Liam's wine grew, wondering about their lost parents buried beneath them. Had they got there by illness and accident, or by Liam's hand? But Cam knew that his lost parent was under the sea, long gone. Like the whales.

'That explains a lot,' he said eventually.

Banjo began to talk softly. 'If Whale Mob hadn't found out the truth, we'd have carried on believing what we were told, and our kids would have believed the lies and their kids too, and the truth would have been snuffed out forever.'

'That's why you've got to break some rules,' Petra said. 'To see why they're there in the first place.'

They made the rest of the journey downhill in silence, and Cam wondered if the exhaustion of the battle with Liam might be too much for him. He couldn't celebrate, when such terrible truths had been revealed; his mind and body needed to rest. But when they reached the outskirts of the town, something in the air changed his mind. There was a vibe. A thrumming in the streets that was pure carnival, a kind of freedom. And it was infectious. As they got closer to the centre and the music, Cam's energy came roaring back, and on the horse next to him, he saw Petra and Banjo – grins big as bananas. They slid off the horse and tugged at each other. *Let's go!*

Cam wanted to go with them. But he needed to check on his mother. So much had happened – he didn't know how much she knew or if she'd be worried and confused. Making promises to find each other later, they tethered the horses and then parted ways.

Cam entered his house, his mind and body buzzing, tears appearing for no reason he could work out. Was it relief? Happiness? Or was it just being home? He ran upstairs, calling for her, but her room was empty, the bed neatly made. Cam felt a cold lump in his stomach as he stepped inside, but there was a note on the bedside table.

Come and find me! Mumma.

He noticed that her wardrobe door was open and her dress was gone – the one she'd secretly made when she was working in garments, with rags of tunics, all different colours. She was okay. She was happy! Grinning as if he'd eaten his weight in mango, Cam thundered back down the stairs and out of the house. He ran into the festival, letting the music and laughter fill him up. Activity bubbled like lava. Children leapt like wallabies. Adults stood on street corners, laughing and talking.

Teachers found teachers, zoologists found biologists, folk who hailed from the same old cities of Adelaide, Perth and Sydney gravitated towards each other to talk about the Old World and familiar neighbourhoods. Their eyes crinkled with happiness and they clasped their hands in joy. Cam realised how lonely and sad they must all have been before, this older generation. Since the Birth of Cetacea, they had lived with their secret history burning in their hearts, letting slip tiny details to release the pressure, knowing it could get them killed.

Some *had* been killed. But was it any wonder Arlo had made so many friends?

Cam looked out for his mother, but found himself drawn towards the art district, to Arlo's home. Perhaps he had been hoping that it was all a mistake – that somehow Arlo had got away and there he'd be, sitting by his inks, smiling in that knowing way.

The door had been broken in by the Watchers, but

for the first time ever, there was colour. To honour his life, artists had covered the outside and inside with paint and decorations. It was the celebration Arlo deserved.

Rosemary was on her doorstep, talking to other neighbours. When she saw Cam she winked, and Cam ran and gave her a hug, because he realised it was the small part that everyone had played that had saved him, and saved Cetacea. He only wished Arlo's part hadn't been so big.

'I do a little tattooing, myself,' Rosemary whispered, tapping his chest. 'I told Arlo I'd complete the colouring for you. Want to do it now?'

Cam thought. His whale tail was missing a spot of blue, it was true . . .

'No thanks. Whenever people ask why it isn't finished, it'll give me an excuse to talk about Arlo again.'

Rosemary smiled. 'I understand.'

He drifted away, flowing with the currents as crowds surged across the town to seek out music and friends. Everywhere Cam went, he was forced to stop and retell the story of his discovery. To gaggles of kids who pulled at his tunic, and to grown-ups who surrounded him with kind expressions. After a while, he hardly felt the hands that slapped him on the back. The words 'Well done, mate' bounced around his ears.

Banners and flags swirled like fog. Throngs of entertainers tumbled and rolled across his path, whooping. There were shouts of 'Day of the Whale!' It made him dizzy. The snatches of colour and faces, like a feverish dream. Lindy called his name and waved, her smile full and bright. Pip, too. Dean fist-bumped him like an old friend. And out of nowhere, Keith picked him up and swung him round. 'Brilliant, buddy. You did your dad proud.'

A headache brewing, Cam slipped from the chaotic main street into a shady passage to catch his breath. But he was being followed. He looked up to see a girl with feathers in her hair.

'Cam! It's brilliant, Cam. It's bloody brilliant!'

Petra's eyes were wild and her cheeks were dotted with yellow and green face-paint, like a parakeet.

'This is amazing!' she sang to the air above his head, then she pirouetted and grinned. Cymbals clashed somewhere in the lanes. 'I've got to go!'

'Have you seen Banjo?' Cam shouted over the deafening clatter.

'What?'

'Banjo?'

She shook her head and was gone, sucked into the madness. Cam turned his back and slid down the wall. He closed his eyes and breathed in deeply, allowing his imagination to drift to a place that was soft and blue, to find some peace.

In his mind's eye, he looked around at the endless sea, with its steely depths below and fanned sunlight above. It was a place he'd visited so often in his dreams to meet Big

Blue, but there were no whales now. He was alone. His ribcage contracted suddenly, and his stomach folded. A grief that he'd pushed so far down now rose to the surface.

He cried. For the fear he'd felt and the whales he'd loved, and for Arlo and his father. And he cried for the painful realisation that life and loss could be lonely. He cried until there was nothing left, and drifted into sleep.

When he woke, the afternoon had become evening and the atmosphere had mellowed. He got to his feet, disorientated, and stumbled out of the alleyway and back through the streets. Wherever he went, guitars strummed quietly. People lay on blankets in the square, telling stories and laughing. Cam saw some of them heading to Terra Beach. The stars came out, but the party went on, with candles and song.

Cam washed his face at a water pump and went in search of his mother, looking for a flash of her multicoloured dress. He eventually found her in a courtyard by the canteen quarter with a group of people who, like her, had originated from Western Australia. He stood in the shadows and listened to them talk. Nearly all of them had boated east towards higher land when the sea level rose. *We were all in the same boat!* they joked. His mother's laugh was the loudest. Her hand-waving the grandest. She was herself again.

'Cam!'

When she saw him, she took him in a hug that had the strength of his mother and father combined. She pushed him back and looked at him, her eyes sparkling.

'You remarkable boy,' she said. 'You bloody remarkable boy.'

'Mumma!' Cam laughed.

'Dad would have been so proud of you. Come here, my darling.' She hugged him again and pulled him to meet her friends.

Cam stood with them a while, holding her hands and watching her face dance as she talked about herself and Poppy, her sister: 'Daisy and Poppy! We were the flower sisters of Kalgoorlie.' They had been singers, entertainers, small venue actors. She talked about the pain of losing Poppy to the floods, the joy of finding David Solomon on a rescue boat, the excitement of the future on an island they thought might be paradise.

She was better. And more than that.

Cam kissed her cheek and strolled back into the night, weary but not ready for bed. He ached for the comfort of friends. He stepped through the groups of people still gossiping in the gloomy light of Eden Place, and meandered into the eastern districts, where neighbours had pulled tables, chairs and oil lamps into the streets. He felt as if he'd seen every single member of Cetacea, apart from the ones that mattered. Where were they?

As he turned to go home, a soft hand slid into his.

'Come with me,' Dana said. Her other hand held the reins of her horse.

Where? He didn't care where.

She helped him on to the horse, and they rode slowly down to Terra Beach, round the perimeter to the far end, and then south, past the farmlands. The sway of the horse rocked him towards sleep, and he hardly noticed the sea wall looming out of the darkness ahead.

He stared at its intimidating height. It seemed so long ago he was last here, but it was just a few days. So much had happened in so little time. His mind crumpled with fatigue.

Dana helped him dismount. He shook his head. 'I can't climb it. I can't.'

'You don't have to,' Dana said. 'Come this way.'

Further along, a section of the wall had been smashed through with a mallet, creating a ragged hole. There was a flicker of light on the other side, down by the sea. They left the horse tethered to a piece of farm fencing, and climbed through. A trail of moonlit footprints in the sand showed them the way to gaps cut in the rolls of spiked wire.

Down the beach, at the water's edge, a few figures sat round a campfire. His friends, Petra, Banjo and Matteo, and an old woman whose wrinkles were lit up by the fire's glow. They were quiet, stoking the flames, deep in thought.

'I've got him,' Dana called.

Banjo leapt up and ran across the sand to Cam, grabbing his hand and pulling him back to a log seat. Banjo pointed at the sky, right above their heads. 'The star patterns. I found out they're called conspidations –'

'Constellations,' Dana corrected.

'Yeah, constellations. My one's called the Southern Cross. Do you see it?'

The five twinkling blue lights. Banjo's stars. 'Yeah, I see it, Banjo.'

'Shows you where home is.'

'So home is here.'

'That's right. Home is here.'

Across the flames, Dana's hair gleamed bronze and gold. Her blue eyes looked red and sore and Cam remembered that, despite everything, she had lost a father. She pushed a stick into the fire, making sparks hiss like snakes. She caught Cam's eye.

'Dad's speedboat was found two miles out. It got stuck on the kelp. No one on board. We think he tried to swim.'

'We can find him. Greg can drive a boat,' Cam started.

Dana shook her head. 'He was bleeding.' There was a silence as everyone considered what that could mean. Cam remembered the sharks he'd seen cruising the murky depths. 'If he's found his ending, it's only right that it should be at sea.'

Then there was a moment of peace. Banjo poked the fire so it crackled, occasionally looking up at the stranger he'd brought along with him. His gaze was curious and affectionate. The woman was sitting on a log, her legs apart, arms resting on her knees like a bridge, still and settled as if she was part of the landscape.

Cam was too tired to ask who she was. It didn't matter this very minute. He had his friends, and for now that was all he needed. Sometimes questions could wait.

He kicked off his shoes and wriggled his toes in the sand. It was cool and soothing, like silk. He sank his hands in too, thinking of the trillions of grains pouring through his fingers. Shells ground down over millennia, as old as time. His fingers brushed against a buried kelp ribbon and he tugged it free and held it in front of him. This was the brown-green rubber he'd scrubbed since he was seven. He'd always imagined it growing in natural forests, waving like dancers to the whales, the turtles and the seals . . .

'We have to pull down the kelp farms and get rid of the algae. We need to make things clean again,' he said.

'It'll be Cetacea's new purpose,' Dana said softly. 'What we all work for. No matter where we go from here, our priority will be to put things right. We'll meet first thing tomorrow to talk about how.'

'Not *first* thing,' Banjo corrected.

'Of course.' Dana paused. 'First, we must have the ceremony.'

'What ceremony?'

'I'm very glad you asked that question,' Banjo said, winking a big brown eye at Cam.

Banjo got up and squatted in the sand next to the

quiet old lady. 'Cam, this is Arabella. I met her at the feast. She's a descendant of the Yuin nation from the South Coast. She says we should do a whale ceremony.'

'I don't understand.'

'Saltwater people performed ceremonies to wish the whales safe passage. Humpbacks, mainly.'

'But they're gone. The whales are *gone*.' Cam sighed. 'We have to accept the truth.'

Arabella leant across and wrapped a hand around his wrist. Her light brown skin and amber eyes glowed in the firelight. Her voice was soft and slow.

'There's a whale out there or else we wouldn't be here. Our existence is intertwined with theirs. That's what my people would say. So, we must let the whale know that this is a safe place to return to.'

'And if he comes, will it be the start of a new Dreamtime?' Cam asked.

Arabella's face crinkled in amusement. She smiled, shook her head and stared into the fire. 'Dreamtime is always what was, what is and what will be.'

Cam realised he didn't quite understand. Maybe one day he would. He wanted to learn. But for now, he liked the comforting thought that *what was, what is and what will be* had always been part of life's plan. He closed his eyes and thought of his father, his time imprinted on the Earth forever. Part of Everywhen.

Cam felt a long arm wrap around his neck, warm as the breeze on a salt-baked pontoon. As if he could read

Cam's heart, Banjo placed a hand on his chest. 'There'll be another whale. There will.'

'Yes, Banjo. I believe it.' Cam turned to look out at the ocean, hoping to see the rise and fall of a humpback or the width of a tail fluke.

Instead he saw a figure. It limped along the shoreline where the sea kissed the sand – a dark silhouette in the white, moonlit froth of the breaking waves. King? No. The figure was taller, leaner; long arms swung at his side as he walked. Cam watched curiously as the man stopped and looked up, his eyes drawn by the fire. There was no mistaking him.

Cam was on his feet, toes churning the cool sand as he sprinted towards the water, making a sound that was almost unhuman – a cry of pain and happiness and relief rolled into one. It was followed by a determined roar as the tiredness left his limbs, his heart suddenly enlarged and strong, adrenalin and hope pumping through his body, making him run faster than he'd ever run before.

He flung himself against the man and pressed his face against his wet shirt.

'Arlo,' Cam sobbed. 'I thought you were dead.'

'So did I.' Arlo folded his arms round Cam's back and drew him close. 'But I wanted to be here when you found the truth.'

'The truth hurts, Arlo.'

'It does. But it also heals.'

They stood with their feet in the shallows and their

arms locked round each other until the shouts from the campfire grew too loud to ignore.

'I think they've guessed it's you,' Cam said, smiling up at Arlo's craggy, tired face, noticing now the blood caked at the side of his head and the missing chunk of ear. 'He nearly got you.'

'He thought he had.'

'Where have you been all this time?'

'Swimming to shore took time. Then I hid. I had to play dead.'

'You've missed so much. Arlo, everything is different now. Come on – I'll show you.' Cam took Arlo's hand and led him slowly up the sand towards the campfire. The silhouettes turned and beckoned.

'Who's there?' Arlo asked, his voice thin and uncertain.

Cam stopped and turned to face his old friend, the tattooist. He patted his chest.

'Whale Mob.'

Acknowledgements

Day of the Whale was written during lockdown, when we were stuck inside with scrolling news and questions about the future. Concerns were churning and burning: the rise of populism and division; disinformation; the climate crisis; how we became separated into groups, nationalists and globalists, left and right, right and wrong; how the rich pulled the strings that ruled the world . . . Then, one day, quite out of the blue, an image came to mind: it was simple – a boy looking at a whale on a giant screen. And somehow, everything that was going on in my head melted together with this image and a story began to take hold. At the same time, I was also thinking a lot about my birthplace, Australia, and how I missed her diverse wildlife and those humbling skies and warragal landscapes. She is a country of extremes, where nature always finds a way. That's why, beneath this tale of human greed and control, she is the wild beauty that refuses to be tamed.

For a book that seemed to come from nowhere, it came to mean everything to me, and so many supported me on its way from first to final draft. Too many to mention. However, I would like to give special thanks to a few.

Firstly, to Linda Canning whose reaction to my first draft made me think I was on to something special, and who subsequently read several drafts! Linda, not only are you generous with your time, supporting authors alongside a teaching career, you are a champion of children's literature and an inspiration to your class. I would like to send whale-sized hugs to Emma Norris, whose ardent love for *Day of the Whale* became so important to me, and to Stu Atkinson, who not only encouraged but created incredible fan art to keep my spirits afloat.

For being the best ever beta-readers, thank you to: Nicki Cleveland, Tris Irvine, Hannah Fazakerley, Fiona Faith Ross, Louise Nettleton, Louise Baker, Wendy Flood, Jo Clarke, Scott Evans and Zillah Bethell.

And I couldn't have done it without others in my writing community, and especially the unwavering support of Jo Nadin, Fleur Hitchcock, Dandy Smith, Sinéad O'Hart, Lindsay Galvin, Gareth P Jones, Martin Howard, Tom Easton, Danielle Breachwood, Jamie Russell, Pete Williamson and Liam James.

A big thank you also to dear friend Hattie Bosnell for being by my side on this journey. To the fabulous

Vanessa Ferret who is my very own champion. To Lucy Wendover, Katie Preedy and Victoria Walker, who are the greatest support group. To Susie Chadwick and Sarah Wratten, who are part of me. To Jill Brierley and Sally Monkhouse, who are always so supportive. To the Harvey family and Stanley family who have always cheered me on. To Michelle Margherita and John Van Duursen, who were put in my life for a reason. To the talented storyteller, Kelly Lefever, whose updates keep me connected to the big country. And to all my friends who regularly check in, knowing just how important this writing life is to me.

I am deeply grateful to Aboriginal Elder, Kevin 'Gavi' Duncan, of the Darkinjung (whale dreaming) people, of the Central Coast, New South Wales, for advising me on the right words to explain the Dreamtime and for sharing with me the Dreamtime story of *Baiyami the Sky Father and Toorongong the Whale*, which shaped this tale and became its wisdom.

For fascinating chats about kelp, thank you to Dr Cayne Layton from the Institute for Marine and Antarctic Studies at the University of Tasmania, and to members of the Seaweed Forum, Wales; also to journalist Sabrina Weiss for putting me in touch with the right people.

As ever, I'm grateful to my wonderful agent, Alice Williams; to my family, for loving me and leaving me alone – and especially Mike, who makes my writing possible; to my parents, the best you could wish for;

to my Aunty Liz; and to Rachel Ward, who drew the marvellous map of Cetacea. Thank you also to wildlife artist Sophie Green for inspiring me and allowing the use of her whale art in my marketing.

Finally, to Roy and Martin at Troika Books: how ever can I thank you enough for falling in love with *Day of the Whale* and allowing Cam, Banjo and Petra to share their important stories? You've given a home to a work that I am so proud of, and I'll be thanking you until the stars go out.

ABOUT THE AUTHOR

Rachel Delahaye was born in Australia where *Day of the Whale* is so vividly imagined. She has written young fiction for Farshore and Little Tiger – her most recent series is *Mort the Meek* – and an animal adventure series with Stripes and a three-book comedy series, *Jim Reaper,* published with Piccadilly Press. There are more middle grade projects on the horizon. Rachel also writes fiction and poetry for accelerated reading schemes and Level Readers to help children gain reading confidence.

Rachel lives in Bath. This is her first book for Troika.

You can visit her website www.racheldelahaye.com